P9-CSE-954

THOMAS CRANE PUBLIC LIBRARY
QUINCY MA

CITY APPROPRIATION

STAR TREK: THE NEXT GENERATION®

DEATH IN WINTER

STAR TREK: THE NEXT GENERATION®

DEATH IN WINTER

---◆---

Michael Jan Friedman

Based on
Star Trek: The Next Generation
created by Gene Roddenberry

POCKET BOOKS
New York   London   Toronto   Sydney

POCKET BOOKS, a division of Simon & Schuster, Inc.
1230 Avenue of the Americas, New York, NY 10020

This book is a work of fiction. Names, characters, places, and
incidents are products of the author's imagination or are used
fictitiously. Any resemblance to actual events or locales or persons,
living or dead, is entirely coincidental.

Copyright © 2005 by Paramount Pictures. All Rights Reserved.

 STAR TREK is a Registered Trademark
of Paramount Pictures.

This book is published by Pocket Books, a division of
Simon & Schuster, Inc., under exclusive license from
Paramount Pictures.

All rights reserved, including the right to reproduce
this book or portions thereof in any form whatsoever.
For information address Pocket Books, 1230 Avenue
of the Americas, New York, NY 10020

Library of Congress Cataloging-in-Publication Data

Friedman, Michael Jan.
    Death in winter / Michael Jan Friedman.
       p. cm. — (Star trek, the next generation)
    "Based on Star trek: the next generation created by Gene
Roddenberry."
    ISBN-13: 978-0-7434-9721-3
    ISBN-10:   0-7434-9721-X
    1. Picard, Jean-Luc (Fictitious character)—Fiction. 2. Missing
persons—Fiction. 3. Space ships—Fiction. I. Star trek, the next
generation (Television program) II. Title. III. Star trek, the next
generation (Series)

PS3556.R529D43 2005
813'.54—dc22

                                2005045898

First Pocket Books hardcover edition September 2005

10   9   8   7   6   5   4   3   2   1

POCKET and colophon are registered trademarks of
Simon & Schuster, Inc.

Manufactured in the United States of America

For information regarding special discounts for bulk purchases,
please contact Simon & Schuster Special Sales at
1-800-456-6798 or business@simonandschuster.com.

*For the Girgentis, the dessert
on the menu of life*

SAN FRANCISCO

———◆———

2348

MANATHAS FROWNED, WISHING HE COULD HAVE enjoyed just a bit more cooperation. After all, he had an assignment to complete, and he couldn't rest until it was done.

Of course, in his line of work, there were a great many hazards, a great many ways for disaster to strike. He had learned long ago to exercise patience and wait silently for his chance—and then pounce on it when it came.

So he stood with his cotton-gloved hands at his sides, along with all the other formally dressed waiters and waitresses, and watched the ballroom's hundred or so wedding guests partake of their dinner as a band played a brassy twentieth-century love song—and hoped fervently that one guest in particular would see fit to sample his chicken cordon bleu.

But the guest—a young man with light brown hair, strong features, and a cleft chin, wearing a cranberry and black captain's uniform—again managed to disappoint

Manathas. He left his entree untouched, the same way he had ignored his one-eighth slice of honeydew, his *saladé niçoise,* his champagne, his sparkling water, and even the black cloth napkin that lay alongside his plate.

Ah, Picard, Manathas thought.

He had already asked the fellow if he would prefer another dish to the chicken, speaking intimately to be heard over the music. But Picard had waved away the suggestion, mumbling something about not being hungry.

Still, Manathas refused to give up hope. *The good captain will eventually relent. He will consume something, either a food or a beverage. And when he does, I will be ready.*

Unfortunately, he couldn't devote all his attention to Picard. There were three other starship captains in the room, and each was as important to Manathas as Picard.

It was unusual to find four such highly decorated officers in the dining hall at the same time. In fact, entire weeks often went by without an appearance by even *one* such officer. And when one of them did happen to visit, it was invariably an individual Manathas had already served.

So this wedding feast, vulgar as it might have been by the standards of Manathas's people, was something of an occasion for him too—although not the kind the newlyweds had in mind. For Manathas, it was a day of great promise, great potential, a day he had worked toward for some time.

Walker Keel. Leo Blais. Marielle Kumaretanga. And the rarely seen but often mentioned Jean-Luc Picard. *Yes, a day of great promise indeed.*

As Manathas thought that, the bride and groom got up to dance. The groom was tall and athletic-looking, with an easygoing manner. His mate was a redhead of uncommon beauty—from a human standpoint, of course.

And as they made their way around the floor, the bride's pearl white dress trailing her as foam followed a wave, her guests cheered and clapped and made what they no doubt believed were humorous remarks. There was no decorum, no restraint, no dignity to the occasion.

It was a bizarre custom, the human wedding celebration—almost Klingon in its excess and its indulgence. But then, there was much about humans that Manathas found bizarre.

Eventually, other couples finished or abandoned their entrees, and joined the newlyweds on the dance floor. As they did this, Manathas paid a visit to one of their tables, bringing along a metal-frame cart with a plastic bag hanging inside it.

Unfortunately, he had a bit of a problem with germs—a phobia, to be completely truthful about it. But it didn't stop him from carrying out his mission, thanks to the sheer, sterile gloves he wore beneath the cotton ones.

Piece by piece, he picked up the guests' used silverware and placed it in the plastic bag, making room for a waitress to lay out a clean set of implements. Then he moved on to the next table and did the same thing.

Most of the silverware went into the bag indiscriminately. However, a few pieces were diverted into a smaller bag, coyly concealed inside the first.

In his mind, Manathas labeled each implement with the name of a captain. The fork was Keel's. The spoon belonged to Blais. The knife had been used by Kuma-retanga.

And nothing had come from Picard, leaving Man-athas's collection still one piece shy of completion. But in time, he trusted, that deficit would be corrected.

He took in the room at a glance, making sure no one was paying him undue attention. And, of course, no one was. No one believed he was anything except a human waiter, carrying out the menial work assigned to him.

But then, who would suspect him of being a surgi-cally altered Romulan spy—an agent dispatched across the deceptively quiet Neutral Zone in support of a pro-gram only the praetor, in his brilliance, could have con-ceived?

A plan to grow clones from the genetic material of Starfleet's most prominent captains and, at some oppor-tune juncture years or even decades hence, replace them with their secret progeny. *Brilliant* was probably an under-statement.

But Manathas wasn't a scientist. His job was only to obtain the required genetic material for the praetor, not to make duplicate humans out of it afterward.

It was just as well. He was rewarded more generously for his work than were the praetor's scientists. Besides, he preferred the intrigue of an undercover assignment on an enemy world to a life spent studying DNA molecules on a computer screen.

Even on those occasions when "intrigue" only meant collecting dirty silverware.

Manathas had cleared off his third and final table when one of the guests got up and raised his champagne glass shoulder-high. He had dark hair, prominent cheek-bones, and wide-set eyes that seemed to demand one's attention.

It was Keel, the much-decorated captain of the *Ambassador*-class starship *Horatio*. A good friend of both the bride and the groom, Keel was the one who had booked the ballroom for them months earlier.

"It pleases me to see all of you today," he said, looking out over the expanse of both uniformed and civilian guests. He grinned. "Well, maybe not *all* of you."

The remark was met with a chorus of jeers. But they were good-natured jeers, the kind exchanged between comrades.

Keel continued. "I'm happy to tell you that I've accomplished a few things in my life. I've established myself as easily the most capable captain in the fleet—"

Again, a tide of raucous disapproval.

"Not to mention the handsomest—"

This time, the groans took a bit longer to subside.

"As well as the best-loved captain in the entire sector. Or is that most *oft*-loved . . . ?"

"You're pushing it," observed Captain Blais, a notoriously affable man.

Keel laughed. "Maybe I am. But with all I've done, my greatest accomplishment by far—" He turned to the bride and groom. "—was bringing together these two very special people, who were meant to spent their lives with each other."

The groom wagged his finger at Keel. The bride just smiled and rolled her eyes.

"Ladies and gentlemen," said Keel, "I ask you to join

me in a toast. To the lovely Beverly Crusher and her un-deserving husband, Jack—may they always be as happy as they are today."

The sentiment was echoed from one end of the room to the other. Then Keel and all the other guests drank to the health of the newlyweds, a common ritual here on Earth.

"And now," Keel continued, "I yield the floor to my colleague Jean-Luc Picard, without whose forbearance Beverly and Jack's romance would never have gotten off the ground."

All eyes turned to Picard, who looked to have been taken by surprise. He waved away the invitation.

"Come on," said Keel, beckoning. "The occasion won't be complete without a word from you."

Others echoed the sentiment. And little by little, it turned into a rhythmic cheer: *Jean-Luc, Jean-Luc . . .*

Finally, Picard gave in to the urgings of the other guests. Rising from his seat, he picked up his glass and made his way to Keel's side. Then he looked out over the assemblage.

Silence ruled for a moment or two. Manathas could hear the sounds of ice tinkling in glasses and heels click-ing on the uncarpeted floor. Finally, Picard cleared his throat, extended his glass in the couple's direction, and got started.

"As Jack will tell you," he said, "I am not much of an orator. My words will certainly pale in comparison to those uttered by our friend, Captain Keel."

There were encouragements to the contrary, but Picard seemed to remain unconvinced.

"I would just like to say how happy I am to be here," he

went on, "and how privileged to have witnessed the marriage of Beverly and Jack, who are very dear to me."

Everyone in the ballroom nodded approvingly. Some even raised their glasses. But they withheld their applause, obviously waiting to hear more.

"*Very* dear," said Picard.

Having lived on Earth for some time, Manathas had become as much of an expert on human expressions as he was on those of his own people. He could tell when a person was angry, or fearful, or amused by something, despite that individual's best efforts to conceal it.

In the same way, he could tell when someone was disappointed with a turn of events. As the Romulan observed Picard, there was no doubt in his mind: this was a man carrying a considerable burden of pain and disappointment.

Sometimes it was difficult to divine the cause of a human's emotional state. But not in this instance. All Manathas had to do was follow the direction of Picard's gaze . . .

Straight to the bride, who was nestled in the encompassing arms of her new mate.

"I . . . wish them all the best," said the captain.

The other guests seemed to expect more. But Picard didn't *say* any more. Without warning, he raised his champagne glass and drank.

It was only then that everyone realized the speaker was done speaking. Gradually, a well-meaning murmur of agreement rose from his listeners, but it wasn't nearly the enthusiastic response that had greeted Keel.

With a smile that had too much grimace in it, Picard

retreated to his seat. And though he was patted on the back by his immediate neighbors as he sat, he seemed to know as well as anyone how lackluster his performance had been.

But then, he was in love with the bride.

Manathas was certain of it. And though he had no reason to take Picard's part, he found himself sympathizing a little. He too had once lost a female he loved to another man. But fortunately for him, the other man hadn't been his friend.

Picard and the groom were quite close, from what Manathas had gathered. What's more, they served together on the *Stargazer*—or more accurately, one served under the other. So every day, the captain stood to be reminded of what he had lost.

And every day, he would have to conceal his pain, lest he destroy his friendship with both bride and groom.

However, there was a bright side to every darkness, and Manathas was quick to find one. As Picard settled into his chair, the Romulan picked up a chilled champagne bottle and moved in his direction.

"Excuse me, sir," he said on arrival.

Picard peered up at him. "Yes?"

"May I refill your champagne glass?"

The captain seemed to consider the request for an inordinate amount of time. Then he blinked and said, "No. That will not be necessary, thank you."

Manathas had hoped that Picard would say yes, and give him the chance to inspect the glass more closely. But it really didn't matter. He could still achieve his objective.

"Sorry," he said, securing the glass and holding it up to the light, "but there's a chip in this. My apologies."

The captain shrugged. "No harm done."

"I will be back with a replacement in a moment," Manathas promised. Then he took the champagne glass and withdrew as inobtrusively as possible.

It wasn't difficult for the Romulan to make off with his prize. Picard's gaze had already drifted in the bride's direction again. And in the process, Manathas had been forgotten.

Making certain no one was watching, he emptied what was left of Picard's champagne into another glass—one that had earlier been the property of the bride—careful not to disturb the smudge where the captain's mouth had come in contact with the transparent rim.

After all, the Romulan didn't want to lose the epidermal cells that the human had deposited there. Beverly Crusher's cells, by contrast, were of no value to him. She didn't command a starship, so she didn't fit into the praetor's plans.

Adding his new bit of booty to what he had already collected, Manathas wheeled his cart into the kitchen. Finding a secluded corner, he broke the stem off the champagne glass. Then he removed the inner bag from the outer one and placed it in an interior pocket of his jacket.

There, he thought. *All I require, tucked away where no one will find it.*

Later, Manathas would meticulously package the items—using another, even more effective set of sterile gloves, lest he come in contact with the humans' assuredly virulent bacteria—and send them back to Romulus through a series of cargo vessels, each of which had a clandestine agent aboard to assure the items' safe passage. And in a matter of weeks, the genetic material of Jean-Luc Picard, Leo Blais, Walker Keel, and Marielle Kumaretanga would become the property of a most grateful praetor.

But Manathas wouldn't reap the harvest of the praetor's gratitude quite yet. After all, he had worked long and diligently to become a trusted employee in Starfleet's main dining room. And with all the interesting conversations that took place in that establishment, there was more than DNA to be harvested . . .

ARVADA III

2339

IF THERE WAS ANYTHING BEVERLY HOWARD HATED more passionately than brussels sprouts, it was Bobby Goldsmith. That night she got to sample both of them at once.

Doing her best to ignore Bobby, who was peering across the oval dinner table at her with his dark brown eyes, she separated one of the round green sprouts from all the others and cut it into the smallest sections she could manage. Then she speared one of them and put it in her mouth.

Beverly would have let the sprout lie there on her plate in its dissected form, but her grandmother wouldn't have taken kindly to that. When she served something, it was either eat it or hear about it for hours afterward.

"Waste not, want not," Felisa Howard was fond of saying, though it had been many generations since a member of the Howard family had actually wanted for anything.

"These brussels sprouts are delicious," said Mrs. Goldsmith, a rawboned woman with a thick, dark ponytail who was sitting on Beverly's right.

"You must have a knack with the replicator," said Mr. Goldsmith, a tall man with close-cropped hair.

"Actually," Beverly's grandmother said with a quirk of a smile, "I grew them in my garden."

As one of the founders of the Arvada III colony, she seemed to feel it was her responsibility to help newcomers feel at home. The Goldsmiths had arrived two weeks earlier on a shuttle from Alpha Sindaari along with three other families.

But none of the others brought teenage kids, Beverly reflected. She wished the same could be said of the Goldsmiths. Not that Bobby had gone out of his way to annoy her or anything. But every time she turned around he was staring at her, making her wonder if she had dirt on her nose or something.

And sometimes she did—not just on her nose, but under her fingernails and in the creases of her hands. After all, her grandmother didn't like to tend her garden alone, and Beverly was the only family around to help her.

She barely remembered her parents. They had died when Beverly was very young, victims of an Ubarrak attack on their research vessel. She had lived with her grandmother ever since, way out there in the Arvada system.

"Your garden?" said Mrs. Goldsmith. "Really?" She glanced sideways at her husband. "I'd *love* to start a garden."

"It's not as easy as you might think," said Beverly's grandmother, her face still strong and handsome despite her age. She looked a lot like Beverly's father. "Not with all the acid you find in the soil around here."

"Mind if we take a look?" asked Mrs. Goldsmith.

"Not at all," said Beverly's grandmother. "Right after dinner, if you like."

Her eyes, which were blue and slightly almond-shaped like Beverly's, seemed to gleam with delight. After all, it wasn't often she had a chance to show off her garden, and even less often that someone *asked* to see it.

Beverly was happy for her grandmother, but hoped the Goldsmiths' tour would be a quick one. The sooner she was able to escape Bobby's scrutiny, the better.

As it turned out, having the garden inspection on the agenda was a good thing. It made dinner move more quickly, so the Goldsmiths could see what they wanted before it got dark.

At least Beverly had *thought* it was a good thing—until her grandmother turned to her and said, "You and Bobby can take a walk if you like. I don't think he's as fascinated by brussels sprouts as some of us."

The Goldsmiths laughed at that. But not Beverly. She wanted to say, "Take a *walk* with him? I don't even want to be on the same *planet* with him!"

However, she couldn't protest—not with everybody looking at her. So she kept her emotions in check and nodded, and said, "Sure." Then the adults went out the back door into the low-slanting rays of the sun, and left Beverly alone with Bobby.

He shrugged his bony shoulders. "Which way?"

Without a word, Beverly led the way out the front of the house—a sturdy silver-white prefab with sleek, rounded corners. It was getting on to evening, so she didn't bother to grab a hat or anything to drink—precautions she would have been certain to take during the heat of the day.

The Howards' domicile was on the westernmost outskirts of the colony, closest to a distant cluster of hills. It was in that direction that Beverly decided to start walking.

Out of the corner of her eye, she could see Bobby keeping up with her. But she didn't turn to look at him. She just kept her eyes on the hills up ahead, which were turning purple as the golden light began to fade.

This was by far Beverly's favorite time of day, when the air cooled down and the breeze died, and she could hear the cries of avians if she listened carefully enough. Unfortunately, her companion didn't give her the chance.

"So," he asked, "do you like it here?"

"It's all right," Beverly said.

"Have you been on Arvada Three a long time?"

"Since I was three," she told him. "Three and a half, to be exact."

"You must know a lot about the place."

"Everything," she said. It wasn't a brag. "Then again, there isn't much to know."

Beverly had often dreamed of living on Earth or one of the Sol-system colony planets, or even on an alien homeworld. They had always sounded so exciting to her, the kinds of places where someone could see something new every day.

But her grandmother had no intention of leaving Arvada III. That was where she had chosen to do her work in exobiology. That was where she had set down her roots.

And as a teenager Beverly had little choice but to remain with her.

Wait until I grow up, Beverly thought, not for the first time. *Then I'll join Starfleet and see all those wonderful places for myself.*

She didn't know anybody in Starfleet, but she was pretty sure that was the place for her. The last thing she wanted to do was live on a far-flung colony world, apart from anything that was of any interest to her at all.

And yet at the same time, she didn't like the prospect of leaving her grandmother behind. For all the woman's devotion to things Beverly found boring and trivial, there was a bond between them as strong as that between any mother and daughter.

Abandoning her grandmother would be like cutting out a part of herself. And while Felisa Howard had never spoken of the day her granddaughter would depart to pursue a career of her own, Beverly was sure the woman wasn't looking forward to it.

"You're lucky," said Bobby.

Beverly turned to him. "What do you mean?"

"You've been here most of your life. Arvada Three is the fourth colony we've been to." The boy breathed a sigh. "I'm just hoping we'll stay at this one for good."

It had never occurred to Beverly that moving around could be a bad thing. It gave her something to think about.

"You walk this way a lot?" Bobby asked.

"Some," she said.

"It's nice out here."

By then, the sun had gone down behind the hills, leaving a pale radiance lingering in the western sky. Everything around Beverly seemed softer, even the rocks.

"I guess," she said.

"It was cold on Sejjel Five," said Bobby. "That was where we lived before we came here. Winter twelve months a year. You didn't dare stay out after dark because you'd freeze to death."

"That's cold," Beverly allowed, though she had a hard time relating to it. Arvada III seldom got any colder than this, and she couldn't remember what it was like anywhere else.

"You don't ever want to be in a place like that," Bobby told her.

Beverly shrugged. "I guess."

Her companion didn't come up with any other questions; he just walked alongside her with his hands stuck into his pockets. But Beverly still couldn't hear the calls of the avians.

After a while, she decided she liked it better when they were talking. In the silence, it was too easy to imagine Bobby staring at her.

She was about to ask him what he thought of their school when he spoke up again. "You know," he said, his voice strangely thick and slow, "you're the most beautiful girl I've ever seen."

It hit Beverly like a blow to the stomach. She stopped and looked at Bobby, not knowing what to say or do. And for a moment, it seemed he was as paralyzed as she was.

Then he took an awkward step toward her and put his hand on her arm. Somehow, it wasn't as unpleasant a sensation as she would have thought. And his eyes, which she had found so irksome, were like warm dark pools drawing her into their depths.

He's going to kiss me, Beverly thought, her heart thudding against her rib cage. *He's going to* kiss *me.*

No boy had ever done that before. And certainly not on the lips. But she could tell by the way Bobby was tilting his head that he meant to do just that.

And with a shock, Beverly realized that she *wanted* him to. In fact, she couldn't wait.

A minute earlier, the very notion would have made Beverly sick to her stomach. But somehow, in the space of just a few seconds, everything had changed. She didn't shrink from Bobby as he brushed her lips with his own, then pressed them against hers with unconcealed yearning.

He's doing it, Beverly thought. And then she remembered what he had said about her. *He thinks I'm* beautiful.

Bobby put his arms around her, drawing her closer ever so gently. And he kept on kissing her, which was good because she wanted to keep kissing him back.

Suddenly, Beverly felt a tickle in her throat. She tried to subdue it, contain it, but she couldn't. In a single breath, it grew too urgent to deny.

Had she yielded to it right away, it might only have been a polite little cough. But her attempt to stifle it had transformed it into something else, something harsh and ragged and ultimately more burp than anything.

Surprised, Bobby pulled back and looked at her, wide-eyed. Beverly wanted to hide, to crawl out of sight. But there on the plain between the colony and the mountains, there was nowhere to hide.

Abruptly, Bobby laughed—and unexpectedly, Beverly found herself laughing with him. It took all the air out of the situation, relieving her embarrassment.

Then Bobby's smile faded and he gazed at her as if he wanted to kiss her again, burp or no burp. But before he could move, something happened in the sky.

The first Beverly saw of it was in Bobby's face, pinpoints of light appearing in the dark parts of his eyes. Turning then, she saw it for herself—a thick streak of golden fire falling from the heights of the dark blue heavens.

She muttered something, an expression of incredulity and terror. A moment later the streak of fire struck the earth beyond the hills, making the ground shiver beneath the girl's feet.

"What was that?" Bobby breathed.

Beverly shook her head, her knees weak with a mixture of fear and—unexpectedly—excitement. "I don't know," she said, "but we've got to get back to the colony."

"There it is," said Beverly's grandmother, pointing to a spot among the darkened hills.

Beverly, who was standing beside her in their sleek standard-issue suborbital craft, strained to see through its forward observation port. "Where?" she asked.

"More to your right," said Felisa Howard.

The girl made the adjustment—and with a shock of morbid fascination, spotted the ship. She was lying at the end of a long, violent furrow in a shallow valley, as dark and dead-looking as a bird that had plummeted from the sky.

The vessel was as big as some older Federation star-ships, though she never would have been mistaken for one—and not just because she was a strange coppery green in color. With her flattened-cylinder shape and closely gathered warp nacelles, she was unlike any star-ship Beverly had ever seen.

"Putting down," said Amihai Zippor, the handsome, dark-haired botanist in charge of the colony.

Manipulating his helm controls, he executed a looping descent that put them on the far side of the downed vessel. Then he opened the hatch, allowing them to join the grim-faced men and women who had preceded them in the colony's other suborbital craft.

In the light of urgently cast palm beams, Beverly could see the damage the ship had taken in her fiery descent and hard landing. Her hull was charred in spots and badly dented in others, and there were places where it looked as if it had been clawed by some colossal predator.

But for all that, the vessel was still intact—both inside and out. Her warp core had been of particular concern to the colonists, but their sensors had already assured them it was stable and uncompromised. It wasn't going to blow up, taking the ship, the colonists' rescue team, and a con-siderable hunk of the surrounding landscape with it.

The best news was that there was life inside the ves-sel—a surviving complement of nearly two dozen beings, all representatives of the same unknown species. But in some cases, they were on the knife's edge between life and death. If they were going to see the dawn on Arvada III, they would need medical attention—and quickly.

Which was where the colony's rescue teams came in.

"Look for an entry hatch!" barked Zippor, his voice thick with concern for the crash victims.

It turned out to be a difficult item to find, thanks to the beating the ship had taken. But after a minute or so, Dar Xarota—whose people, the Ondu'u, had notoriously sharp vision—gave a deep-throated cry of triumph.

Using his light beam as a pointer, he played it over a rectangular shape just forward of the ship's nacelles and a couple of meters off the ground. The hatch cover had been obscured by a long stretch of carbon, but Beverly could see it easily enough now that she knew where to look.

"Phasers," said Zippor.

The colonists who had been entrusted with the devices took them out and trained them on the hatch cover. Then they unleashed their beams, constructing a gaudy crimson display in the dark of night, and began gouging a hole in the metal alloy.

Thick as the hatch cover was, it held for only a couple of minutes against the force of the colonists' barrage. Then it buckled in the center and gave way, exposing the space behind it.

Zippor allowed a minute for the edges of the opening to cool off. Then he and two others, their faces strained with anticipation, used broad-backed Xarota as a stepping-stone to clamber inside.

Beverly glanced at her grandmother in the spill of light. The older woman was frowning deeply, as intent on the rescue effort as if it were her own family in the ruined vessel.

The girl was proud of that, though she couldn't quite say why—almost as proud as she was of her grandmother's insistence that Beverly be allowed to take part in the rescue operation. But then, Beverly wasn't a little kid anymore, and Felisa Howard was too respected a figure in the colony for anyone to balk at her granddaughter's inclusion.

"We're in a main corridor," came Zippor's voice, received by the com system in one of the open suborbital craft and amplified so everyone could hear it. *"There's no sign of any survivors yet."*

As the botanist and the others pursued their search, they reported to their colleagues each step of the way. Apparently, the vessel had been a cargo hauler, built with an emphasis on storage capacity rather than creature comfort.

Beverly tried to visualize it, but she had little to go on. After all, she had been on only one spacegoing vessel in her life, and that was the one that had brought her to Arvada III.

Suddenly, she heard an exclamation over the com link. And then a softer expression that sounded too much like someone feeling sorry for someone else.

"We've found a number of them," Zippor announced, *"on what appears to be their command bridge. Stand by."*

Beverly's heart began to race, her curiosity about the aliens' ship giving way to an even deeper curiosity about the aliens themselves. Sensor data could go only so far in describing a life-form. It couldn't say much about the life-form's appearance, and it certainly couldn't say how it was likely to behave.

Abruptly, the ruined hatch door swung open. As Beverly moved closer to get a better look, Zippor began lowering a survivor to Xarota and the other colonists.

The alien was covered with a hide of beautiful white fur. It was evident on all the exposed parts of her body, even her face. Still, there was something about her that gave Beverly the impression that she was a female.

If the alien had any injuries, they weren't easy to spot. However, she seemed to be in great pain—unable to move, speak, or even breathe without grimacing.

The colonists placed their charge on a stretcher. Then they left the web of light and carried her to one of the suborbital vehicles, Doctor Baroja—a tall, gray-haired man who was the colony's only trained physician—walking alongside them and running a tricorder scan of the victim. Beverly could barely make out the expression on Baroja's face in the darkness, but it seemed to contain as much surprise as concern.

"What is it?" asked Tan, the colony's senior geologist.

Baroja frowned. "She's got a virus—nothing we haven't seen before. But her species must be vulnerable to it, because it's eating her alive."

Then the alien was tucked into the suborbital craft, where Beverly could no longer see her. By then, Zippor had begun lowering another survivor to his colleagues.

The girl felt a familiar hand on her shoulder—that of her grandmother. "Why don't you see what you can do to comfort the injured?" Felisa Howard asked. "They're bound to be a little scared."

Part of Beverly wanted to stay and see the rescue effort. However, she had come to help, not to gawk.

"I'm on it," she told her grandmother, and made her way to the suborbital vehicle into which the first survivor had been deposited.

Doctor Baroja was making the alien comfortable in a seat that had been tilted all the way back. Up close, in the even blue light of the cabin, Beverly could see that she had been wrong about that pure white coat. It actually had a couple of black streaks in it.

"Can you look after this one?" Baroja asked, his blue eyes as intense as the girl had ever seen them.

"That's what I'm here for," she said.

The doctor smiled and said, "There you go." Then he went to help with the other victims.

Beverly hunkered down beside the alien. There was something about the look in her startling multicolored eyes, something that *connected* with the girl.

"What's your name?" Beverly asked.

"Jojael," came the reedy, barely audible response. The alien extended her hand. "Help us . . ."

Beverly accepted the heavily furred appendage. It felt both softer and warmer than she had expected. "You'll be all right," she told the alien as convincingly as she could.

But she had no idea if her assurance would hold water.

Beverly stood in the soft illumination of the medical dome, among a handful of other colonists, and watched Zippor fold himself into the chair beside Jojael's bed.

Up until then, it had been Beverly's place to sit there, keeping the alien company as she had in the suborbital craft. But when Zippor said he had some questions for Jojael—the first of the crash victims to be treated, and therefore the one in the best shape to provide answers—the girl had been happy to move aside.

"How are you feeling?" the colony administrator inquired of their guest.

Jojael shifted her weight in her bed. "Better than before," she said, her voice a good deal stronger since the painkillers took effect. It sounded like rocks rubbing together. "Your Doctor Baroja has been most generous."

Zippor smiled. "It's Baroja's duty to be *generous,* as you put it. He's a medical doctor."

Jojael considered the information for a moment. "Then he has done well in discharging his duty."

"I'll tell him you said so," Zippor promised.

"How are the others?" Jojael asked, still too worn out even to turn her head.

She had asked the same thing of Beverly, but the girl hadn't been able to tell her what she wanted to know. Beverly wondered what the administrator would say.

Zippor glanced over his shoulder at the seventeen other beds distributed throughout the domed enclosure. Another eight of them had been set up in a second structure, formerly used for storing generator parts.

"Some perished in the crash," Zippor said at last, "but the majority managed to survive. However, like you, they seem to be afflicted with a virus."

"Yes," Jojael confirmed solemnly. "The bloodfire."

"The bloodfire," the botanist repeated. "When did you first see symptoms of it?"

Jojael heaved a sigh. "Some of us were sick before we left Kevratas. The rest became sick on the ship."

"Kevratas. That's your homeworld?"

"It is," Jojael confirmed.

"We've examined your ship's navigational logs," said Zippor. "It appears your point of origin is on the other side of the neutral zone we share with the Romulans."

Beverly's mind raced. Jojael and her people were . . . subjects of the Romulan Empire?

"In fact," said Zippor, "it's well within the part of space the Romulans claim as their own."

"My homeworld," said Jojael, "is actually on the fringe of Imperial territory. The logs reflect the origin of our vessel, which was built on a planet a bit closer to Romulus."

"Did the Romulans give you permission to leave?" Zippor asked.

"No," said Jojael. "We did so surreptitiously." Her nostrils quivered. "We had no choice."

"And why was that?"

"Because they would not give us a cure for the blood-fire."

"Did they have one?" Zippor asked.

"Not at the time," Jojael explained. "But the praetor had a cadre of brilliant minds at his disposal, scientists who had cured a great many other plagues. Had they wished to find a cure for ours, they could certainly have done so."

Beverly wasn't sure if that was true or not. She knew little about the Romulans, and even less about curing diseases.

Jojael made a sound of disgust. "The Empire takes from its subject worlds without a second thought. And it doesn't feel the least bit obliged to give back."

"That's not right," Beverly said—surprising herself. She hadn't meant to speak out loud. It just happened.

Tan, a broad man with prominent cheekbones and kind eyes, put his arm around her. The other colonists looked sympathetic as well. But then, they couldn't have approved of the Romulans either.

"It is not right at *all,*" said Jojael. "So we found a merchant captain who would accept our generosity and sell us a vessel in which we could leave the Empire, and looked forward to the help we would receive from the Federation."

Zippor's brow creased down the middle. "You believed *we* would produce a cure?"

"Of course," said Jojael with heartbreaking earnestness. Her multicolored eyes turned bright with hope. "You're not like the Romulans. You're like us. You pride yourselves on what you can give to others."

Beverly saw Zippor and the other adults exchange glances, and her heart sank a little. Clearly, they had less confidence in themselves than Jojael did.

"You have to understand," Zippor told the Kevrata, "even though we want to help you, our medical expertise here is limited. We can treat your symptoms and ease your discomfort, but it'll take a team of Federation specialists to come up with a vaccine."

"And they will need time to get here," Jojael inferred. "I did not expect otherwise."

The botanist looked relieved. "As long as you understand."

Beverly wasn't sure Jojael *did* understand. As Zippor continued to talk with the Kevrata, the girl went to seek out her grandmother. She found her sitting beside another of the aliens, a male whose black-lidded eyes were closed in sedated sleep.

Felisa Howard glanced lovingly at her granddaughter. "Are you as tired as you look?"

Beverly didn't answer the question. "I heard Zippor mention a Federation medical team."

"That's right," said her grandmother. "We sent for one even before we got back to the colony."

"How long will it take for them to get here?"

"A week and a half. Maybe a little more."

Beverly felt a drop of icewater run down her back. "But . . . will they be in time?"

Her grandmother's features hardened. "That's our hope, and it's not an unreasonable one. But no one here can say for sure. Not even Doctor Baroja."

The girl thought about that. She wished the Kevrata didn't have to wait for a medical team. She wished she could cure them of their virus all by herself.

Of course, she didn't have a prayer of doing that. She wouldn't even have known where to begin.

Her grandmother brushed aside a lock of hair that had pasted itself to Beverly's forehead. "You know," she said, "you did well with Jojael, keeping her calm and all. Better than anyone had a right to expect."

The girl looked at her. "Really?"

"I just said so, didn't I?"

Beverly nodded. *Howards don't fish for compliments.* She had heard that often enough.

"Thanks," she said.

"You know," said Felisa Howard, "Bobby Goldsmith

was asking after you. Sounds like you two had a stimulating conversation before the Kevrata arrived."

Beverly wasn't sure how much her grandmother knew, or had guessed. "It was all right," she said.

But it seemed like a long time ago. And the kiss . . . had it really happened? It felt like a dream.

Suddenly the Kevrata lying beside her grandmother started to groan, his eyes narrowing in pain. The girl thought, *His painkiller is wearing off.*

Dr. Baroja was there in a matter of seconds, bending over the alien and administering a hypospray. Almost immediately, the groaning began to subside.

"Damn," said the doctor.

"Is he all right?" Beverly asked.

Dr. Baroja glanced at her. "Sorry about the language. It's just that these people have a high resistance to anesthesia." He held up his hypospray. "And we've only got so much of the stuff."

What if we run out? Beverly wondered.

But she already knew the answer, and it wasn't a happy one: The Kevrata would have to do without it. *At least until the medical team can get here.*

Beverly shook her head, dismayed by the injustice of it all. The aliens were so nice, so polite, so grateful for what the colonists had done for them. After all they had been through, it didn't seem fair that they should have to endure such a burden.

And even less so that any more of them should have to *die.*

2379

1

—◆—

JEAN-LUC PICARD STUDIED THE PARTICOLORED
cluster of stars glittering in front of him, dangling so close
he felt as though he could touch them, and was reminded
of the faery lights of French legend.

His forebears had feared them because they lured
young men to their dooms in the realms of magic. But
Picard, captain of the Federation *Starship Enterprise,* had
no need to be concerned. For one thing, he was no longer
a young man. And for another, he had developed a
healthy resistance to temptation.

Besides, these stars weren't faery-inspired. They were
three-dimensional images, generated by the multitude
of tiny holographic projectors positioned in the walls
around him.

Nor was it this cluster alone they were bringing to life.
In fact, there were thousands of them hanging there in the

cool, dark air, three-dimendional entities so numerous as to make even the *Enterprise*-E's new stellar cartography facility seem crowded.

On the *Enterprise*-D, stellar cartography had been much more modest—a planetarium-like chamber with images of the stars emblazoned on its concave, digitally enabled wall. The original *Enterprise*-E version had been only a bit more sophicsticated, incorporating a few extra bells and whistles.

But this, Picard thought, *is a different approach entirely.*

He turned to the fellow standing beside him on a high, safety-railed platform. "And you say this is wrong?"

"Completely wrong," said Lieutenant Paisner, Picard's new chief of stellar cartography. "Beta Diomede, second from the top, is supposed to be a healthy young stud, not even an adult yet. It should be as bright yellow as they come. And yet it looks red enough to go nova at any second."

"Really," said the captain.

"And that's just one example."

Paisner pressed a button on his handheld device and the expanse of stars whirled about them. It made the captain feel as if he were standing in a spinning top.

"Here's another," said the cartographer, as the galaxy mercifully stopping revolving. "Archandra, second star from the bottom on the left side."

Picard searched the cluster in front of him. "Yes, I see it. Too red again?"

"Not red *enough,"* said Paisner. "And it's got no planets. The real Archandra's got *three* of them."

The captain frowned. "Unfortunate."

"You can say that again."

Paisner's previous posting had been on *Voyager,* the *Intrepid*-class vessel that had been lost for seven years in the Delta Quadrant. In addition to charting any number of previously uncharted systems, he had assisted in the assimilation of alien technologies into the ship's long-range sensor functions.

Once back on Earth, he had drawn up plans for a pet idea—a three-dimensional approach to the study of stars. Starfleet had liked it well enough to give it support. And it had chosen to implement Paisner's idea on the *Enterprise*-E, which was undergoing an overhaul after her near-destruction in Romulan space.

Which explained the lieutenant's determination to get everything right as quickly as possible. Like any new parent, he wanted his baby to be perfect.

Picard, on the other hand, was willing to accept a few gaffes in the beginning. Especially when so many more critical systems were also in the midst of overhaul.

"What can I do to help?" he asked.

Paisner smiled a conspiratorial smile. "I could use another set of hands, if you can spare them. Preferably someone who has experience with holoemitters."

The captain gave it some thought. "Larson has repaired a few holodecks in his day, and they can spare him for a while in engineering. I'll send him down as soon as possible."

"Thank you, sir." Paisner included the entire depicted galaxy with a sweep of his arm. "And imagine how much better this will look when we work all the kinks out."

Picard nodded. "Indeed."

Moments later, he was on his way to the botany lab.

From there he went on to visit the cargo transporter and the main shuttlebay. And everywhere he went, he received the same report: The ship was coming together. One lieutenant told him the *Enterprise* would be so beautiful he would hardly know her.

Perhaps, he allowed. As it was, he hardly knew her crew, including the woman who had made the remark.

Picard had barely returned to his ready room when his door mechanism chimed. "Come," he said, wondering who wished to speak with him.

It turned out to be Commander Rager.

She smiled at him. "Good morning, sir."

Knowing why she was there, Picard did his best to smile back. "Good morning, Sariel."

Rager had served under the captain for more than a decade, having joined him on the *Enterprise*-D as a raw ensign only a few years after the ship was commissioned. In that time, she had distinguished herself as a top-notch conn officer, plying the helm as few others could.

Now she was leaving to serve as second officer on the *Hedderjin,* a *Galaxy*-class vessel like the *Enterprise*-D. And she would be doing so under one of Picard's former officers, the ever-impressive Gilaad Ben Zoma, who had taken over command of the *Hedderjin* a couple of years earlier.

It had long been Rager's ambition to move up the chain of command. The only reason she had remained with Picard as long as she had was out of loyalty to him.

Like so many others, he thought.

"Is it that time?" he asked.

"It is," Rager confirmed. And with a lift of her chin, she added, "Permission to disembark, sir."

"Granted," said Picard. "Of course. Where is the *Hedderjin* off to?"

Rager looked very much at ease with the lieutenant commander's pips on her collar, as if she had been wearing them all her life. But then, she had already visited with her new ship and captain. If she had had any jitters, she had long ago gotten them out of the way.

"The Neutral Zone," said Rager. "We'll be there for the next couple of months, reinforcing existing patrol routes until the Romulans sort things out."

"Really," Picard said.

It was a pivotal time in the history of Federation-Romulan relations. Thanks to the *Enterprise*'s role in the defeat of the tyrant Shinzon, the Romulans seemed inclined to put aside the centuries-long history of animosity between the two interstellar powers.

The praetor herself—a former senator who had swiftly and decisively filled the void left by Shinzon—had suggested that the Federation and the Empire revisit the Treaty of Algeron, calling it antiquated and long in need of restructuring. That seemed like a step in the right direction.

On the other hand, the Empire was on shaky ground these days, its resources severely depleted by the Dominion War and its institutions—the Romulan Senate in particular—left by Shinzon in disarray. The cynic in Picard wondered whether these were the real reasons for the praetor's overtures.

More often than not, it was the hand of the needy and

uncertain that extended the olive branch. History had shown the truth of that over and over again.

But the more important question wasn't why the praetor was pursuing conciliation. It was whether she could be trusted to continue in that vein, when her predecessors had so often proven treacherous in the past.

Picard had no idea. Neither did the admirals who composed Starfleet Command, which was why they were still mulling the praetor's suggestion.

The other element to be considered was the Romulans' philosophy with regard to imperialism. Though their efforts at expansion had been interrupted by the exigencies of the war, they were by nature a species of conquerors—which put them at odds with the Federation principle of self-determination.

But then, Klingon philosophy often clashed with Federation principles, and the Federation had managed to embrace the Klingons as allies. Perhaps it could overlook the Romulans' less attractive qualities as well.

"Sir," said Rager, "I want to thank you. For the recommendation, I mean. If not for you, I wouldn't have—"

Picard waved away the suggestion. "No thanks are necessary, Sariel. If I was doing anyone a favor, it was Captain Ben Zoma. Good officers are difficult to come by."

Rager looked at him for a moment. Then she said, "I also want to thank you for . . ." She seemed to have some difficulty finding the words. "For everything."

Picard nodded. "You are quite welcome. Good luck. And give my regards to your captain."

Rager stood there a moment longer. Then she left the captain's ready room as dozens of others had left it over the last few weeks, each of them bound for some other ship or Starfleet facility. And Picard was left alone.

Slightly more than half of the uniformed personnel who had ventured into Romulan territory with him had remained on the *Enterprise*. The others had either perished in the battle with Shinzon or accepted positions on other vessels.

Riker was among the latter. Troi as well. Though they were still enjoying a well-deserved honeymoon at the moment, they would soon be taking the *Luna*-class *Titan* on her maiden voyage as captain and counselor, respectively.

And just before the newlyweds left, Riker had asked Picard's permission to speak with Security Chief Vale. Apparently, Riker wanted her on the *Titan* as his first officer. Naturally, Picard had granted his comrade's request. If Vale had a chance to become an exec, who was he to stand in her way?

Picard sat down in his desk chair and sighed. How many times had he said good-bye in the last couple of weeks, since the *Enterprise* was towed into drydock? And how many more times would he say it before his ship returned to the void?

The captain missed those who had departed. He missed their courage and their optimism, and the dedication they had brought to their work. He missed Shimoda in engineering, who had made such a mess of the isolinear chips when he was infected with the Psi 2000 virus, and Dean, who was the only fencer on board capable of giving Picard a run for his money. He missed Prieto, who had ferried poor Tasha to her death on Vagra II.

And how he missed Data, who had perished in the battle against Shinzon in one of the greatest displays of courage and sacrifice Picard had ever seen. Nor was it any the less poignant for the fact that Data was an artificial life-form. If anything, it was more so.

But there was one face that Picard missed more than any of the others. After all, it was the first time in many years that he had been separated from Beverly Crusher.

She had been his chief medical officer and one of his closest advisors for nearly two decades. However, she had also been a great deal more than that. Long before Beverly appeared on the bridge of the *Enterprise*-D with her twelve-year-old son, Wesley, in tow, Picard had fallen deeply in love with her.

But he had never let Beverly know it, and for good reason. She was betrothed and later married to Jack Crusher, one of Picard's best friends. And even after Jack died, Picard couldn't bring himself to tell Beverly how he felt— not when it would seem as if he were trampling on Jack's grave.

The day Beverly assumed the mantle of Picard's CMO, it had been the captain's intention to keep his relationship with her strictly professional. But it wasn't long before that changed, if not quite in the way he might have expected.

They became friends—the very best of friends. They came to enjoy each other's company so much that they shared breakfast once a week. And for the sake of their platonic friendship, Picard had submerged his deeper feelings.

Then came the *Enterprise*'s mission to Kesprytt III, a politically divided world where one faction wished to join the Federation and the other wished to prevent it.

Picard and Beverly were rigged with devices that created an unintentional telepathic link between them, leaving each one's mind open to the other.

It was then that Beverly realized how much Picard loved her, and for how long. And it was then as well that she admitted her previously concealed feelings for *him*, recoloring in his mind every moment they had ever spent together.

But they had been friends for so long, Beverly didn't want to take a chance on jeopardizing that relationship. And at the time, Picard had been comfortable with her decision. As Beverly had pointed out, there was time for something more than friendship to develop. There was no need to rush it.

And they hadn't. They had continued to have their breakfasts together, looking forward to the time they shared even more than before. They had allowed the emotions that drew them to ripen like plump, dark grapes, unhurried and undisturbed.

The captain might have been content to let life go on like that forever. Then, without warning, Beverly pulled the rug out from under him. She informed him that she was taking an assignment on Earth as head of Starfleet Medical, in which capacity she had served once before.

Picard was hurt by Beverly's decision, no question. But he couldn't have stood in her way, any more than he could have stood in Riker's or Troi's or Vale's. If that was what Beverly needed to be happy, he would accept it and carry on.

Brave words, the captain thought.

Little had he known how lost he would feel without Beverly, how hollow and uninspired. That realization waited until she was already in San Francisco, immersed in her new job, and it was too late to see if she would change her mind.

Apparently, Picard's feelings for Beverly were as powerful as ever. He just hadn't been compelled to examine them as he was examining them now.

Of course, he could still talk to her. With the *Enterprise* so close to Earth, communications would be virtually instantaneous. It would be almost like speaking in person.

Yes, the captain thought, *that is what I will do.* He activated his computer, work on which had been completed only the day before. And since there was no com officer on duty, he punched up a channel to Starfleet Medical on his own.

Almost instantly, a face appeared on the screen—that of a thickset officer with a dark beard. "Starfleet Medical," he said. "With whom would you like to speak, sir?"

"Doctor Beverly Crusher," said Picard.

"Just a second, sir."

A moment later, Beverly's face appeared on the screen. She was even more beautiful than the captain remembered, and he hadn't seen her so very long ago.

"Jean-Luc," she said, "how nice of you to call!"

Her voice was different from the way he remembered it. There was more laughter in it. It bothered him that he could have forgotten in so short a time.

"You must be bored up there," Beverly said. "You were never one for sitting in spacedock."

"A *little* bored," he confessed. But he wanted to know about *her.* "How is Starfleet Medical? Still the way you left it?"

"Not in the least. For one thing, there's an internship program here now—a way of encouraging young talent."

"Not a bad idea," he observed.

Beverly rolled her eyes. "You can't imagine them, Jean-Luc. They're kids!"

He could, actually. He had his share of young officers on the *Enterprise* as well. But he was so pleased to see and hear her, he didn't comment.

"All with advanced degrees in xenobiology," Beverly continued, "and out to conquer every disease in the quadrant."

Picard couldn't help smiling. "Reminds me of a young doctor I used to know."

"They're running me ragged," she told him. "Nothing but questions day and night . . . I love it!"

He should have been happy for her without reservation, but instead he felt a pang of resentment. After all, she had never told him how much she loved serving with him on the *Enterprise*—though she must have, if she had spent all that time doing it.

"Come to dinner," she said, her eyes sparkling, "and I'll tell you all about it. There's a Bajoran band playing at the officers' mess this evening."

Picard was touched that Beverly recalled his appreciation of Bajoran music. He had only mentioned it once before.

Still, his better judgment told him that he would do well to turn down the invitation. It was difficult enough trying to move on with his life. It would make it that much *more* difficult if he reminded himself of what he had lost.

"I would love to," he said, "but I have so much work to do here."

Was that a glimmer of disappointment in her eyes? Or was it merely his imagination?

"Soon then," said Beverly. "I'll save the last dance for you."

Again, he smiled. They weren't quite the words he wished to hear at this juncture, but they warmed his heart nonetheless.

He was still drinking in the sight of Beverly when she ended the transmission. Her image was replaced by the Federation insignia—leaving the captain feeling worse than if he hadn't called in the first place.

Damn, he thought.

He shook his head, then crossed the room to look out his observation port. He had a good view of the single-man vehicles that were swarming around the *Enterprise,* continuing the refitting of sizable sections of her hull.

Taking notice of Picard's scrutiny, one of the technicians waved at him. The captain waved back.

It reminded him that what he had told Beverly was the truth—he *did* have work to do. Perhaps as much as Riker would on the *Titan.* Picard didn't have a new ship to break in, but he did have what was largely a new crew.

Of course, some positions were already spoken for, Worf's and Geordi's among them. Picard was grateful that they had decided to remain with him. Both had received offers to go elsewhere—tempting ones, no doubt—but they had seen fit to turn them down.

On the other hand, a number of other posts had yet to

be assigned. And conspicuous among them was the rather significant position of chief medical officer.

It wasn't that there was any shortage of applicants for the job. Picard had a padd containing more than a dozen of them, each one eminently qualified. Any of them could have come aboard and hit the ground running.

But the captain couldn't bring himself to choose one over the other—because in doing so, he would have been compelled to acknowledge that Beverly was gone.

So he had procrastinated—for days, and then weeks. However, it was time a decision was made. And if Picard couldn't do it, he would have to delegate the job to someone who could.

What's more, he had just the individual in mind. Glad that he was finally taking action of some sort, the captain looked up at the intercom grid hidden in the ceiling. Then he said four words that he would no doubt repeat many times before his stint on the *Enterprise*-E was over . . .

"Picard to Commander Worf."

"Worf here," came the response.

"I have a job for you. . . ."

Praetor Tal'aura took a sip of the wine brought to her only the day before, shifted her lithe, long-legged form in her gilded, high-backed chair, and regarded the individual on the viewscreen in front of her.

His name was Braeg. Until recently he had been an admiral in the Imperial Defense Force. He was tall, broad-shouldered, and good-looking, with a strong jaw and piercing hazel eyes. And though he had made a career of winning space battles, which implied a certain degree of ruthlessness, every word he spoke in public seemed to reek of fairness and common sense.

A compelling combination, to be sure.

"You know me," Braeg began in a deep, resonant voice, as he addressed a crowd in one of the capital's busier public plazas, "and you know also that my loyalty to the Empire is beyond question. I have demonstrated that in a hundred battles in more than a dozen star systems, risking all I have for the enduring glory of Romulus."

Perhaps not a hundred, Tal'aura thought, *but close enough.* And the admiral had certainly been unstinting when it came to valor.

"Yet now," Braeg continued, moving across the dagger-like shadow of a nearby obelisk, "there looms a threat greater than any posed before. Greater than the Federation, greater than the Klingons—greater even than the once-mighty Dominion. Because this time, it is no foreign enemy clawing at our borders. This time, the Empire threatens itself."

"He doesn't waste any time," said Tal'aura, "does he?"

"No, Praetor," said her companion, a slender, unattractive nobleman named Eborion.

"On our farthest outworlds," said Braeg, "places like Daasid and B'jerrek and Sefalon, natives dissatisfied with their treatment at the hands of Romulus have for some time huddled in secret, whispering of rebellion and secession. But in recent days, my friends, they have done more than whisper. They have taken their objections to the streets and challenged imperial authority."

Tal'aura winced. In filling the power vacuum created by the demise of the Praetor Shinzon, she had been prepared for any number of challenges. The situation developing on the outworlds had not been among them.

"The praetor," Braeg continued, "has amply demonstrated her inability to deal with the growing list of rebellions. Perhaps she hopes the problem will take care of itself, given enough time. But as you and I know, that will not happen. It will fester like a badly treated wound and grow worse."

Eborion made a sound of disdain. "His rhetoric is crude, to say the least."

"You think so?" asked Tal'aura. *She* didn't. In fact, she thought it was most impressive.

So did the crowd, apparently, or what she could see of it on the screen. The Romulans nearest the admiral shook their fists and roared their approval of Braeg's remarks. The display struck an unexpected chord of envy in the praetor.

She had come to power by using the political allies she had acquired as a senator, and by wooing families like Eborion's. Or rather, not the families entire, but the individual in them who would most covet association with a praetor. It was they who had delivered the people of Romulus to her.

However, a part of her wished she had done it on her own. It would have been infinitely more satisfying that way.

"Shall we allow Tal'aura to lose the outworlds and diminish the Empire?" Braeg demanded of his audience. "Or shall we advise this praetor of the people's displeasure?"

The crowd's enthusiasm jumped a notch. Tal'aura took another sip of her wine and found she didn't like it so much after all. She made a mental note to take her wine purveyor to task for it.

Eborion leaned closer to her. "You know, Praetor, it would not be an especially difficult thing to eliminate this admiral-turned-insurrectionist."

"Perhaps not," she said. "But if Braeg were to meet with an untimely end, the people would know it was an assassination—and that would make a martyr out of him. Then someone else would come along to stir up the masses in Braeg's name."

Eborion made a sound of disgust. "So he's to proceed unfettered, free to say and do as he wishes?"

Tal'aura glanced at him sideways. "That is a most patrician way of looking at it."

Eborion smiled, though his long, narrow features were clearly not made for it. "I am a patrician, Praetor."

"So you are, Eborion." Tal'aura herself had come from humble beginnings, being the daughter of an innkeeper. But Eborion's family was one of the Hundred—the five score clans whose wealth was almost as old as the Empire itself.

She watched Braeg lift both of his hammerlike fists in the air, bringing his diatribe to a crescendo. Then she rose and turned her back on the screen.

"We'll allow this upstart to have his day," she said. "Then, when he feels most secure, we'll cut his legs out from under him, and his movement will collapse under its own weight."

Of course, even if there were no Braeg, the outworlds

would still be a matter of heated debate. They were critical components in the imperial economy, keys to a thousand fortunes.

And their continued submission to Romulus was in jeopardy, just as Braeg so eloquently proclaimed. Tal'aura acknowledged that, if only to herself. It was why she had sent her best operative, the half-blood, to Kevratas—the outworld where the currents of rebellion ran the strongest.

The half-blood would hunt down the rebel movement and attack it like a hungry warbird. She had done such work before, for Tal'aura's predecessors, earning a name for herself with her cold and ruthless efficiency. Surely the Kevratan rebels, crude as they were, would prove no match for her.

But because Tal'aura was no longer an innkeeper's daughter, she had also dispatched a second operative to Kevratas—a veteran spy, who was there without the half-blood's knowledge.

Between the two of them, the praetor told herself—and *only* herself—firebrands like Braeg would soon have precious little to rant about.

Beverly Crusher sat in the ruddy light of a wall torch at a scarred wooden table, huddled in a *nyala*-skin coat like everyone else, and sipped at her pitted metal mug. It contained a frothy, bitter liquid as dark as her son's eyes, and vaguely reminiscent of a beverage she had sampled on Delos IV when she was doing her medical internship with Dalen Quaice.

But Delos IV had been an arid, dusty place. Rainfalls there had been few and far between, and her throat had sometimes been so parched that she would have drunk anything at hand—even her own perspiration, she had joked on occasion.

Kevratas, where Beverly now found herself, wasn't even remotely hot and dusty. In fact, it was the coldest, bitterest, most snow-clogged frozen vault of a world on which she had ever set foot, a vicious snowstorm shaping and reshaping its powdery white terrain every day for half the year.

My luck, she thought, *it had to be* this *half.*

Still, she continued to sip at the beverage—something the natives called *pojjima*—because every other patron was doing the same between exhalations of thick white vapor, and she didn't want to stand out from the crowd. Besides, if she held her mug up high enough she could peer over its brim at three of the tavern's four entrances— one directly before her, one to her right, and one a little farther back to her left.

Beverly didn't know why the place had been built with so many doors. Maybe the people she had come to meet would be able to explain it to her.

Of course, she had never met them before, so she didn't know what they would be able to do. If not for the infor- mation she had received regarding their appearances, she wouldn't even have been able to identify them.

Nor would they be able to identify *her. After all,* the doctor thought, allowing herself a shadow of a smile, *I'm not quite myself these days.*

It was a corny joke, the kind her husband Jack might

have made. Strange—it had been so long since his death. *When did it stop seeming like yesterday?*

She was still pondering the question when the door directly in front of her swung open, affording the doctor a glimpse of swirling, diamond-dust snow. Then a couple of Kevrata came in and pulled the door shut behind them.

It's them, Beverly thought, as she saw the colors of their coats. One was a rich blue with silver highlights, the other black with red patches. Though there were others in the tavern wearing the same colors, there weren't many— and none of them, as far as Beverly could tell, had walked in together.

No, these were her men—or rather, her Kevrata. She would have staked her life on it. *In fact,* she added musingly, *I will be doing just that.*

For their part, they had been told to look for a female of their species, one who would be unremarkable except for the color of her facial fur. Whereas most Kevrata were pure white, a few had brown or black streaks mixed in. Beverly's streaks, which were black as pitch, were located just under her eyes, making it look as if she had been crying black tears.

She thanked Macrita Helleck, her immediate predecessor at Starfleet Medical, for coming up with the subdermal holoprojector technology that allowed field personnel to impersonate a different species without undergoing surgical alteration.

Until a few years ago, anyone who wanted to go unrecognized in an alien milieu—either to study it or spy on it—had been forced to go under the laser scalpel. In the course of Beverly's Starfleet career she had been on both ends of the procedure, performing it as well as having it performed on her.

She hadn't liked it in either case. It was a time-consuming operation, and the surgically implanted prosthetics never felt quite right. That was why assignments that entailed surgical alteration had become such objects of dread among the rank and file. And though the patient's original features were restored when the mission was over, that required surgery as well.

Now, Beverly was pleased to say, it was different. All one had to do was come up with an alien image, and a network of projectors the size of dust motes, strategically inserted under the skin, did the rest. And they didn't just create an appearance; they generated a tangible surface, using electromagnetic fields.

The basic technology wasn't new. It had been employed in holodecks for nearly twenty years. But Helleck had miniaturized the emitters, making the idea a practical one.

Good thing, Beverly thought, as she considered her reflection in the rounded surface of her mug. Building brow ridges was one thing. Fur implantation was quite another.

And it wasn't just the fur. It was the obsidian skin underneath it, invisible except under close inspection. Surgically altering her to look like a Kevrata would have been a nightmare for one of her colleagues, no question.

It took the males in the blue and black coats a few seconds to pick her out from the crowd. Once they did, they waddled purposefully in her direction, jostling a dozen or more of their fellow Kevrata on the way.

No one seemed to mind. But then, the Kevrata liked

physical contact. Beverly had learned that a long time ago.

The males stopped in front of her, pulled their hoods back, and sat down. Like all their kind, they had sloping foreheads and wide, flat noses with gaping nostrils.

But it was their eyes that drew Beverly's gaze. They were riots of color, their irises dark purple at the fringes, green farther in, and a ruddy gold around the pupils.

Just like the eyes of the Kevrata who had crash-landed on Arvada III. Beverly could still see Jojael peering imploringly at her through the haze of her illness, begging her for something she couldn't give them.

But with a little luck, she would be able to give it to *these* Kevrata. That was why she had come all the way from Earth, wasn't it? To do as an experienced physician what she hadn't been able to do as a helpless teenager.

"Have you been waiting long?" asked the male in the black coat, uttering the words that confirmed his identity for her.

"Not long at all," Beverly responded, her voice roughened to the level of a Kevrata's by another device, implanted in her throat. *Now for the countersign.* "How is your mother?"

The male shrugged his rounded shoulders. "Fearful, like everyone these days. She sees those around her falling victim to the plague and wonders which of us will be next."

His voice was steady, unaffected. But neither he nor his companion could entirely conceal their desperation. Beverly had seen their expressions on a hundred different worlds. It said they would do anything, risk anything, *sacrifice* anything if it might translate into a cure.

There were times in her career when she had felt bad bringing hope to such people, because hope was all she could bring. But this time she was confident she could do more than that.

"So," said the Kevrata in the blue-and-silver coat, lowering his voice to a conspiratorial whisper, "do you think you can help us?"

"I do," Beverly said in the same barely audible tone. "But I'll need a place to work. And blood samples. And a little time."

"We can provide a place and blood samples," said Blue Coat. "Those will be easy. But time . . ." He tilted his head to one side. "That may be in short supply."

"I understand," she said. Indeed, she understood that as well as anyone in existence, after what she had seen on Arvada III.

"When can you start?" asked the Kevrata in the black coat.

"I was about to ask you the same thing. If you've got a place in mind, I can move in tonight. Otherwise—"

Beverly stopped in midsentence, seeing a crinkling in the black skin around her companions' eyes. It was a sign of apprehension. And they were looking at something directly behind the doctor.

Beverly very much wanted to know what was going on back there. But she also didn't want to attract attention, so she refrained from turning around.

"Problem?" she asked softly.

"Possibly," the Kevrata in the black coat told her. "Sit still and perhaps it will go away."

Beverly did that. But as the seconds wore on, she could

see by the lift of her companions' chins that the problem *wasn't* going away. It was getting closer.

By then, everyone in the doctor's part of the tavern was turning around. It would have seemed strange for her not to do so as well, so she swiveled about in her wooden chair—and saw that there was *indeed* a problem.

A squad of armed Romulans had entered the tavern. There were six of them in all, the goggle-equipped hoods of their white thermal suits tossed back to reveal their brow ridges, the severe cut of their hair, and their tapered ears. It was impossible to mistake them for any other species—even the Vulcans, with whom they shared a long-ago common ancestry.

"No one move," said a hard but decidedly feminine voice.

At first, Beverly couldn't see where it had come from. Then the Romulans opened a path, and the doctor realized that there was a seventh figure in their group.

She had expected to see the severe, dark features characteristic of most every Romulan she had ever encountered. The features she saw were neither severe nor dark.

But they were hauntingly familiar.

The piercing gaze, the strong but feminine features, the close-cropped blond hair, and the determined jut of her chin . . . if Beverly hadn't known better, she would have said she was looking at her old comrade Tasha Yar, who was killed shortly after she became security chief on the *Enterprise*-D.

But this was the Romulan Empire. That considered, it made much more sense that the woman giving orders in the tavern was Sela, the half-Romulan daughter of a Tasha

Yar who had survived in a rogue timeline. Sela bore an uncanny resemblance to her mother and, with the exception of her pointed ears, almost none to her Romulan father—an ironic twist, considering the fact that she was entirely her father's daughter under the surface.

Sela had first reared her head more than a decade earlier as a player in the Klingon civil war—one whose support of the Duras faction nearly turned the tide against the newly established Chancellor Gowron. Thanks to an armada led by the *Enterprise*-D, Duras's bid for power was crushed, and along with it Sela's plan to manipulate the Klingons.

The next time Sela turned up was on Romulus, where she was engineering an invasion of Vulcan under cover of a "reunification" initiative. Fortunately for Vulcan and the rest of the Federation, the scheme was stymied by Captain Picard, Data, and the legendary Ambassador Spock.

Despite such setbacks, Sela was one of the craftiest and most dangerous individuals Crusher and her colleagues had ever encountered. If the woman was there in the tavern, it meant two things: first, that the Romulan praetor suspected Federation intervention on Kevratas and had dispatched Sela to deal with it; and second, that the Romulans had somehow gotten wind of Beverly's meeting with the Kevrata.

Sela looked around the tavern, her eyes like tiny, hungry predators. "There is an offworlder among you," she barked. "Give him to me and none of you will be punished. Try to protect him and you will have occasion to regret it."

Him, Beverly thought. *So she doesn't know everything.*

No one in the tavern responded to Sela's demand. But then, most of the Kevrata didn't know of Beverly's presence there.

Sela looked around a moment more. Then she said, "Very well," and trained her disruptor on a tavern patron at random.

There was a flash of pale-green energy and the Kevrata went hurtling backward out of his chair. He was dead before he hit the floor, a plume of oily, dark smoke rising from a wet black hole in his chest.

Sela's voice cut through the sudden tide of fear and dismay. "The offworlder—*now.*"

Beverly felt the weight of a hand on her forearm and turned to the Kevrata in the black coat. With his other hand, he was poking a furred thumb in the direction of the door by which he had entered. And his comrade's fingers were inching inside his coat for something—a weapon, no doubt.

They wanted her to go while they stayed and covered her escape. She hated the idea of accepting their offer, but what choice did she have? As the only person on Kevratas who could stop the plague, she had to do what she could to preserve herself.

And that included letting others die so she could survive.

Of course, there would be Romulan centurions posted outside the tavern—Beverly was certain of it. Otherwise, those who had entered with Sela would have moved immediately to block the exits.

Taking a deep breath, she shot her companions a look

of gratitude. Then she grasped the edge of the table, coiled, and launched herself over it.

Her foot caught something as she shot between the two Kevrata, but it was only for a fraction of a second. Then she was bolting for the door, a green energy beam sizzling over her shoulder and striking the wall ahead of her.

Beverly heard a cacophony of voices, and knew by the savage strobe of green light on the wall that her friends were returning the Romulans' fire. But she didn't stay in the tavern long enough to see the results. She swung the door open, taking a stinging blast of snow in the face, and lurched into the storm-choked street.

At the same time, she pulled out the smuggled phaser concealed beneath her coat. Squinting against the stinging, white lash of the weather, she looked for a target—and didn't find any.

Suddenly Beverly caught something out of the corner of her eye. She whirled in time to see the flash of a green energy beam—but it shot past her, missing its target.

She returned fire, her ruby phaser beam turning the snow the color of human blood. Then, her heart pumping, she pelted through the drifts in the opposite direction, hoping the storm would give her a chance to get away.

The snow was deep in spots and Beverly's boots were big, clumsy things, and she couldn't help anticipating a disruptor bolt between her shoulder blades. But she was in good shape and she had the urgency of fear driving her forward, and every plunging stride down the street took her farther from the prospect of danger.

After a few minutes, she allowed herself to entertain the possibility that she had eluded Sela's centurions. If that was so, she had to find shelter. She couldn't go back to the inn where she had been staying—not if there was the slightest chance that Sela had tracked her there.

Fortunately, this wasn't the first clandestine mission the doctor had undertaken. She had known enough to take with her everything she brought to Kevratas, which wasn't much at all.

Glancing back over her shoulder, she reassured herself that there was no one in close pursuit. Then she slowed her progress to a measured jog. By then, her breath was coming in fiery gasps and freezing on the air like tortured wraiths, and her heart was pounding painfully against her ribs.

But none of that mattered. She had gotten away from the tavern unscathed.

Thank goodness, she thought. For a moment, she had been afraid that she would perish there in the cold and the snow, and never again see the people who mattered to her. She imagined how Wesley would have felt—and Jean-Luc as well—if she had died on this frozen, faraway world.

The same way she had felt about Jack . . .

Quickly, Beverly thrust the image away from her. She wasn't safe from Sela's centurions yet—not completely. The last thing she needed was a distraction.

I'm still alive, she thought. *But I'll need a little luck to stay that way.*

It was then she heard something to her right—or thought she had. *A voice? Or was it just the wailing of the wind?* She whirled to see, her phaser held out in front of her.

But there was nothing there—just the vague, hulking outline of a building. Beverly felt a wave of relief.

Then she heard something else, from a different direction entirely. And this time, when she turned to investigate, she saw something loom out of the storm—something that looked altogether too much like a Romulan thermal suit.

Beverly squeezed off a phaser blast, digging a red tunnel into the falling snow. Then she started running again, hoping to elude the Romulans as she had before.

It was harder this time. The air had begun to tear the lining of her throat, and her legs were becoming more leaden with each stride, and her coat was a heavy, stifling burden. But she forced herself to ignore it all.

The Kevrata need me, the doctor told herself. *I can't let them down.*

She had barely completed the thought when something ripped into her shoulder, spinning her and dropping her into a drift. As she lay there, stunned, her shoulder raged as if it were on fire.

A disruptor bolt, she thought. If it had hit her more squarely, it would have killed her.

Through sheets of silent, falling snow, she saw man-sized shapes advancing on her. It occurred to her to fire back at them, but the disruptor bolt seemed to have knocked the phaser out of her hand, and her arm was numb from the shoulder down anyway.

Beverly wrenched herself about and got to her feet, despite the agony it cost her. Cradling her arm with her opposite hand, she tried to get away, to find a hiding place. But it was no use. The pain in her shoulder was too great and the energy blast had taken too much out of her.

Before long, she noticed a third thing working against her. Without realizing it, she had run into a cul-de-sac formed by three shadowy walls.

Turning, Beverly saw the Romulans had filled the mouth of the dead end, their weapons leveled at her. But they didn't fire. They just stood there, waiting for something.

Or someone.

Beverly was cold all of a sudden, so cold she couldn't stand it. Her body began to shiver, coat or no coat. *I'm going into shock,* she thought.

Then she saw a figure move through the rank of centurions and stop a couple of meters in front of her. It was Sela. Beverly could see enough of the woman's face to be sure of that.

Raising her weapon, Sela trained it on her captive. She didn't bother to see who might be lurking beneath the Kevratan hood. She just smiled and squeezed the trigger.

Closing her eyes, Beverly said a silent good-bye to Wesley and Jean-Luc. It looked like they would be learning of her death after all, as much as it hurt her to think so.

Then, at point-blank range, she felt the splintering impact of Sela's disruptor beam.

2

———◆———

"TEA," PICARD SAID OPTIMISTICALLY. "EARL GREY. HOT."

He watched with interest as something took shape in his replicator's alcove. It took a while, but it finally manifested itself as a cup and saucer. *Ah,* the captain thought with a feeling of satisfaction, *now we are getting somewhere.*

The day before, his request had produced the required beverage sans cup—which made for rather a mess. This was progress. He made a mental note to thank Chief Heyer, who had assumed the responsibility of getting all the replicators into working order.

Removing the simple white china from the alcove, Picard watched the steam rise lazily, even sensuously from his cup. Then he brought it to his lips and took a sip.

And regretted it.

Had the carpet not been laid so recently, he might have spit out what was in his mouth—that was how vile it tasted. As it was, he took pains to return the liquid to the cup whence it came, and then—with a shiver—returned the cup to the replicator.

Progress, perhaps. But it was far from a *fait accompli.*

Just then, he heard the voice of his chief engineer over the ship's intercom. "Captain," he said, "this is La Forge. There's a communication for you from Starfleet Command."

Picard smiled, his experience with the tea forgotten. "Are you also our com officer now, Mister La Forge?"

The engineer chuckled. "Whatever it takes, sir."

The captain had always admired that attitude in Geordi. "By all means, Commander, put it through."

Sitting down at his desk, he watched as the Federation graphic was replaced with another image—that of Admiral Edrich, the gray-haired elder statesman of Starfleet Command. Picard hadn't met the man until after he took command of the *Enterprise*-D, but he had taken a liking to Edrich instantly.

"Admiral," he said. "What can I do for you?"

Edrich frowned, accentuating the wrinkles around his mouth. "I'm afraid I have bad news, Jean-Luc."

Picard recalled a time when he had heard a similar remark, albeit from a different admiral. However, he had never expected the news to be *that* bad. To lose his brother, his sister-in-law, and his beloved nephew all at once . . . it had almost broken his heart for good.

The captain cringed a little, wondering what the news would be on this occasion. *Not as devastating as that other time, certainly.* It couldn't be.

Then Edrich said, "It's Beverly Crusher. She's been declared missing in action."

Picard found himself shaking his head, unable to wrap

his mind around the information. "Missing . . . ?" he repeated numbly.

"The likelihood," the admiral said softly but unrelentingly, "is that she's been killed."

It has to be a mistake. The captain said as much. "How could Beverly be missing when she's back at Starfleet Medical?"

Edrich sighed. "She left Starfleet Medical a week ago, Jean-Luc, on a covert mission. Top clearance only."

How is that possible? Picard had spoken to her only . . . he counted the days. *Has it been an entire week already?* "Where did she—" Feeling his throat begin to constrict, he paused to get himself under control. "Where was Doctor Crusher sent?"

"A world called Kevratas," said the admiral, "on the edge of the Romulan Empire. An epidemic is ravaging the native population. Doctor Crusher had experience with it a long time ago, on Arvada Three. We hoped she would be able to develop a vaccine."

Picard remembered Beverly telling him about Arvada III. She had been but a girl, helping to treat the victims of a crash—not only for their injuries, but also for a virus they seemed to have brought with them.

And she *had* developed a vaccine—for Federation member species, at least. He remembered her flush of triumph when she told him about it from her office at Starfleet Medical. And that, he admitted grudgingly, made her the perfect candidate to find a cure for the epidemic on Kevratas.

"Of course," said Edrich, "this was more than a humanitarian gesture. As you know, the Empire has been in disarray since Shinzon destroyed the greater part of the Romulans' leadership. Some of their outworlds have taken advantage of the situation to reach out to the Federation. Kevratas is one of them."

And Kevratas isn't just a single planet, Picard noted. It was the homeworld of the entire Kevratan species, which had established itself on a dozen previously unoccupied planets before the Romulans conquered them all and took control.

The other Kevratan worlds took their cue from Kevratas. If the Federation could gain Kevratas's trust, the effect would spread among the outworlds like wildfire.

"You understand the implications," said Edrich, "I'm sure. The praetor may have sent out feelers, extending the promise of improved relations. But this is a bird in the hand—a chance to take the Empire down a peg and liberate the outworlds at the same time. It's of the utmost importance that we jump on this while the opportunity presents itself. If it weren't, we would never have sent the head of Starfleet Medical."

"Why," Picard asked, "are you so quick to assume that Doctor Crusher is dead?"

The admiral looked apologetic. "We haven't heard from her or the Kevrata who were supposed to help her for three days now. Seldom do operatives remain missing that long and turn up alive. You know that as well as I do."

Seldom, the captain echoed stubbornly in the privacy of his mind, *but not* never. There was still a chance, no matter how slim, that Beverly had survived.

"I wish I could be more sanguine," said Edrich. "Unfortunately, those are the facts."

Picard shook his head. "No."

The admiral regarded him, his eyes full of sympathy. "I know how hard this must be for you."

That wasn't what the captain meant. He wasn't in denial of the facts. He was in command of them. "Beverly Crusher is alive. I am certain of it."

Edrich straightened in his chair. Clearly, it wasn't the response he had expected.

"And," Picard continued, "I will do whatever it takes to extract her from the trouble she appears to have encountered."

The older man hesitated for a moment before responding. "I had a mission in mind for you, all right. However, it doesn't involve a rescue operation."

The captain eyed him. "What then?"

"Doctor Crusher's mission was exceptionally important, and we're still determined to pursue it. Obviously, she was our first choice with regard to stopping the epidemic, our best chance at success—but there *is* another option."

And he told Picard who it was.

In one way, it was the logical conclusion, no question. In another, it was anything but that.

"We want you," said Edrich, "to get this doctor to Kevratas and put him a position to find a cure. Then we want you to see to the distribution of it." He scowled. "In retrospect, we should probably have gotten you involved from the get-go. No one knows the Romulans better than you do."

It was true. Picard had been the first to make contact with the Romulans when they came out of their fifty-three-year period of isolation. He was the one who had gone to Romulus to look for Ambassador Spock. And more recently, he was the one who had dealt with Shinzon.

"Also," Edrich continued, "no one knew—" He stopped himself. "—knows Doctor Crusher better than you do. Having worked alongside her all these years, you're in the best position to steer clear of whatever went wrong for her."

The admiral's features softened. "And after you've helped the Kevrata, if you want to push your luck and stay to look for her, you'll be in the best position to do that as well."

Picard didn't like the idea of allowing Beverly to languish in what might be desperate circumstances while he pursued another objective. He wanted desperately to extricate her from whatever snare had taken her.

But she would have been the first to remind him that the welfare of the Kevrata came first—before hers, before his, before that of any single individual, no matter how important or beloved. That was where his duty lay.

"Unfortunately," said Picard, "the *Enterprise* is in no condition to take me to the Empire. I will need an alternative means of transportation."

"You'll have one," said Edrich. "I've made arrangements in that regard with an old friend of yours—Pug Joseph."

Joseph had served on the *Stargazer,* the captain's first ship. The fellow had left the fleet years earlier to pursue a career in commercial shipping, but for a mission like this it couldn't have been difficult to lure him back into service.

"In addition," said the admiral, "you'll be accompanied by a Romulan named Decalon—one of the first defectors the Romulan underground spirited out of the Empire. He lived on Kevratas for a while. He'll know his way around."

Beverly would have benefited from such support, Picard reflected. Obviously, Starfleet Command was being careful not to make the same mistake twice.

"I'm sending you the details now," said Edrich. "Good luck, Jean-Luc . . . on all counts."

The captain nodded. "Thank you, sir."

Then Edrich's visage vanished from the screen, leaving Picard alone with his thoughts. They were gray and ponderous, and they threatened to drag him down. But he wouldn't allow it.

Beverly is alive, he told himself. *I know she is. And in time, I will find her.*

Tomalak, the newly appointed commander-in-chief of the praetor's Imperial Defense Force, watched his servant splash a bit of Romulan ale into his spiced fish casserole.

The dish's aroma had been most tantalizing to begin with. Mingled with that of the ale, it was irresistible.

"My compliments," he said.

"The commander is too kind," said his servant as he replaced the flagon of ale on the commander-in-chief's table. Then he inclined his head and backed out of the room.

No, thought Tomalak, stabbing a juicy chunk of fish meat on the end of his metal dining implement. *Not too kind. Many things, but never that.*

He tasted the morsel. It was every bit as intriguing as its scent promised, every bit as succulent. As was the next morsel, and the one after that.

A victory, he thought. And there was nothing Tomalak liked more than victory.

Savoring each bite, Tomalak took his time consuming the loaf of spiced fish. Finally, with a pang of regret, he swallowed the last piece of soft, white flesh and used a finely finished cloth napkin to wipe his mouth.

Then he set the napkin down, swiveled in his chair, and considered the oval monitor screen that was now in front of him. It was a shame that he had to follow such a delectable meal with such an unappealing sight, but he had little choice in the matter. With a sigh, Tomalak activated the screen.

It showed him a vast array of warbirds, a bit more than sixty at last count. They had gathered just outside the edge of Romulus's star system like airborne scavengers, waiting for some earthbound beast to make its kill.

Among them were the vessels commanded by Donatra and Suran, a fiery young female and a crafty veteran respectively. Originally the leaders of the Imperial Third and Fifth fleets, they had ever so briefly taken the reins of the entire Defense Force by tying their destinies to that of Shinzon.

At the time, Tal'aura had been their ally, their co-conspirator. But it was only their common allegiance to Shinzon that held the three of them together, not any real affinity for one another. When Shinzon fell, leaving the praetor's chair empty, Tal'aura swept in to seize power on her own.

Of course, she could have thrown Donatra and Suran a bone, leaving them in charge of the military. However, they had already betrayed one praetor all too gladly. What would stop them, Tal'aura had asked herself, from betraying her as well?

Hence, the appointment of Tomalak as head of the Imperial Defense Force. But Tal'aura had underestimated the influence of Donatra and Suran on the Romulans who had served with them. Almost without exception, every ship's commander in the Third and Fifth Fleets remained loyal to his or her superior and—casting aside a millennia-old tradition of fealty—refused to recognize the legitimacy of the praetor.

It was this wave of sentiment that had created the rogue force on Tomalak's screen. Nor was it inconsequential, by any means. Sixty warbirds were sixty warbirds.

But Tomalak had nearly a hundred ships under his command, and only a third of them were dispersed throughout the Empire. That left him with a fleet at least equal to the rogues'.

He laughed softly to himself. All he had ever needed in the past was a fighting chance. For someone as skilled as Tomalak, equal odds were a rare and heady luxury.

One that would, in due course, prove the undoing of Donatra and old Suran.

And so it goes, Tomalak mused, *around and around like a child's spinning toy*. The great became the least and the least became the great, over and over again, so quickly sometimes that it made him dizzy to contemplate it.

Only Tomalak always kept his place in the firmament,

because he knew better than to reach for something as high as a throne. Instead, he identified the favorite of the moment—Tal'aura today, someone else tomorrow—and inured himself to them.

Naturally, he had political preferences. One of them was that the Empire stay as far away from the Federation as possible—a policy from which Tal'aura seemed increasingly ready to diverge. But that didn't mean Tomalak would stint one iota in his support of the praetor or her regime.

Until another one came along.

That was what it meant to be a rock in a tempest. That was the price one paid to remain a survivor.

He would never have done anything so rash as to stand in defiance of authority, like the swarm of warbirds on his monitor screen. And he would certainly never have laid his sword at the feet of anyone as politically inexperienced as Braeg.

Without question, the fellow had been a great military commander in his day, a hero of the Empire. But leading a fleet into battle wasn't nearly as difficult as marshalling the loyalty of a senate, or manipulating a congress of merchants, or holding sway over the backstabbing, bickering Hundred.

Unfortunately for Braeg, he would never have the opportunity to learn that lesson firsthand. Depressing a button with his forefinger, Tomalak called up a different image—that of his own powerful, well-prepared fleet.

The one that would defend Romulus when the rebels came. The one that would, in the end, prevail.

If Donatra and the others wanted a fight, he would give them one—and remind Tal'aura that, of all those who served her, no one was more valuable than Tomalak.

Carter Greyhorse's life had become much fuller since the head of his penal settlement retired and was replaced by a new, more liberal administrator.

The woman's name was Esperanza. She had been in charge for only a couple of days when she granted Greyhorse access to a series of monographs published by Starfleet Medical.

Her predecessor, a fellow named Dupont, had repeatedly refused Greyhorse that privilege. It wasn't that there was anything in the monographs he could have used to hurt anyone—not even himself. But Dupont had denied them to Greyhorse all the same.

It had seemed unnecessarily cruel. Greyhorse had, after all, been a doctor. Despite everything that had happened, his mind still moved in that direction.

But he was a prisoner these days, at the mercy of others in every way. There was little he could have done about the administrator's stubbornness except continue to make his requests, and hope that Dupont changed his mind.

He hadn't, of course. But he had removed himself from the equation, which was even better.

Now Greyhorse could read a monograph whenever he wanted. In fact, he was poring over one of them at that very moment, following the research of a Doctor Bashir who had done groundbreaking work in the field of biomimetics.

Intriguing, he thought—as the door to his quarters slid open, revealing his guard. In actuality, McGovern—a hatchet-faced man with a shock of red hair—was but *one* of the guards who worked at the penal settlement. However, Greyhorse had come to think of McGovern as his own.

"Yes?" said the doctor.

"It seems," said McGovern, "that you have a visitor."

A visitor? the doctor thought. "There must be some mistake. I'm not expecting anyone."

"Nonetheless," said the guard, "he's on his way. Figure five minutes." And he withdrew, allowing the door to close behind him.

Greyhorse turned back to his computer screen, where the biomimetics monograph was waiting patiently for him. He saved it, clearing the screen. Then he got up and smoothed the front of his standard-issue, pale blue coveralls.

It still seemed like an error to him. There was only one person who visited him these days, and it wasn't like her to surprise him this way.

Still, he supposed anything was possible. As someone who had served as the chief surgeon on a starship, he was in a position to know that as well as anyone.

Greyhorse had been incarcerated for more than a decade, and he had never complained about the passage of time. But now, as he waited for his visitor, time seemed to drag. He began counting his heartbeats, wondering how many it would take.

Finally, his door slid open again. McGovern stuck his head in, just to double-check that everything was all right, which it clearly was. Then he withdrew and someone else entered the room.

A short, small-boned man with straw-colored hair and watery blue eyes, wearing the gray-and-black uniform of a Starfleet captain. The doctor noted the maroon stripe of command on his sleeve.

"Doctor Greyhorse," the man said warmly, "my name is Jefferson. I work for Starfleet Command."

He extended his hand for Greyhorse to shake. The doctor looked at it as if it were some rare variety of alien fauna.

After all, it was a long time since he had shaken hands with anyone. In all the years he had spent in the Federation's penal settlement in New Zealand, his counselors and physicians had never once initiated physical contact. Neither had his fellow prisoners, whom he had seen only on the rarest of occasions.

As a result, it was a little daunting for Greyhorse to contemplate the touch of flesh now. However, he didn't want to give his visitor any indication that he was still unstable, so he clasped the proffered hand.

It felt cool and dry. And ridiculously small. The doctor had forgotten how big and strong he was in comparison with other humans, almost as if he were a member of another species. He did his best not to squeeze too hard.

Finally, Jefferson took his hand back. Greyhorse found that he was sorry about that.

"You're probably wondering why I'm here," said the captain, "so I'll get right to the point. We need your help."

The doctor blinked. "To do what?"

Jefferson laid it all out for him. When he got to the part

about Doctor Crusher and what had happened to her, Grey-horse must have made a face, because his visitor paused.

"I hope this news doesn't come as too much of a shock," he said, a note of concern in his voice.

It did. In fact, it cut Greyhorse to his core. But he was determined not to show it.

"Please," he said, "go on."

As he absorbed the rest of what Jefferson had to say, he began to understand why he, of all people, had been asked to help. Outside of Doctor Crusher, he was the Federation's only real authority on the disease in question.

"What would you like me to do?" he asked.

"We are sending a team to Kevratas," said the captain, "to pick up where Doctor Crusher left off—to find a cure for the virus and distribute it among the Kevrata. I've come to ask you to be part of that team."

Greyhorse could barely contain his excitement. The idea of leaving the penal settlement, leaving Earth entirely . . . it was so exhilarating as to be overwhelming.

Calm yourself, he thought sharply. "I will be happy," he said in a carefully measured way, "to help in any way I can."

"I'm glad to hear that," said Jefferson.

But he had reservations, and Greyhorse knew what they were. He would have been an imbecile otherwise.

"Unfortunately," said his visitor, "there is the matter of what happened on the *Enterprise* several years ago . . . your attempts to murder Captain Picard and others."

"Which were unsuccessful," Greyhorse noted.

"Of course they were, and we're all happy about that. But the attempts were made nonetheless."

Greyhorse didn't know what to say to that, so he said nothing.

Jefferson smiled. "Some people would claim it's the height of foolishness to put someone like yourself in the thick of a complex interplanetary situation."

The doctor nodded. "I can understand that."

"But Admiral Edrich doesn't hold with that point of view. He's studied your record as an officer and a physician, and reviewed your progress here, and he thinks Command can depend on you to help the Kevrata. The question is . . . what do *you* think?"

Greyhorse licked his lips, doing his best not to seem either too eager or too hesitant. "I want," he said simply, for he felt simplicity would serve him best, "to be useful again."

The captain nodded, obviously pleased with the doctor's answer. "I was hoping you would say that."

Of course there was much that Greyhorse did *not* say, a great deal of information that he kept to himself. But then he didn't wish to deprive himself of this most remarkable and unexpected opportunity—and if he spoke everything that was on his mind, he would surely do just that.

He had been convicted of crimes, it was true. However, stupidity wasn't one of them.

"I think you'll be pleased when I tell you with whom you'll be working," said Jefferson.

When Greyhorse heard, he was *quite* pleased. But he wondered how Captain Picard and the others would feel about *him*. . . .

3

————◆————

PICARD HAD HOPED IT WOULD BE HIS OLD SECURITY
officer who greeted him as he materialized in the cramped,
dimly lit transporter room of the Barolian trader. He wasn't
disappointed.

"Captain," said Pug Joseph, a smile stretching across
his stubbly face. "Welcome to the *Annabel Lee.*"

He was perhaps a bit stockier than the last time Picard
had seen him, a bit less toned. However, there was no mis-
taking his sandy, close-cropped hair and small, flat nose—
the latter being responsible for the designation "Pug,"
which had affixed itself to Joseph well before the captain
met him.

"I am not your captain any longer," Picard reminded
him.

"Old habits die hard," said Joseph. "Come on. You look
like you can stand something to eat."

In point of fact, Picard hadn't eaten anything for several hours, but he wasn't hungry. He was too intent on what lay ahead of him to think about food.

Still, he didn't want to insult his old comrade. "I could do with a cup of tea."

Joseph chuckled. "And some habits die harder than others."

Gesturing, he led the way out of the room into the corridor beyond. It was narrower than those on the *Enterprise*, but not so narrow that two old comrades couldn't walk side by side.

The captain glanced at Joseph. "What did you tell your crew?"

"That I had some private business to attend to. They knew better than to ask what it was."

"Discreet of them."

Joseph nodded. "Discretion is a virtue when you're hauling cargo."

"I suppose so." Picard put a hand on his companion's shoulder. "It is good of you to do this, Pug."

"Hey," said the freighter captain, "it's the least I can do." His features straightened, became solemn-looking. "I mean, after what happened with Jack."

It took Picard a moment to remember what Joseph meant. But then, it was a memory the captain had done his best to put aside—for many reasons.

The *Stargazer* had been caught in a previously unknown space phenomenon, one that struck at all her essential systems. Before the captain or any of his officers realized what was happening, the ship was deaf, dumb, blind, and utterly defenseless. And to make matters worse, the phenomenon was creating an overload in the starboard warp-field generator.

Picard had his chief engineer shut down the warp drive, to keep the situation from spiraling out of control. But there was still a lot of energy cycling through the starboard nacelle—enough to blow it up and perhaps take the rest of the ship with it.

Unfortunately, the *Stargazer* couldn't separate into a saucer section and a battle section like later starship designs. The captain had only one choice: to sever the nacelle.

However, the ship wasn't capable of firing on herself, even if her phaser banks had been operational at the time. And there was no way Picard could approach the problem area through the power transfer tunnels, which were full of energy that had leaked from the warp-field generators.

A team would have to go outside the ship and do the job with phaser rifles. Jack Crusher was the first to volunteer, and Joseph was chosen to go with him. It made sense. Both men had experience performing hull repairs and had proven they could negotiate the ship's exterior.

That last part was important. After all, the transporters weren't working, so Picard couldn't provide them with a lifeline. They would have to make the trip to the nacelle and back on their own.

Crusher and Joseph looked cool and determined as they climbed out an airlock and started their journey. With the sensors down, the captain couldn't watch them. He could only keep track of their progress via their helmet communicators.

It took a long time to cut through the nacelle assembly,

but that was understandable, considering the thickness of the ship's skin. Then they sliced into the transfer tunnel, and the energies collected there shut down their communicators—forcing Picard and his remaining officers to *guess* how the expedition was faring.

And the guesses grew more dire as time elapsed. Too *much* time, they decided after a while. Over the objections of Ben Zoma, Picard's first officer, the captain donned a containment suit and went after his men. Minutes later, he discovered Joseph drifting alongside the hull, unconscious.

Picard could have gone after Crusher and tried to bring *both* men in. However, he chose to bring Joseph in first—and because of that decision, both he and Pug survived.

Because he had barely negotiated the curve of the *Stargazer*'s hull, putting her nacelle out of sight, when the ship bucked savagely beneath his feet.

There was no air in space to carry the noise, but something had exploded. At first, Picard thought it might have been the warp-field generator, but that would have been massive enough to destroy the entire ship. Later he would find out it was just a pocket of accumulated energy.

When it went off, it completed the job Crusher and Joseph had started, jerking the nacelle free. But Picard couldn't see that from where he was crouching on the hull. For the moment, all he knew in his heart was this: that his friend Jack Crusher had perished.

The captain brought Joseph back inside the ship, then went back out to find Jack. And he found him, all right. But as he had feared, his friend was dead.

When Joseph came to, he said he had blacked out in the face of all that energy. At the time, no one guessed that it was just a story, and that Joseph had lost his nerve. He had run, abandoning Jack, leaving him alone to carry out their assignment.

That was why, in the end, Joseph had survived and Jack had not—because the security officer had escaped the blast when the energy pocket finally exploded, severing the nacelle.

On the *Stargazer*, no one suspected that Joseph had panicked. No one knew that Jack's death might have been avoided—that he might have survived if his colleague had remained alongside him a little longer.

Joseph kept his guilt over Jack's death locked inside him for years, allowing it to eat at him like a Regulan bloodworm. He might have kept it there the rest of his life except for a visit to Picard's *Enterprise*-D.

Joseph and others who had served on the *Stargazer* were reunited there for the coronation of one of their colleagues—a D'aavit named Morgen, who had become a captain by then. And for the first time since Jack's death, Joseph was placed in the company of Jack's widow, Beverly.

At the urging of Guinan, Picard's El-Aurian bartender, Joseph told Beverly the truth about her husband's death. But far from hating him for it, Beverly forgave him.

"That was a long time ago," the captain pointed out.

"Still," Joseph insisted. With what seemed like an effort, he smiled. "On top of that, Doctor Crusher's been good to me. I'd like to pay her back a little."

Picard looked at him. "Good to you . . . ?"

Joseph shrugged. "You remember that problem I had for a while—with alcohol?"

"Yes, of course," said the captain, wondering what that had to do with Beverly. "But my understanding is that you managed to overcome it. Unless . . ."

Joseph waved away the notion. "No, I haven't fallen off the wagon. But I'd still be a drinker if I hadn't had help from Doctor Crusher. She's the one who contacted me after I left the *Enterprise* and convinced me that I needed treatment."

Picard didn't know a thing about it. He said so.

"That's not all," said Joseph. "She spoke to some people she knew and got me into a rehab center. She even spent a shore leave there once, playing a miserable game of *sharash'di* and listening to my old *Stargazer* stories."

"Really," said the captain, feeling vaguely discomfited.

He had believed he knew Beverly better than any man alive. But as it turned out, there was more to his friend the doctor than met the eye—even *his*.

"So I've got even more reason to want to get her out of there," Joseph explained.

No more than I, Picard reflected. *However, that is not the reason we were dispatched.*

"Our priority," he said by way of a reminder, "is the Kevrata. Starfleet did not send us on a rescue mission."

Joseph chuckled in a decidedly conspiratorial way. "And Queen Isabella didn't send Columbus to discover the Americas. But he managed to pull it off anyway."

For the sake of his duty to the Kevrata, the captain frowned. "Columbus found the Americas by *mistake.*"

"That's *his* story," said Joseph.

———◆———

Commander Donatra didn't know whether to curse Tomalak's arrogance or just laugh.

"Not even the Second Fleet?" she asked.

"Not even that," confirmed Suran, who was sitting across the wardroom table from her. His gray-haired presence had always been reassuring to Donatra, especially in the days when she first served beneath him. "No Defense Force ship has made a move toward Romulus in days. It seems Tomalak is determined to defend Tal'aura with the forces already gathered about him."

"That is good news," said Donatra. "In a numerically even fight, we will certainly prevail."

Suran shrugged beneath the weight of his severe, linked-metal tunic. "Perhaps."

Donatra regarded her comrade—no longer her superior these last few years, but her peer—with undisguised wonder. "Our command personnel are a hundred times more vital than Tomalak's. We have firebrands in our center seats, hungry to take back the Empire by any means necessary. Tomalak has elder statesmen, more adept at charming the wives of the Hundred over expensive wine chalices than giving orders in the heat of battle."

"True," said Suran, who wasn't above playing the role of an elder statesman himself when circumstances called for it. "But I know Tomalak. He is not a risk-taker. If he appears content with the sea-stones dealt him, there is a reason for it."

Donatra considered the insight. "Is it possible that he would like to bring the First and Second Fleets home—but can't? Because something else demands their attention?"

"Anything is possible," said Suran, "but I do not know what that something might be. There is unrest among the rim worlds, no question—but not enough to occupy both the First Fleet and the Second. And at the moment, neither the Federation nor the Klingons seem inclined to threaten our borders."

It was true. If anything, the Federation appeared eager to build on the alliance they had cobbled together.

"Perhaps some other threat, then," Donatra suggested. "Something of which we are as yet unaware."

Suran's expression told her he didn't believe that. He was just too considerate to say so.

Donatra decided to change the subject. "In the meantime, I have been in contact with Braeg. He assures me that the people are responding to his rhetoric, both in the capital and the countryside. Every day, he shakes the foundations of Tal'aura's authority a little more."

Suran smiled. "You sound like a centurion who beamed aboard my warbird twelve years ago, saying she couldn't wait to destroy the enemies of the Empire."

"Was I that eager?" Donatra asked.

"Every bit," her comrade said. "And do you remember the counsel I gave you at the time?"

All too well. "You told me to slow down—there would be no shortage of enemies for me to destroy."

"Nor is there a shortage now," said Suran, "even if they originate within the Empire rather than without. That is why my advice today is the same as then: Temper your eagerness. In time, I believe, Braeg will prevail. If I thought otherwise, I would not be here. But it will not happen overnight, no matter how promising the admiral's reports may be."

"Shinzon's coup took a few seconds," Donatra pointed out. "Just long enough to turn the Senate to dust."

"Yes," said Suran, "and look what became of it. Shinzon's reign lasted hardly any longer than his victim's cries of terror. We would do better to move slowly and make certain of our support before we reach for Tal'aura's throat."

Donatra smiled, grateful for her comrade's advice. "You are too wise for your own good, Suran."

"On occasion," he said, "that is true. But fortunately, I am wise enough for yours."

Abruptly, a third voice filled the room—one that came to them over the warbird's communications system. *"I sorely regret the interruption, Commander, but Commander Suran's first officer wishes to speak with him."*

Donatra glanced at Suran. He nodded.

"By all means," said Donatra, "put him through."

A moment later they heard from Vorander, Suran's second-in-command. Apparently, there was a discipline issue aboard the *T'sarok* that required Suran's attention.

"It's an epidemic," said Donatra.

"So it would appear," Suran responded.

It was perhaps the tenth incident that had cropped up in the last few days, and it seemed unlikely it would be the last. But then, Romulan centurions weren't accustomed to playing the waiting game. They craved action.

And their commanders are no different, Donatra mused.

Suran rose and said, "I should take care of this. We will speak again later."

But not in person, Donatra reflected. And that made it less satisfying, somehow. "Long live the Empire."

"The Empire," Suran echoed, and left Donatra sitting there alone in her wardroom.

With her colleague gone, she could hear the rhythmic throbbing of the *Valdore*'s engines through the bulkheads. It was a good sound, as reassuring as Suran's presence in its way, and even more so considering how recently the engines had been rendered silent.

Donatra remembered every detail perfectly—the flash and hull-piercing impact of Shinzon's torpedoes, the way she had been thrown across the deck, the metallic taste of blood in her mouth. She remembered too how helpless she had felt after she realized the extent of the damage.

No propulsion, no weapons, not even a forward shield. All she could do was contact her ally, Captain Picard, and let him know he had to fight on alone.

But Donatra's engineering team was among the canniest in the Empire. It hadn't taken long for them to get the engines running again and return the *Valdore* to fighting form.

So she can take part in the struggle against Tal'aura, the commander thought. So she could shake the pretender free of the throne she had claimed so quickly, and to which she clung now with such consummate stubbornness.

Of course, Braeg was doing all the fighting for now. Once again he had whipped a crowd into frenzy, inflaming it with his criticisms of Tal'aura's misguided regime. And once again, the praetor had demonstrated her weakness by declining to send her centurions to arrest him.

Donatra sympathized with the crowd in the capital.

She appreciated how difficult it was to ignore Braeg, how difficult it was to turn one's back on him.

The first time she encountered Braeg had been years earlier, in the D'nossos System, when she was still serving as Suran's first officer. As head of a special task force, the admiral impressed Donatra with his courage and his cunning.

Not to mention his dark good looks.

Braeg had occasion, as it turned out, to notice *her* virtues as well. During the battle in which they finally routed the Tellati, Donatra came across a warbird whose command staff had perished. Beaming aboard with a couple of her subordinates, she returned the vessel to the fray and launched a critical assault on the enemy's flank.

Suran boasted about her brilliance in the affair as if she were his own daughter. But that wasn't the highest praise she received for her effort—because shortly thereafter, Braeg offered her command of one of his ships.

Any officer in the fleet would have given a limb to command a warbird under Admiral Braeg. Donatra, to the surprise of even Suran, turned the offer down.

At the time, she was too devoted to Suran to accept a berth anywhere but on the *T'sarok*. There were those who told her that her loyalty had destroyed a potentially splendid career, and she wondered if they weren't right.

But Braeg wasn't insulted. Far from it. Never having met anyone self-possessed enough to disdain his largesse, he wanted to know more about Donatra. He delved into her military files and whatever else he could find, studying her as he might study an adversary on the field of battle.

Finally, having learned all he could from secondary sources, the admiral made arrangements to confront Donatra in person. That was the only way, he explained later, that he felt he could truly plumb her depths.

Their "chance" encounter at an imperial training facility in the Reggiana system, where Donatra had been invited to lecture, began as a polite give-and-take on matters of military philosophy. However, it evolved into a heated discussion, and soon became even more heated—though it could no longer be called a mere discussion.

Until then, Donatra would not have believed that an encounter between two accomplished military combatants could result in a victory for both parties. But that night, it was exactly what happened.

And from then on, Braeg became her lover.

It wasn't public knowledge that they were so entwined. It couldn't be, or both their careers would suffer. Braeg made Donatra pledge to keep their secret even from Suran, a vow she made reluctantly but had yet to violate.

It was difficult enough for Donatra and Braeg to meet while Donatra was a first officer. When she became a full commander and received the *Valdore,* it became even more so. But in her worst moments of longing and frustration, she pacified herself with the promise that someday she and Braeg would be together.

It was only a matter of time.

And now, strangely, that time was nearly at hand. Days ago, Braeg resigned his position in the Imperial Defense Force—something he had never imagined himself doing—and dedicated himself to Praetor Tal'aura's downfall.

Braeg had never had a taste for politics before. He had been content to leave that serpent's nest to the noble Hundred who claimed it as their birthright.

However, he had grown disgusted watching Tal'aura degrade the Empire with her ineptitude, squandering what he had fought so hard and so long to attain. The praetor's only true talent, it seemed, was in the area of self-preservation.

So Braeg had decided to offer himself to the people as an alternative. Not forever, of course. Just until someone better suited to the job could take over, leaving the admiral free again to do what he did best.

In Braeg's eyes, he was still fighting for the glory of the mighty Romulan Empire. He was just doing it in a new theater of operations.

And Donatra hadn't hesitated to become Braeg's fiercest ally—not because she was his lover, but because she believed in his cause as much as he did. In no time at all, the praetor had allowed the rim world crisis to spiral out of control; she had to be replaced before she could do any more damage.

How could I ever have aligned myself with someone like Tal'aura? Donatra wondered with a flush of embarrassment. *Someone so selfish, so insane for power?*

Then again, Donatra had sided with Shinzon, and he was even worse. Clearly, her judgment had been lacking in the area of political alliances. *But not this time,* she thought. Braeg was an honorable man, a leader who would restore prosperity to the Empire.

All he has to do is prevail over Tal'aura, Donatra

reflected. It was a difficult task, to be sure, but hardly an impossible one. And once he accomplished it, they would be together, finally and for always.

It is just a matter of time. . . .

Worf shook his massive head and rumbled, "I do not like it."

Geordi considered the *Enterprise*-E's newly refurbished mess hall, with its free-form seating arrangements and its long, narrow observation ports. Somehow, the place had looked better in the blueprint stages.

"It'll take some getting used to," the engineer conceded. "But after a while, we'll probably forget it was ever—"

Worf turned to him, his dark eyes narrowing beneath his brooding ledge of a brow. "I am *not* talking about the interior decoration. I am speaking of Doctor Crusher."

Geordi felt as if a weight had been placed on his shoulders—or rather *re*placed. "Right."

Ever since the captain told them about the doctor's disappearance, the engineer had done his grudging best to put his concerns about his friend aside. After all, he had a duty to make sure the ship was outfitted correctly. A single oversight could cost a crewman his life some day.

He couldn't do anything about Doctor Crusher. However, he *could* make sure the *Enterprise*-E was everything it needed to be.

Worf, on the other hand, wasn't an engineer. He didn't have as many critical decisions on his hands, which left his mind free to dwell on Beverly's plight.

"The captain should never have gone after her without

us," the Klingon insisted, his voice echoing raucously throughout the mess hall.

"He didn't have a say in the matter," Geordi noted calmly. "Apparently, Starfleet Command was pretty clear about that."

Worf's lip curled in disgust. "Every last official at Starfleet Command should be dipped in honey and spread-eagled naked on a mound of fire ants."

Geordi was tempted to agree. He and his colleagues from the *Enterprise*-E were still a family, no matter what anyone thought. Data might be gone and the rest of them might have been dispersed to the four corners of the galaxy, but that didn't mean they cared any less about each other.

If Beverly had gone incommunicado in the midst of a clandestine mission, it wasn't the captain's business alone. Geordi and Worf should have been brought in on the matter, and their friends on the *Starship Titan* as well.

Worf made a sound of exasperation. "We do not even know the nature of Doctor Crusher's mission."

In recent years, Captain Picard had shared everything with them. But all he said this time was that Beverly was missing in action, and that he had been asked to lend a hand. Then he boarded a shuttle for parts unknown.

"What if the captain goes missing as well?" Worf asked. "Will they send us *then?*"

Geordi turned to an observation port and peered out at the stars. "I'd feel better if I just knew where she was."

"You would *not* feel better," Worf shot back. "Because if you knew her whereabouts, you would be tempted to join the captain and provide assistance."

"Me?" said the engineer, turning to look back over his shoulder. "What about *you?*"

Worf lifted his bearded chin. "I learned much in serving as a diplomat. Restraint, for example."

Geordi looked at his friend askance. "So if you knew where Doctor Crusher and the captain were, you wouldn't go charging in after them?"

Worf's eyes smoldered. "I said that I had learned restraint, not cowardice. Knowing what I know now, I would take a moment to learn about the situation at hand—to immerse myself in its complexities, to appreciate the motivations of all involved. *Then* I would go charging in."

Geordi couldn't help smiling a little. His friend really *had* learned something in his stint as a diplomat.

"The question," said Worf, "is whether you would follow your impulses and accompany me."

The engineer felt an unexpected chill climb his spine. "We're still talking about the hypothetical here, aren't we?"

Worf's brow furrowed. "I do not know. Are we?"

Geordi looked askance at his friend. "You mean you'd go after the captain? For real?"

The Klingon hesitated for a moment—but *just* a moment. "Given the opportunity, yes."

"Come on," said Geordi, trying to inject some reason into the conversation. "Going after Captain Picard without official sanction—it could get us court-martialed."

"Without question," said Worf. "But," he continued in a softer yet more emotionally charged tone, "there are more important things than one's rank."

Geordi couldn't argue with that. Beverly wasn't just

another reported missing-in-action. She was his friend, his comrade, someone in whom he had confided things he would have told no one else. She had given him strength when he needed it, stood by him through his greatest trials.

Hell—she had saved his *life*.

What if she's really dead? asked a voice inside him.

No, he insisted stubbornly. The captain hadn't believed it and neither would he. Beverly might have been gentle and caring, but she was tougher than most people might believe.

Not dead, he told himself firmly. *Alive.* But clearly, operating in perilous conditions, or the report wouldn't have gone out in the first place. *And if that's so, the captain may need a hand getting her back.*

Geordi looked around. There was still the question of the retrofit, which had a long way to go. "I'd hate to leave the rehab crew by itself."

Worf rolled his eyes. "Do you think everything would grind to a halt without you?"

The engineer started to protest that it might.

"The truth is," Worf said peremptorily, "you could be gone for days before anyone realized it."

"Maybe not days . . ."

"You understand my point."

Geordi realized he couldn't argue that either. The retrofit *could* go on without him. All he had to do was leave someone in charge to answer any questions that came up.

"Well?" said Worf.

Geordi whistled softly. It was a crazy idea, no doubt about it. Maybe the craziest he had ever considered.

But for Beverly, he would do it.

"I'm in," he said. "But first, we've got to find out where the captain went."

The Klingon nodded. "Any ideas?"

Geordi had a few of them. After a couple of decades in Starfleet, a lot of people owed him favors. It seemed like a good time to cash in on them.

4

AS PICARD'S SHUTTLE SOARED OVER A SURF-WREATHED
beach, he got a better look at the lush expanse of forest
that stretched beyond it. Nestled within the greenery was
a low, clay-colored compound.

"That's it?" he asked.

"That's it," his pilot confirmed.

She headed for the compound, found an open patch of
relatively level ground, and gently set their craft down on
the grass. Then she turned to the captain and said, "Go
ahead, sir."

It would have been quicker and easier for Picard to
simply beam down from Pug Joseph's cargo vessel. But
like many high-security installations in the Federation,
the penal settlement was protected by a transparent but
highly active energy field that made site-to-site transport
impossible.

Picard moved aft through the shuttle, pressed the

hatch control on the bulkhead, and watched the door slide open. It admitted a warm, pine-scented breeze and an unexpectedly raucous chorus of bird cries. Stepping outside, the captain shaded his eyes against the afternoon sun and looked around.

A stocky, dark-haired officer was walking out to greet him, the buildings behind her barely visible through the trees. Her smile was so big she seemed to squint.

"Good to meet you," the officer said when she got close enough to be heard over the birdsong. She extended her hand. "I'm Monica Esperanza."

"The pleasure is mine," said Picard.

"Please," said Esperanza, "follow me."

The captain allowed her to lead him up a path that meandered among the trees. It was cool there, shaded as it was from the sun, and the fragrance of pine was even stronger.

"How is Doctor Greyhorse?" Picard asked.

"Eager to see you," said Esperanza.

"Yes," said Picard, "I imagine he would be. But that is not what I am wondering about."

The woman turned to him. "You want to know if it's wise for him to participate in a mission of this magnitude. Or for that matter, any mission at all."

The captain nodded. "That is correct."

"Well," said Esperanza, "I'm the one who cleared Doctor Greyhorse for Admiral Edrich, so that should tell you something. The doctor has come a long way, Captain. He's no longer the man who tried to kill those people on your ship."

"I am pleased to hear that," said Picard. "After all,

Greyhorse was my friend and a great talent as a physician. What's more, there is no mission without him. But we will be in constant peril on Kevratas. If Doctor Greyhorse is likely to buckle under the strain, I need to know that in advance."

"I understand your concern," said Esperanza. "However, in my professional opinion, Doctor Greyhorse is no more likely to do that now than when he served on the *Stargazer.*"

It made Picard feel better to hear that.

"Have you ever had occasion to visit a penal settlement?" Esperanza asked.

"I have not," said the captain. It was something he supposed he should be thankful for. "It is more pleasant here than I would have imagined."

Indeed, it was the sort of place he might have chosen for a picnic, had he been inclined to have one, and if there were someone to join him. *An idyllic locale,* he thought, *without question.* But it was still a prison.

And Greyhorse had spent the last fourteen years of his life there, enjoying only those limited freedoms he could earn by cooperating with his therapists. A man who had traveled the vast, majestic distances between stars, confined to such a small and unchanging place . . .

It was difficult for Picard to imagine. Almost as difficult to imagine as what the doctor had done to compel the Federation to put him there.

"When the compound was originally built," said Esperanza, "more than a century ago, it wasn't nearly this pleasant. Prisoners—as they were called then—lived in small, stark cells instead of freestanding cottages. Security systems were much more visible. The overall atmosphere was one of mistrust."

As she said that, she and the captain emerged from the embrace of the forest and gained an unrestricted view of the compound. He could see now that it was actually a collection of unconnected buildings with smooth, silicon-composite walls and large, airy windows.

"Things have changed," Picard observed.

"Indeed they have," said his guide.

Walking up to the first building in their path, Esperanza ascended a series of steps and went through an arched entranceway. Picard followed her into an anteroom furnished with exotic flowers, leathery-looking furniture, and evidence of the tribal culture that had originated in this part of the world.

There was a security officer stationed at a desk to one side of the entrance. At a sign from Esperanza, he tapped a command into the panel in front of him. Then he looked up at Picard and said, "He'll be right out, sir."

"Thank you," said the captain.

As a student of archaeology, he had some interest in the Maori artifacts on the walls, and under other circumstances would have inspected them more closely. But at the moment, he was too eager to see Greyhorse.

After what seemed like a very long time, an interior door slid aside and two men walked into the room. One was a security officer whom Picard had never seen before. The other had once been his chief medical officer on the *Stargazer*.

Picard didn't know what he had expected to see. Greyhorse had been incarcerated for so long, it wouldn't have surprised the captain if the doctor had been diminished in some way.

However, Greyhorse was every bit as impressive as Picard remembered, his shoulders jutting like boulders from a mountainside, his features as proud as if they had been chiseled from stone. And despite all he had done and tried to do, the captain was still glad to see him.

"Doctor Greyhorse," he said.

Greyhorse didn't smile. But then, he never had, not in all the time Picard had known him.

"You look well," the doctor observed in his deep, cultured voice.

Truthfully, the captain wouldn't *feel* well until he had found Beverly. But he accepted the remark without objection.

"Is Mister Joseph with you?" asked Greyhorse.

"No," said the captain. "Mister Joseph—Pug—is in orbit, awaiting our arrival. It appears we will all three be working together again."

Greyhorse nodded. "Just like old times. An unlikely prospect, I grant you, and yet one I eagerly embrace."

Picard couldn't help smiling a little at the doctor's enthusiasm. "Come on then. Let's not keep Pug waiting."

Decalon gazed out the observation port, mesmerized by what he saw there. *Stars,* he thought. *So many stars . . .*

One of them, too far off to discern with the naked eye, bathed Romulus in its warmth. Decalon remembered watching that star diminish behind him as he made his way to a new life in the Federation, certain that he was seeing it for the last time. And yet, in a few days he would be watching it wax larger again, welcoming its native son to its embrace as if he had never left.

As if nothing had changed.

It was a disconcerting thought. *I have changed,* Decalon insisted. *I am not the man who left the Empire more than a decade ago. I am calmer now, more contemplative.*

I am at peace.

In truth, he was more like a Vulcan now, though he had mixed feelings about that association. One could reject the Empire and all it represented without aligning oneself with the particular principles of Vulcan logic. Surak, wise as he was, did not have a monopoly on serenity.

Ignoring the stars for a moment, Decalon focused on his reflection in the observation port. As far as he could tell, he didn't look any different from the day he had left Romulus. The crow's-feet at the limits of his eyes were no deeper, the loose skin at the corners of his mouth no looser.

Appearances, he thought, quoting a Romulan adage, *are the glimmer of sun on water.* It was one of the few bits of homeworld wisdom to which Decalon still clung.

I am different, he insisted. *I must be. Otherwise, what was the point of leaving?*

As he thought that, he saw someone else's reflection loom behind him. It was that of Captain Momosaki, the commanding officer of the *Starship Zodiac.*

"This must be difficult for you," Momosaki observed, smiling in apparent sympathy.

Decalon shrugged his shoulders. "A small adjustment."

"It's understandable," said Momosaki. "You risked your life in order to leave Romulus."

"Others risked their lives as well," the Romulan noted.

Indeed, dozens of his people had died helping to set up the network that would smuggle Decalon and others like him out of the Empire. And it wasn't just Romulans who had given their lives. Starfleet officers had done so as well.

Decalon had thought many times about their sacrifices, their courage. They never knew the identities of those whose lives they were saving, and yet they were willing to put everything on the line for them.

It was the reason Decalon had agreed to assist in the mission at hand. If those others could place themselves in deadly jeopardy for a stranger, how could he fail to return the favor? Especially when the Starfleet admiral who approached him had asked so nicely?

To that point, Decalon had been quite content living in the enclave established for his people on Santora Prime. He had become a senator, albeit in a very small and humble imitation of the homeworld Senate. He had grown a summer squash garden that was the envy of his neighbors.

Then Edrich had come to him and described the circumstances. Captain Picard, he said, needed Decalon's help. And Picard, along with his Betazoid counselor, had been instrumental in delivering that first trio of Romulan defectors to freedom nearly fifteen years earlier, paving the way for dozens of other defections.

Including that of Decalon himself.

"Are you familiar," he asked, "with the writings of a human named Thomas Wolfe?"

Momosaki thought for a moment. "*You Can't Go Home Again? That* Thomas Wolfe?"

"One of my neighbors on Santora Prime brought his work to my attention. I found it most eloquent when I read it—and even more so now, considering the circumstances in which I find myself."

"Don't think of it as home," said Momosaki. "It's just where your mission happens to be taking you."

It was an interesting approach, Decalon had to admit. But he doubted that it would work. Romulans were not transient by nature. They became attached to their domiciles in a way it was difficult for non-Romulans to understand.

Nonetheless, to be polite to Momosaki, Decalon said, "I will remember that."

Eborion entered the stone chamber beneath his family's palace early enough not to be late, but late enough not to be confused with someone who was concerned about what others thought of him.

Faces turned in the soft, artificial light, all of them familiar. But then, each of them bore at least a passing resemblance to Eborion—not surprising, perhaps, considering they were all aunts, uncles, and close cousins.

The nobleman did a quick count. Apparently, he was the last of the sixteen in the family council to have arrived. *Only fitting,* he thought, *for one who has the ear of the praetor.*

Clabaros, the eldest of Eborion's three long-faced uncles, second in age only to Eborion's long-deceased father, cast a vaguely reproachful glance at his nephew. It was Clabaros who had, in his brother's stead, taken it upon himself to tutor young Eborion in the ways of Romulan society.

"Thank you for coming," Clabaros grumbled in his courtly but understated way, his voice echoing slightly among the stones. "If you will be seated, we can begin."

Eborion's uncles, aunts, and cousins took their places around the long, crimson-and-cream-colored marble table that had served their family for hundreds of years. Though a stranger might not have noticed, each seat represented a different level of importance in the family hierarchy.

Claboros, for instance, sat at the head of the table, at its northern extremity. His brothers Rijanus and Obrix sat on one side of him and his sister Cly'rana sat on the other.

Cly'rana, a great beauty by all accounts, alone seemed to bear no resemblance to the rest of the family. She was either a throwback to some recessive set of genes or the product of an extramarital dalliance, as was rumored about the capital. Even if the latter explanation was based in fact, it had not diminished her standing in the family's stone chamber.

But then, Cly'rana was not just beautiful. She was also exceedingly clever, and there wasn't a family among the Hundred that could not benefit from a little more cleverness.

Eborion's place, which was nearly at the opposite end of the table from Claboros's, was not one of advanced status. Only his cousins Tinicitis and Solops, who were seated to his right, enjoyed less of a say in family matters.

But that will change soon enough, Eborion thought.

After all, he had secretly made himself one of Tal'aura's confidants. And he would shortly be her very *closest* confidant, if all the pieces fell into place for him.

First, Claboros called for reports on the family's holdings throughout the Empire. These were rendered by the youngest relatives in attendance. Solops described the profitability of their agricultural ventures, which he had lately extended to a fifteenth colony world. Tinicitis spoke proudly of their investment activities, which had allowed them to participate in the successful businesses of less wealthy families.

When it was Eborion's turn, he brought everyone up to date on developments in their weapons manufacturing plants. As usual, their technology was ahead of their competitors', allowing them to maintain their position as the foremost supplier of disruptor systems to the Empire's warbird fleets.

"Naturally," said Rijanus. "We have the best engineers working for us." It was a reference to a precept put forth by Inarthos, Eborion's paternal grandfather: *Gather the brightest and most innovative individuals in their field, and make yourself wealthier on the strength of their gifts.*

Inarthos's insights into the armaments business were used as touchstones around the marble table. After all, it was Inarthos who had supplied the Empire with directed-energy weapons during the war with Earth some two hundred years ago, trebling his family's already considerable fortune.

"Yes," Eborion said in response to his uncle's remark, "we *do* have the best engineers."

What he *didn't* say was how thoroughly the weapons

business bored him, and how glad he would be to give it up some day. Were it not for its place in the family's history, he would have lobbied for another assignment long ago.

"We have also made inroads into the hand weapons market," Eborion went on. "Before the year is out we hope to be the second biggest supplier of such items, and a year later we should be at the top of the mountain."

"Excellent," said Claboros. He glanced at Eborion's cousins as well. "All of you."

The last three words got under Eborion's skin. He wasn't like his cousins in the least, and he hated being lumped together with them. But out of deference to Claboros, he kept his objections to himself.

The young ones' reports made and accepted, the family's *real* agenda got under way. It was at this time that they would identify threats to their accumulated wealth, as well as unexplored opportunities to expand it.

"As you know," Claboros said soberly, "the praetor has to this point managed to put down any serious threats to her rule. However, Admiral Braeg seems to represent an exception."

"The people love him," Obrix observed.

Rijanus dismissed the remark with a gesture. "The people are fickle, brother. Today they love Braeg. Tomorrow they will love someone else."

"I don't think so," Obrix insisted. "Braeg is a war hero, remember. And he comes from common stock."

"*And* he has the loyalty of many of his old comrades," said Cly'rana. "Enough, some believe, to hold his own in a civil war, if it comes to that."

"It won't," Rijanus argued.

"But what if it does?" Claboros asked. "How will it affect us? In the long term? The short term? And what measures should we take to protect our assets?"

"In the short term, it will bolster our weapons business," Eborion reported dutifully, though it was a rather obvious conclusion.

"In the longer term," said Solops, "there may be food shortages. The price of our grain will go up."

"But our security costs will go up as well," Obrix noted. "There will be widespread looting, and the occasional mob of commoners who have gotten their hands on a weapons cache."

"Yes," said Rijanus, "civil conflicts always bring out the worst in the common people."

"Perhaps we should speak with Admiral Braeg," said Cly'rana, "to get a sense of his intentions. Surreptitiously, of course. We wouldn't want Tal'aura to imagine our unmitigated support for her has diminished."

"Our father dealt with a rebel once," said Obrix. "And that fact preserved us when other families fell."

Claboros made a face. "It would be a delicate maneuver. And a dangerous one."

"It might be *more* dangerous to assume a posture of complacency," said Cly'rana. "If we are precise, we can play both sides with a minimum of risk."

"We need to find out what the other houses are doing," Claboros told them. "We don't want to inadvertently put ourselves at odds with any of our allies—or in league with any of our enemies."

"Would Braeg even be receptive to an overture from one of the Hundred?" asked Obrix. "Sometimes these rebels are too idealistic to accept help from a noble house."

"Or too stupid," added Cly'rana. "But I don't believe Braeg is guilty of either charge. If it pleases the council, I will personally see to the—"

"The praetor will deal with him," Eborion announced, though it was customary for the family's elders to resolve their differences of opinion before anyone else had a say.

It was as if he had dropped a pebble into a still mountain pool. Everyone turned to him, eyebrows raised in surprise and—in the cases of Cly'rana and Rijanus, at least—amusement.

"How can you be so certain?" asked Claboros.

How indeed, Eborion thought, feeling a cold drop of perspiration make its way down his back.

He had resolved not to reveal his position in Tal'aura's court until he knew it was perfectly secure. He had promised himself that he would keep his mouth shut. But he was sorely tempted now to tell his uncle everything he had done and where it had gotten him, and where it would get *all* of them if they accorded him the respect he was due.

No, he insisted inwardly. It was not the proper time. And as his uncles were fond of pointing out, Inarthos had been a great believer in timing.

"I have observed the praetor," was all Eborion said in the end, "and I am confident in her abilities."

"I wish *I* were so confident," said Obrix. A ripple of laughter followed on the heels of his remark, turning Eborion's cheeks a hot, dark shade of green.

"What about the rim worlds?" asked Claboros, mercifully turning the conversation in a different direction. "Braeg seems to mention them often enough in his diatribes."

"They are in turmoil," said Obrix, "by all accounts."

"However," said Rijanus, "our exposure there is minimal. We have few interests on the planets in question."

"What if the spirit of rebellion spreads?" asked Obrix. "We have interests on planets in the next tier."

Rijanus shrugged. "Rebels are always poorly armed and poorly organized. They are not visionaries. They are simply opportunists, taking advantage of the confusion that inevitably follows a change in regime."

"So you discount them as a threat?" asked Claboros.

"To *our* house," said Rijanus, "yes."

Cly'rana shook her head, loosening her nest of braided black tresses. It was all it took for her to gain everyone's attention.

"Need I remind you," she asked Rijanus sweetly, "that what affects one house often affects another? Three of our closest friends among the Hundred will be profoundly affected by what transpires on Kevratas."

Rijanus laughed scornfully. "We have no allies with substantial holdings on the rim."

"I did not say they were our allies," Cly'rana replied in the same inoffensive tone. "I said they were our *friends*. What else would you call someone who furthers your interests and adds to your wealth . . . whether he is aware of it or not?"

Claboros nodded, then looked around the table, wordlessly soliciting further comment. No one spoke—Eborion least of all. He was not about to make the same mistake twice.

"It seems," said Claboros, "that the situation on the rim worlds requires investigation. Braeg as well, if he is as formidable as some of us appear to believe."

"You will receive full reports on both matters at our next meeting," promised Tinicitis, presuming to speak for everyone at his end of the table.

Eborion wanted to rebuke him, to tell him what a sniveling rodent he was. But he held himself in check.

"I am glad to see you take the initiative," Claboros told Tinicitis. "However, considering the urgency of these matters, I think we would be ill advised to wait until our next scheduled meeting." He looked around the table. "I will see you all back in this chamber in four days."

It was not the first time Claboros had convened the family on short notice. However, it was a rare occurrence, and a measure of his concern. Of course, that was how their house had risen to prominence and remained there—by dealing with problems before they became full-fledged disasters.

"Until then, good health to you all," said Claboros, "and long live the Empire."

"The Empire," everyone echoed.

The meeting was over. In twos and threes, Eborion's relatives pushed their chairs out and got to their feet.

Only Eborion remained in his chair, reluctant to face the patronizing looks he knew he would get from his relatives. He had been made to look the buffoon because he couldn't divulge his dealings with the praetor.

But that would not be the case forever. Eventually, he

would let them know what he had accomplished. And after that, he would be *listening* to business reports instead of giving them.

As he thought that, Eborion felt a hand alight softly on his shoulder. Turning, he saw that it belonged to Cly'rana.

"You appeared overeager today," she noted, looking at him askance. "It was unlike you, nephew. Usually, you are much more measured in your actions."

Eborion swallowed. "It seems I was not myself."

His aunt looked at him a moment longer. Then she said, "That is one explanation," and walked away.

She suspects something, he told himself, as the hiss of Cly'rana's slippered footfalls marked her departure. *I must be more circumspect in her presence.*

He remained seated at the crimson and white table until he was certain Cly'rana and everyone else had left the underground level. Only then did he get up and head for the circular stair that led to his family's palace, and the light of the sun.

As Decalon materialized on the transporter platform of the *Annabel Lee,* he looked to Picard much like any other Romulan. His eyes were dark and inquisitive, his ears pointed, his hair severely cut. It was unmarred by strands of gray despite his inclination toward what was—for Romulans, at least—late middle age.

"Captain Picard," said Decalon, stepping down from the platform. "I am pleased to meet you."

Romulans usually remained distant in their dealings

with other species, giving away nothing of their inner thoughts. However, Decalon's tone betrayed undeniable enthusiasm.

"After all," the Romulan continued, "it is largely because of you that I was able to emigrate from the Empire. One might say I owe you my life."

Ah, the captain mused. *So* that's *it.* "Do not give it a second thought. I am glad I had the opportunity to help."

"No more than I," said Decalon.

"If you will follow me," said Picard, gesturing to the exit, "I will introduce you to Captain Joseph and Doctor Greyhorse, the other members of our team."

"Actually," Decalon said peremptorily, amid the beginnings of a frown, "I would like to ask you a question, Captain. Concerning Doctor Greyhorse."

The captain had a feeling he knew what the question would be. However, he allowed Decalon to frame it.

"Admiral Edrich seemed to believe that Doctor Greyhorse was as capable as Doctor Crusher of devising a cure for the Kevatran plague. Is that your estimate as well?"

It wasn't at all the question Picard was expecting. It made him wonder how much Edrich had told Decalon, especially with regard to Greyhorse's past.

"It is," the captain assured Decalon. "Doctor Greyhorse is a brilliant individual, and he worked with Doctor Crusher on a cure for other variants of the disease."

The Romulan nodded. "That is good to know."

Perhaps it was better that Decalon didn't possess any other information about Greyhorse. If Starfleet was right about the doctor, he was no longer capable of committing

the crimes he attempted on the *Enterprise*. He had reha-
bilitated himself, wiped the slate clean.

And if that was true, who was Picard to scrawl warn-
ings across it? "Come," he told the Romulan. "Joseph and
Greyhorse will be eager to meet you."

5

———◆———

I'M ALIVE.

It came as a surprise to her. But if she was capable of being surprised, it had to be true: *I'm alive.*

Opening her eyes, Beverly Crusher saw that she was lying on a bed, her Kevratan disguise gone along with her holo-unit. Without it, no one could have mistaken her for anything but human.

The room in which she found herself was small and square, perhaps three meters across. It was bounded on three sides by gray stone walls that looked worn enough to be hundreds of years old. The fourth "wall" was a shimmering, yellow-white energy barrier.

A prison cell, she concluded.

Not that Beverly was complaining. Being in prison was still a significant improvement over what she had expected when she felt the kick of that point-blank disruptor.

Obviously, whoever had shot her had set his weapon on a lower energy level—one that would knock her out, but fall short of killing her. Romulans didn't often settle for that option. Most of the time, they preferred their enemies dead.

If they had diverged from that policy, it was because they had questions to ask her—for starters, what was an offworlder doing on Kevratas disguised as a native?

Romulans were experts at getting answers to their questions. That much was common knowledge. But some of them were more expert than others. And if one in particular had taken an interest in Beverly's case . . .

No, she thought. *I'm not going to go down that road. I'm going to take this one step at a time.*

Beverly tried to get up, but found her right shoulder was too stiff to be of help in that regard. It was the shoulder that had been torn up by the *first* disruptor blast she absorbed—the one that *hadn't* been taken down a level of intensity.

Under the circumstances, Beverly would accept a little stiffness. *Gladly.* It beat losing the arm altogether, which had been a real possibility.

Whoever had administered to her had done a good job—one she could appreciate as a doctor. She made a mental note to thank the person if she ever got the chance.

Rolling onto her left shoulder, she tried to get up again—this time with a bit more success. Wrestling herself off the bed and onto her feet, she experienced a wave of vertigo—a vestige of the punishment her nervous system had taken. She stood there a moment, feet spread wide, until the dizziness went away. Then she approached the energy barrier.

Beyond it was a corridor, also made of stone, also ancient-looking. And all along it were cells just like Beverly's. But they were empty, their barrier projectors inactive. At the moment, it seemed, she was her captors' only prisoner.

Looking around, she saw a sensor high on the wall opposite her cell. Obviously, her captors didn't trust their energy barrier completely. But then, Starfleet personnel had been known to defuse such things on occasion.

And who knew that better than the Romulans?

The doctor felt another wave of dizziness, even worse than the first. She felt like retreating to her bed and lying down until the discomfort went away, but she knew that her captors would be watching her.

It wasn't wise to let a Romulan know you were hurting. It would only encourage him—or her—to take advantage of the fact. Better to make her think you had your wits about you. Then there was at least a chance she would leave you alone.

It was Jean-Luc who had told her that, wasn't it? And a number of other things as well. But then, he had had a lot more experience with Romulans than she had.

Beverly remembered surgically altering his features before he left the *Enterprise*-D to look for Ambassador Spock. How silly he looked with his Romulan brow ridges, though of course she had refrained from saying so. . . .

Just then, she heard something—a clatter of boot heels, echoing sharply from the stone walls. Obviously someone was coming to see her, having taken note of the fact that she was awake.

And Beverly knew who it was, without the slightest doubt. Pulling herself up to her full height, she forced her pain aside and waited—and saw that she was right.

Her visitor was tall, slender but strong-looking, and more fair-haired than any other Romulan Beverly had seen. And even with the shadows in the corridor obscuring the woman's features, Crusher knew them almost as well as her own.

Of course, back on the *Enterprise*-D, she had seen that face every day for nearly a year.

"Sela," she said.

Regarding her from the other side of the energy barrier, the blond woman feigned delight. "I'm so glad you haven't forgotten me, Doctor."

Beverly hadn't forgotten her first compound fracture either. Things like that tended to stay with you.

"You shouldn't have come here," said Sela, her tone only vaguely remonstrative. "The last thing the Kevrata need is a human stirring up unrest."

"I didn't come here to stir up unrest," Beverly said. "I came to find a cure for the disease that's ravaging the Kevrata, which is more than the Romulans have done for them."

Sela smiled. "Perhaps. But it won't be difficult to make it *appear* that you came here to start trouble. That would make you a provocateur. And those convicted of such a crime in the Empire are made to pay dearly for their transgressions."

"Even if the charges have to be trumped up a little."

"Even then. And you couldn't have arrived at a more propitious time. Your death will make the Kevrata see they can't take Romulus lightly—not even after the reorganization precipitated by the demise of the Reman praetor."

Now it was the doctor's turn to smile. "Is that what you call it? A *reorganization?*"

Sela shrugged. "Call it what you like. It has happened before and it will happen again. The old is burned away in favor of the new. Things change."

"Some do," Beverly allowed. "And others remain the same. The intrigues, the infighting—"

"Are part of what makes us strong," said Sela, apparently unperturbed. "Like two muscles pulling in opposite directions—the exercise improves both of them."

"If you're so strong, why don't you let me help the Kevrata? Surely they can't—"

Sela interrupted her, her gaze suddenly hard and unyielding. "We both know what they can do, Doctor. They can start a chain reaction that will destabilize the entire outer rim and jeopardize our hold on it—which is why it's so important for me to keep you from carrying out your mission."

Beverly's teeth ground together. *Politics.* "How many Kevrata, do you think, will die because Romulus is worried about losing its subject worlds? Fifty thousand? A hundred?"

"If I were you," said Sela, "I would be more concerned about my *own* future." Her eyes took on a softer, more reasonable cast. "As you can imagine, most Romulans in my position would simply have killed you and left you to rot in the snow. I opted to bring you here instead, to treat the injury you sustained—and to give you a chance to avoid death."

Beverly looked at her askance. "How?"

The Romulan leaned forward until her face was almost touching the barrier. "If you were to tell me which vessel brought you to Kevratas, it would improve your situation considerably."

Beverly met Sela's gaze. "In other words, you want me to betray the people who risked their lives to get me here."

"The people who broke Romulan law, and imperiled the security of the Empire? Yes, *those* people."

The doctor controlled the anger she felt rising inside her. "Go to hell."

Sela straightened, as if she had been slapped across the face. Then she found it within herself to chuckle. "Romulans," she said, "have no hell."

Then she left Beverly standing in her cell and went back the way she had come, heels clacking on the stones. It seemed to take a long time for the echoes to fade—and even then, the doctor seemed to hear them reverberating in her mind.

Geordi swiveled away from his computer monitor and considered what he had just learned. Then he touched his combadge and said, "La Forge to Commander Worf."

"*Worf here.*"

"Can I see you for a second? I'm in my quarters."

"*On my way. Worf out.*"

Geordi closed his eyes and massaged them. His optical prosthetics had reduced the concept of vision to a computer-driven series of mechanized procedures, but there were still muscles involved, and his got as tired as anyone else's.

Moments later, he heard the chime that told him Worf had arrived. "Come on in," he said.

The doors slid aside, revealing the Klingon's imposing presence. "What is it?" Worf asked, an unmistakable note of eagerness in his voice.

"I've got something," said Geordi. But he waited for the doors to whisper closed before he went on. "I don't know where the captain went yet, but his mode of transportation was a Barolian trader called the *Annabel Lee.*"

Worf shook his head. "It does not sound familiar."

"To me either," Geordi told him. "So I looked it up. It's registered in the name of Peter Joseph."

The Klingon's eyes lit up. *"Pug* Joseph!"

"That's right," said Geordi.

Pug Joseph had been Picard's security chief when he commanded the *Stargazer.* Geordi had met the guy only once, a few years after the launch of the *Enterprise*-D, when Joseph was working through some personal problems.

"What does Pug Joseph have to do with Beverly's disappearance?" Worf asked.

Geordi shook his head. "I don't know. Maybe nothing."

Worf's eyes narrowed. "Nothing . . . ?"

"Maybe the captain needed Pug's ship. It's a trader. That means it can go places a starship can't."

"True," the Klingon allowed.

"I received another piece of information," said Geordi, "but I'm not sure how trustworthy it is. You remember Carter Greyhorse?"

Worf nodded. "The doctor on the *Stargazer.*"

"If my source is correct, Greyhorse was released recently from a penal facility in New Zealand—into the custody of Captain Picard."

"Interesting," said Worf. "But why would—?" He stopped himself. "Greyhorse worked with Doctor Crusher at Starfleet Medical."

"That's what I was thinking," said Geordi. "So if it's true that Greyhorse was released, the captain may have a bit more on his plate than we thought."

"He may have to address the medical crisis Doctor Crusher was sent to address." Worf stroked his beard. "If we can determine what sort of crisis it was—"

"We may be able to figure out where the captain went."

"There would be a record at Starfleet Medical of everything Doctor Crusher and Greyhorse worked on together. I do not suppose you have any friends *there?*"

"Not anymore," Geordi said ruefully.

Worf dismissed the remark. "There is another way to approach this. If Joseph and Greyhorse are involved, they may have confided in one of their *Stargazer* comrades."

"Makes sense," said Geordi. "But even if they know, will they tell us? Their first loyalty is to Captain Picard, and it'll be clear that he didn't want us to know what was going on."

Worf considered the matter for a moment. "Actually," he concluded, "there is *one Stargazer* officer who might be inclined to see it our way."

"Who's that?" asked Geordi.

It was only after Worf provided an answer that he understood what his friend meant.

Eborion regarded the gray-haired individual standing before him, sandwiched between two of his personal guards. The fellow's name was Poyaran, and he had been a servant in Eborion's family for as long as Eborion could remember.

Eborion's uncles, and perhaps even his father, would have taken the length of Poyaran's service into account as they considered his punishment for attempted theft. But Eborion was not nearly so inclined toward clemency.

"What do you have to say for yourself?" he asked, his voice a bit too shrill for his liking as it echoed through the airy, columned chamber.

Poyaran averted his eyes. "I ask for your understanding, master. I did not intend to steal the chalice, only to admire it in the sunlight. It belonged to my family when I was small, and I had not seen it in many years."

It was true that the chalice had once been the property of Poyaran's father, a merchant trader who had enjoyed ties with several of the Hundred. And it was certainly possible that he had shown it to Poyaran in the days when his every finger bore a ring of jewel-encrusted gold.

But Poyaran's father had gotten greedy and tried to increase his fortune at the expense of his clients. *A bad idea*, Eborion reflected. His underhanded practices exposed, Poyaran's father was executed in a public plaza, and the executors of his estate were directed by a tribunal to make reparations to the houses he had wronged.

Unfortunately, Poyaran's father wasn't wealthy enough to pay off his debts in their entirety. The tribunal was compelled to pursue its only other option—breaking up

Poyaran's family and distributing its members to the injured houses as bond servants.

Which was how Poyaran came to work for Eborion's father. And for a long time, his service had been quite satisfactory. However, Eborion would not tolerate stealing. If he were lenient with Poyaran, it would only encourage other servants to try their luck.

"Is that all?" Eborion asked. In the Empire, even servants enjoyed the right of statement.

Poyaran looked up, his face pale and his eyes sunken in their sockets. "It is the truth, master."

Eborion was relieved. He had expected a long, drawn-out defense, which would ultimately have been of no avail anyway, and there were more pressing matters that required his attention.

"I do not believe you," said Eborion. "You are hereby sentenced to a year at the penal facility on Assaf Golav. When you return, it will be with a renewed appreciation of how fortunate you are to serve in this house."

Poyaran's mouth twisted, as if he were about to utter a curse. After all, Assaf Golav was not a pleasant world, and its overseers were reputed to be among the cruelest in the Empire. But in the end, Poyaran restrained himself.

"My master is kind," he said, choking on the last word as if it were something tangible.

At a gesture from Eborion, the guards took Poyaran away. The aristocrat watched them until they had left the chamber. Then he rose from his seat, meaning to take care of one of those more pressing matters.

And he would have, had his aunt not chosen that moment to make her presence known.

"Cly'rana," said Eborion, inclining his head as she approached him. "I am sorry you had to witness that."

"I have witnessed worse," she told him. "But I wonder . . . was Assaf Golav the best choice in this case?"

Eborion stiffened. He did not like to be criticized. Again, he had to remind himself that the day when others questioned him would soon be coming to an end.

"And," Cly'rana continued, "was it appropriate for you to pass judgment on a servant when one of your elders is present in the house? In other words, *me?*"

"It was my chalice," he said.

"So it was," his aunt allowed. "And I am certain it meant the Empire to you. I have seen," she said, with naked sarcasm, "how attached you are to it. But it is costly to send servants to Assaf Golav, nephew, no matter how much we are offended by what they may have done."

Eborion shrugged. "I see it as a lesson to the other servants."

Cly'rana smiled. "And we must not miss out on an opportunity to teach our servants."

He let the comment go unanswered. What was Cly'rana doing there anyway? Wasn't she supposed to be in the midst of a holiday on the Apnex Sea?

"If you will pardon me," he said, "I have research to do. I do not wish to disappoint Claboros."

"Who would?" asked Cly'rana.

Another provocative remark. She used them to draw people into conversational traps, wherein they would make revelations they did not really wish to make.

But Eborion was clever enough to avoid taking the bait. All he said was "Indeed."

Then, before Cly'rana could get in another comment, he got up and left the chamber. Heels clacking on the ancient marble underfoot, he made his way down a corridor to the palace's back door.

There a suborbital craft was waiting to convey him to a weapons research laboratory in the mountains—one of many owned by his family. Without a word to the pilot, he got in, settled back, and watched the palace withdraw into the distance.

Eborion had not lied to his aunt. He was indeed pursuing the research that his uncle had required of him. But he was also pursuing a rather bold and daring plan.

Tal'aura, obviously uncomfortable about pinning all her hopes on the much-vaunted Commander Sela, had hedged her bet with the services of a spy. Sela didn't know this, of course—she was too far from the praetor's palace these days to know much of anything.

But Eborion knew. He had more informants at court than he could count on the fingers of both hands, and he paid them all well. There were no secrets from him, nothing that went on in Tal'aura's palace of which he did not eventually learn.

Certainly, there was a risk in knowing Tal'aura's secrets. *A considerable one.* However, Eborion hadn't stopped there. Once he knew that there was a clandestine agent, he made it his business to find out which one it was. A costly endeavor, that—but then, spies were in the business of being *difficult* to identify.

Fortunately, Tal'aura had used go-betweens in hiring her spy, and at least one of them was not above selling the information. It was in this manner that Eborion learned who the fellow was, and the role he was playing on Kevratas.

And then, in a master stroke of which Eborion was immensely proud, he hired the spy to serve *him* as well.

He wondered now how much progress the fellow was making. People in the espionage profession tended to move slowly and carefully, reluctant to take too many chances. After all, exposure wouldn't just portend the failure of their mission—it would mean death.

Eborion knew how they felt. It was an immense chance he was taking, operating behind the praetor's back this way. If she were to discover his machinations, his life would certainly be forfeit—no doubt, in a most public and humiliating manner.

However, Eborion was an ambitious individual. He believed he was meant for the highest places in the Empire, if only he could find it in himself to scale them.

That was why he had been so careful in deciding which senators to support with his wealth. That was why he had remained their patron even during the time of Shinzon, playing a hunch that the clone wouldn't remain in power very long.

And that was why he was so determined now to discredit Sela, his chief rival at Tal'aura's court. Because as long as Sela appeared useful, Eborion would never become the praetor's sole, unchallenged source of counsel.

The aristocrat couldn't confront Sela on his own. She was too forceful, too crafty, too well connected. However, his spy on Kevratas was in a position to undermine Sela's effectiveness, to find the hairline weaknesses in her regime and expand them into gaping crevices. And he would, if he was even half as good as he was reputed to be.

He would drag Sela down into the mire of her failure, centimeter by helpless centimeter. And in the process, he would help Eborion raise himself up.

"Shall I take the mountain route or the coastal route?" asked his pilot.

The coastal route was the less direct of the two, but Eborion was developing more of a taste for the indirect with every passing day. "The coastal route," he replied, and sat back in his seat to enjoy the view.

Of the seventeen worlds in the mammoth Arbitra Tsichita system, the one called Kevratas was by far the closest to its tired red beacon of a star and therefore the only one even remotely capable of supporting life.

However, Kevratas's surface was so cold it challenged that life on a daily basis. Even in its equatorial belt, the region that had given birth to the planet's only sentient species, temperatures only occasionally crept over the freezing mark.

At certain times of year—this being one of them—it was even worse. A nearly unbroken mantle of clouds stretched from pole to pole, making sunlight as rare as hail on Vulcan's Forge.

"Hope you all like a good winter storm," said Pug as they came within orbital range of the planet. He leaned back in his captain's chair. "Looks like a humdinger brewing right where we'll be beaming down."

From his seat at the helm station, Picard considered the cloud-swaddled sphere on the modest, rectangular viewscreen before him. "I trust the weather will not exacerbate the difficulty of our transport?"

He had already heard about the planet's myriad magnetic fields, which made transporting anywhere a tricky operation. That was why he and his comrades would carry concealed, miniaturized pattern enhancers for the return trip, which promised to be a hasty business indeed, and would almost definitely not be carried out in cooperation with the authorities.

"It shouldn't be an additional impediment," said Decalon, who was sitting at the bridge's operations station, "unless our transporter system is hopelessly antiquated."

"Which," Pug said with just a hint of resentment, "it's not. I made a point of overhauling it just a couple of years ago."

Greyhorse, who was standing behind Picard, refrained from contributing to the exchange. But then, transporter mechanics were hardly his specialty. And in any case, he had been a man of few words since he came aboard the *Annabel Lee*—no doubt the effect of having lived in confinement for so long.

"They're hailing us," said Pug. He punched a response into the black control panel at the end of his armrest. "And we're answering, like any trader with nothing to hide."

A moment later, the image of Kevratas was replaced on the viewscreen with that of a hawk-faced Romulan officer. He regarded Picard and the others on the cargo vessel's bridge with unconcealed suspicion.

Fortunately, all four of them were disguised. They had

loose gray skin, startling blue eyes set deep into their skulls, and noses that spread almost from ear to corkscrewed ear. If not for the significant differences in their statures—Pug being stocky and of medium height, Decalon being somewhat taller and narrower, and Greyhorse towering over all of them—Picard would have had a dickens of a time telling them apart.

Then again, he wasn't a Barolian, despite the appearance his subdermal holoprojector enabled him to assume, so he wasn't sensitive to any of the details that distinguished one member of that species from another.

"What is your business here?" the Romulan demanded.

"Trade," said Pug. Thanks to the implant in his throat, his voice boomed as deeply as any true Barolian's.

The Romulan eyed him for a heartbeat. Then he said, "You have permission to enter orbit. Be advised that you must submit a request before you may beam yourselves or your cargo to the surface. If the request is acceptable, you will be assigned a checkpoint."

"I understand," said Pug.

Without any warning, the Romulan cut the communications link. Pug turned to Picard and said, "That didn't go too badly."

Picard agreed. "Let us submit our request. The sooner we beam down, the better."

For Beverly's sake, he added silently, *as well as that of the Kevrata.*

6

AS BEVERLY LANGUISHED IN HER CELL, SHE WASN'T optimistic about her chances of escape.

Had she been captured by a Romulan with a less thorough knowledge of Federation prisoners, she would have stood a better chance. But Sela was hardly what one might call ignorant on that count.

More than likely, the doctor would be executed. That was the standard fate of prisoners who refused to cooperate with the Romulans. The method of execution might vary, but not the result.

It was all right. Beverly had expected to perish when she absorbed that disruptor blast. In that one moment, she had said all the good-byes she could ever hope to say. Whatever happened to her now, she was prepared for it.

What nettled her, keeping her from the peace that should have come with resignation, was the prospect of what would happen to the Kevrata. According to the intelligence supplied by the underground, the plague had already claimed the lives of nearly five percent of the native population, and another twenty-five percent were afflicted to one degree or another.

And the situation would get worse before it got better. Beverly knew that from the work she had done at Starfleet Medical. The Kevrata would be decimated—a population of more than a million reduced to perhaps a couple hundred thousand.

All because they had been denied the proper vaccine— a vaccine Beverly could easily have developed for them if only she were allowed to do so. It was too hideous to contemplate.

Fortunately for the Kevrata, the Federation wouldn't give up on them. Once it became apparent that something had happened to derail the doctor's mission, Starfleet Command would huddle and come up with a backup plan.

First and foremost, they would need another physician to deal with the epidemic. Unfortunately, there weren't a great many options to pick from. The only other person who had had any real experience with the disease was Carter Greyhorse, the former chief medical officer of the *Stargazer* and Beverly's colleague in her first go-round at Starfleet Medical.

It was she who had made the disease a research priority. However, Greyhorse had plunged into the work as deeply as she had, making major contributions along the way. Beverly might have come up with the cure without him, but her path would have been more arduous, and it would have taken a good deal longer.

So there was no question about Greyhorse's viability as a scientist. But his viability as a clandestine agent? That was an iffy proposition, at best.

That means he'll have to have someone dependable with him, she thought. *Someone he'll respect. And someone who's had experience with the Romulans.*

To her mind, there was only one person in the universe who fit that description—Jean-Luc Picard. Of course, he was also the last man Greyhorse had tried to kill. But that was many years and thousands of hours of therapy ago.

As far as Beverly knew, Greyhorse again saw Jean-Luc as he had during his earliest days on the *Stargazer,* as someone who deserved his loyalty and respect. If that were so, the two of them might do what Beverly had been prevented from doing—find a cure for the Kevrata's plague.

Part of her prayed that it would be so. But another part feared for her friends. Sela had a grudge against Jean-Luc, the product of more than one stinging defeat at his hands. If she had even an inkling that he was on Kevratas, she would do everything in her power to get her hands on him.

And squeeze until he begged for mercy.

On the other hand, Beverly allowed, *I may be way off base.* It was possible that neither Jean-Luc nor Greyhorse would wind up anywhere near the Romulan Empire, just as it was possible that she would be the last doctor sent to help the Kevrata. But her knowledge of Starfleet told her otherwise.

As she thought that, she heard the sharp report of footfalls on the naked stone. *Sela?* she wondered. Had the woman come back to obtain the answers she had failed to get last time?

Beverly moved forward in her cell until her face was almost touching the energy of the barrier. It allowed her to see all the way down to the end of the corridor.

Moments later, someone turned the corner, all right—but it wasn't Sela. It was one of her centurions. Probably the one who had looked in on her every hour or so since she woke up.

No, Beverly thought as he got closer. *This is a different one.* The other centurion had been tall and broad-shouldered, with high, aristocratic cheekbones and a thin, cruel mouth.

This one was shorter, slimmer, more wiry-looking. And his features were less remarkable—downright bland, in fact. As good as the doctor was with faces, she would have been hard-pressed to describe his with any accuracy.

Like the other centurion, he approached her cell and gave it a visual inspection. When he got to Beverly, she returned his scrutiny. She might have to endure it, but she certainly wasn't going to be meek about it.

In any case, the centurion wasn't likely to linger. There was nothing amiss in her cell, nothing to address. The doctor expected him to do what his predecessor had done—cast a final warning glance at her and go back the way he came.

Until he spoke.

Beverly was so surprised and his voice was so low, so soft, she couldn't make out a single word. Her expression must have communicated the fact, because the centurion spoke again—a little more distinctly this time.

"Not all of Commander Sela's centurions are eager to follow her orders," he breathed. "Some believe the Kevrata deserve their freedom."

Beverly studied him, trying to decide why he would say such a thing. If anyone overheard him, his life would surely have been forfeit. And yet he had taken the risk.

"Right now," she whispered back, "they need freedom from their plague."

The guard eyed her for a moment. Almost imperceptibly, he nodded. Then, without another word, he went back down the corridor and disappeared around its bend.

Strange, Beverly thought.

She had dealt with Romulans enough to know that even the humblest of them had his own agenda—and that it might not be the one he professed. Nonetheless, she embraced the hope that the guard was willing to help her.

As her grandmother had said often enough, beggars couldn't be choosers. And at the moment, the doctor felt very much like a beggar.

Kito wasn't sure when or where or how the wave of Kevrata started moving through the city, but it had reached mammoth proportions by the time he caught sight of it flooding Wophan Square.

"What is this about?" he asked.

A female in a red robe turned to shout to him through the pelting snow. "A physician was dispatched to help us, but the Romulans imprisoned her!"

A physician? "From what place was she dispatched?" Kito wondered out loud.

"From the Federation!" called a male. "She was sent here to stop the plague!"

Hands of the generous, Kito thought, a spurt of anger climbing his throat. Could even the Romulans be that cruel? If they could not—or would not—come up with a cure for the killing sickness, why not permit someone else to do so?

It was but one of the questions he would have asked if given the opportunity. Unfortunately, the Romulans were not in the habit of discussing their policies with the species they oppressed. They were more inclined to deal with questions across the length of a disruptor rifle.

Joining the broad, moving flow of Kevrata, Kito pressed closer to a fellow in a black and red robe. "Is there any way we can liberate this physician?"

A gust of wind tore away most of the fellow's response. However, Kito caught enough of it to understand.

The mob was on its way now to the wrought-iron gates of the Romulan compound, where it would demand the physician's release. Not that it would do them any good. If the Romulans had meant to take the Kevrata's misery into account, they would have done so a long time ago, when the plague claimed its first victims.

Still, it was better than doing nothing. That way lay only despair and slow death.

So Kito added his indignation to that of the others and moved with them through the snow-choked thorough-fares of the city, crying out against the tyranny of the Romulans until his throat was raw. And though it was difficult to see much of anything in the swirling chaos of the storm, he could tell by the buildings they passed that they were getting closer to the oppressors' compound.

They had only two streets to go when the female in front of Kito fell and nearly tripped him in the process. Helping her to her feet, Kito caught a glimpse of her face under her hood.

It was ravaged by the plague, the black flesh beneath her fur stippled with tiny bumps. Kito didn't know where she had found the strength to come even this far.

Part of him wanted to run, to escape the fate that had overcome the female, because the plague was highly contagious. But there was no escape. Every Kevrata in the city had been exposed many times over. It was just a question of how long Kito had until his immune system succumbed.

As he thought that, something moved overhead—a shadow, blotting out even the faint light descending through the filter of the storm. Then Kito heard the moan of an engine, growing louder as the shadow grew denser and more distinct.

And someone yelled, "Romulans!"

A hovercraft, Kito thought, his blood pumping hard through his veins. He had seen its kind before, moving through the air above the city like a slow, patient predator.

It was equipped with disruptor cannons. He had heard they could reduce a living being to a soup of burning flesh, though he had never seen it. But he had also never seen a hovercraft confront a crowd so large and defiant.

Kito couldn't have been the only one who noticed the danger overhead. But the crowd didn't do anything to get away from it. It just kept moving in the direction of the Romulans' compound, caught up in its own momentum.

And then *everyone* knew the craft was overhead, because it started firing disruptor bolts into the crowd.

Suddenly, death was wading among the Kevrata on long legs of green fire, grinding victim after victim under its heels. There were shouts of astonishment and horror, and the river of Kevrata eddied violently in confusion.

Kito reached for the female who had fallen, hoping to get her back on her feet. But before he could get ahold of her he was forced backward, pushed that way by the fleeing mob. And amid cries of fear, some of them regrettably his own, he was swept in a direction he could neither predict nor control.

Somewhere along the line, he realized there was more than one hovercraft—as many as three, perhaps. Not that it mattered. One was enough to get the Romulans' message across.

Kito spun and struggled to maintain his balance, knowing that if he fell he would be crushed beneath the boots of his neighbors. But at the same time he couldn't help tracking the progress of the Romulan craft, their beams stitching death from one end of the square to the other.

The smell of burning fur filled Kito's nostrils, sickening him, making him want to empty his stomach into the wet, churned snow. However, he blocked out the stench and kept moving with the crowd—because if he failed to do so, he wouldn't have to worry about the plague taking his life.

Finally, Kito felt the pressure of his people's bodies begin to fall away from him. He could see past a hundred hooded heads that the crowd was dispersing, releasing itself into the half-dozen streets that projected from the square like spokes.

As the mob thinned out, it began to run. And Kito ran too, knowing the Romulans could skewer him at any moment.

He didn't notice anything about the streets he ran through, or who was running beside him. He just ran. But the energy beams kept touching down behind him, harrying him, striking some Kevrata and driving the others like a herd of burden beasts.

Kito's breath rasped harder and harder in his throat. His body grew warm and heavy beneath his clothing, his legs burning with the intensity of his effort.

He didn't dare stop running, not even for a second. However, he couldn't keep up such a pace forever. *Eventually,* he thought, *I will simply collapse.*

Then his house deities smiled on him.

An alleyway opened to his right, a few meters up ahead. *If I slip inside it,* he thought, *the Romulans may overlook me.* Then again they might dig him out like a stubborn parasite, but there was no telling when another such opportunity might present itself.

Veering in the direction of the alley, Kito maneuvered himself inside it. Then he planted his back against one of the walls and hoped against pursuit.

The Romulans' green energy beams kept on hunting the Kevrata, illuminating the street outside with their fury. But mercifully, none of them came down inside the alley. And after a while, it seemed to Kito none of them *would.*

I'm safe? he wondered, unable to believe it.

Then some of the other Kevrata began slipping into the alley as well. Kito winced as they joined him, knowing there was a chance they would draw the Romulans' attention. Of course, they had as much right to the alley as he did.

And as it turned out, they *didn't* attract attention. The pulses of green disruptor energy receded into the distance, and Kito's hiding place gradually fell dark. Dark and quiet. He and the other Kevrata in the alley exchanged glances.

Was it possible that their ordeal was over? That they could go home now? It was starting to appear that way.

Plodding through the snow drifts that had accumulated in the alley, Kito emerged into the broader environs of the street. It was littered with heavily robed bodies, more of them than he could make himself count.

There were flecks and streaks of blood all over the place, hissing as they ate their way down through the snow. It wasn't Romulan blood. Theirs was a virulent green, the color of their death-beams. This blood was red, as red as ripe snowberries, as warm as the coals at the bottom of a hearthfire.

"Hands of the generous," Kito breathed.

It was one thing for the Romulans to let his people die of the plague. But to kill them this way . . . it was intolerable. Kito couldn't just let it be. He had to do something about it.

And he knew exactly what he would do.

Leaving the human prisoner in her cell, the centurion—who in truth wasn't a centurion at all—made his way to Commander Sela's office and waited in front of her desk until she was ready to speak with him.

He didn't know what Sela was looking at on her computer screen, but he couldn't interrupt her. The last centurion to do so had been executed on the spot, or so the story went.

And every story, he knew, had at least a kernel of truth.

Finally the commander looked up at him, her strangely human eyes, as blue as the midday sky on Romulus, glinting in the light of the overhead fixtures.

"Report," she demanded, as if it were *she* who had been waiting for *him*.

"The prisoner is secure," he informed her.

"All that means," Sela said, "is that she's still planning her escape. Make certain you are not lulled by her into dropping your guard."

The centurion nodded. "I will remain vigilant, Commander."

She eyed him. "See that you do."

Then, with a gesture, Sela dismissed him. There was something about the way she flipped her wrist, the way she held herself, that he found unspeakably attractive. However, he kept that fact very much to himself.

She must have had lovers over the years, but the centurion hadn't heard about any of them. That portended badly for anyone who served her in that manner.

And yet, she was delectable. Undeniably so.

It wasn't the first time he had had a chance to appreciate her beauty. He and Sela had met twice before—once on Romulus at an advanced training facility and once on a warbird, where she was serving as second officer.

But then, in his work as one of the Empire's premier spies, Manathas often encountered people he had met before. Senators, ships' captains, noblewomen, arms merchants—even, on a rare occasion, the bride in a Starfleet wedding celebration in San Francisco.

Not that Crusher would ever have recognized him now. The day he served her and her groom their grotesque dollops of wedding cake, he was wearing a different face—one of perhaps a hundred guises Manathas had assumed over the years. His features had been surgically altered so often even *he* barely remembered the visage with which he had been born.

But Manathas had recognized the doctor. The moment Sela and the other centurions brought her in, he knew who she was. And in that same moment, he understood the magnitude of the opportunity that had been presented to him.

And of course, to his employers. *Both* of them.

Ironic, he thought, *isn't it?* Decades earlier, he had all but ignored the doctor, his assignment for the praetor compelling him to focus on the captains assembled in her honor. Now, with the praetor's cloning scheme long since abandoned, those captains weren't nearly as important as the woman they had feted.

Tal'aura would be displeased when she received news of Crusher's presence on Kevratas. She had made overtures to the Federation, and the Federation had answered them with duplicity.

Yet she must have known that was a possibility. And with Crusher in her grasp, she would be able to respond to the Federation's move with one of her own—based on whatever information she could squeeze from the doctor. And Manathas would have done his job, justifying the generous fee he would receive.

As for Eborion—he too would be served. Rather than

allow Sela to take credit for Crusher's capture, Manathas would spirit her out of prison and then off Kevratas altogether. And in the process, he would let the praetor know how badly the half-blood had failed her in the matter of the Federation operative.

So badly, in fact, that Manathas had himself been forced to bring Crusher to Romulus. Sela's standing with Tal'aura would be crushed. And Eborion would survive as her favorite—thus giving the patrician his money's worth as well.

Seldom did such complicated affairs work themselves out with such beauty and symmetry. Just thinking about it brought a smile of satisfaction to the spy's face.

Of course, he still had to facilitate Crusher's escape. But with the majority of Sela's troops patrolling the city, there would be only a few centurions left to stop him.

He just needed to move quickly, before his commander had a chance to damage the human with her interrogation techniques. Tal'aura would be a good deal more appreciative if the prisoner still had her wits about her when she arrived on Romulus.

So appreciative, perhaps, that Manathas could make this his last bit of espionage. He was getting older, after all, and age was the enemy of covert agents. He had seen his rivals push themselves too far and eventually falter—with fatal results.

When he quit this life, he wanted to do it with the knowledge that his needs had been provided for. He wanted to know he had accomplished something he could not have accomplished as a child's tutor, which was what his father advised him to become.

He hadn't joined the Tal Shiar—the Romulan secret police—like so many individuals with his skills. But then, he had never felt comfortable in a bureaucracy.

Just as well. The Tal Shiar, in its arrogance, had run into a trap laid by the Founders during the Dominion War. As a result, virtually the entire organization had been wiped out.

And so the wheel turns, Manathas thought. *And, turning, raises those who are low.*

It was a line from *Warrior's Dawn,* the best-known work of Dezrai, an ancient Romulan poet. Manathas might have changed his appearance and his employer more than other people changed their underclothes, but his taste in poetry had remained unwaveringly the same.

As Picard joined Pug, Greyhorse, and Decalon on the *Annabel Lee*'s transporter platform, he looked them over one last time.

It was one thing for them to fool someone who could only see them on a viewscreen and quite another to carry off the deception in person. However, as far as Picard could tell, he was among a group of bonafide Barolian traders.

Of course, a halfway thorough sensor sweep would have penetrated their disguises and exposed them as impostors. But according to Starfleet intelligence, their destination—a place that had never experienced a single threat from outside the Empire—possessed no sensor equipment.

"Ready?" asked Pug.

Picard nodded. "Energize."

The former security chief pushed back the sleeve of his thick, black thermal suit to reveal the control band secured to his wrist. Punching in the requisite sequence, he remote-activated the nearby transporter mechanism.

For a moment, nothing happened. Then, with a suddenness to which the captain had grown accustomed over the years, he found himself in an expansive, domed chamber made of large, black stones, illuminated by silver globes hanging from the ceiling.

He and his comrades were standing on one of more than a dozen pattern enhancer-equipped transporter platforms scattered across an ice blue marble floor. But then, according to Decalon, a large percentage of Kevratas's ship-to-surface traffic was funneled through this particular checkpoint.

Clearly, the facility had been there for some time, long before the Romulans occupied the planet. Picard didn't know what role it had played in Kevratan society, but it was certainly large and important-looking. *An indoor marketplace?* he ventured. *Or perhaps a hall for state social gatherings?*

Now there were at least fifty armed Romulan centurions positioned about the place in silver-mailed tunics, most of them lining the walls. One of them approached Picard and his party, his disruptor rifle held across his body.

"Come with me," said the centurion, his tone as impatient as it was imperious.

"Of course," said Picard.

Stepping down from the platform, he fell into line

behind the Romulan, knowing that his companions would be doing the same. Picard followed the fellow to one of several black, functional-looking kiosks at the far end of the chamber, beyond which he could see the exit—a wide, well-guarded doorway marked in both the Romulan and Kevratan tongues.

Thanks to Admiral Edrich's briefing packet, Picard could read a bit of both—though not as much as Decalon, who had lived for more than a year among the Kevrata. The others would be relying on Barolian translation devices to help them communicate.

When the captain reached the kiosk, the Romulan official there held out his hand. "Your documentation," he said brusquely and without inflection.

Picard turned over a display device with the requisite information. It was all fabricated, of course, made up of whatever lies the Romulans seemed most likely to swallow.

The official studied it. He had the look of an individual who had long ago grown bored with his job.

"What is your business here?" he asked, though the display device would have answered that question for him.

"We are traders," Picard replied dutifully, "dealing in impulse engine parts."

Pug's ship had containers full of them, just in case. But then, they didn't know how seriously the Romulans might be taking their security these days.

The official scrutinized Picard for a moment, as if he could detect a clandestine agent simply by looking at him. Then, proving he wasn't nearly as perceptive as he might have believed, he waved the captain on.

One by one, the others passed muster as well, and joined Picard at the exit. *So far, so good,* he thought.

One of the guards there gave them a once-over and then touched a metal plate built into the wall. A moment later the door slid aside, revealing a luridly lit passage beyond.

There were guards there as well, their features cast into sharp relief by the blood-red heat lamps lining the walls. As the captain and his comrades moved forward into the passage, they could feel a distinct chill in the air, lamps or no lamps.

But then, they were in a necessary buffer zone between the temperature-controlled environment of the checkpoint and the arctic cold of the outside. It was bound to be a little cooler there.

Wordlessly, Picard and his comrades made their way past the guards to the door at the far end of the passage. As they got closer they saw it was actually two doors, each an intricately carved slab of rich dark wood.

Obviously, thought Picard, *relics of the original structure.*

The carvings displayed scene after scene of open-handed benevolence—Kevrata gracing each other with food, drink, gems, furs, and other gifts. The Romulans, of course, were absent from these depictions. But if they had been included, it wouldn't have been for their generosity.

The captain was surprised that the imperial authorities had left the doors intact, considering how thermally inefficient they had to be. The natives must have taken a great deal of pride in them, or the Romulans would simply have torn them out and discarded them.

"Bundle up," said Pug, "it'll be chilly out there," and pulled forward the formfitting hood of his thermal suit.

Picard did the same. Then he positioned a pair of attached goggles over his eyes. Without them it would be too easy to go snow-blind. Finally, he pulled a flap of thermal material across the lower portion of his face to protect it from frostbite and fastened it on the other side.

It would have been nice if the guards in the passage could have opened the wooden doors as they had the others. However, whatever impulse had persuaded the Romulans to preserve the carved hunks of wood as artifacts had also persuaded them to leave them unmechanized. To get outside, the captain and his party would have to use a little elbow grease.

Girding himself for the cold, Picard leaned against one of the doors and shoved, while Pug did the same thing. The pieces of wood were heavier than they looked, but after a moment they swung open, giving the three humans their first glimpse of Kevratan civilization outside the checkpoint.

The briefing material sent by Admiral Edrich had been exhaustive, including any number of Kevratan images captured by Federation-friendly traders. And yet, they paled in comparison with the sight that met the captain's eyes.

He had expected to see a bleak terrain of crude stone edifices all but buried in the wild, gray drifts of winter, with only the occasional pale gleam of sunlight for relief. Indeed, the buildings that sprawled before Picard were covered with snow, and soft flakes were even then falling from the sky.

But it wasn't as dreary as he had anticipated, because in the midst of it all was a moving sea of coats representing every bright, warm color in the rainbow. The captain couldn't help smiling in appreciation.

He had seen other societies, both on Earth and on worlds beyond, where people worked hard to ensure the beauty of their garb. But in those societies, clothing was an indicator of status.

Not so in the case of the Kevrata.

They didn't believe in the sort of class distinctions that hinged on what a person possessed. Quite the contrary. In Kevratan society, social standing was based entirely on what someone was capable of giving away.

Picard was reminded of a custom embraced by some of North America's ancient tribal cultures. Known as the potlatch feast, it was an occasion on which some of the more affluent members of the tribe went so far as to bankrupt themselves in order to demonstrate the extent of their openhandedness.

It is better to give than to receive. The potlatch peoples certainly lived by that code. And so, apparently, did the inhabitants of Kevratas.

Or rather, they had lived that way *once*. Then, nearly fifty standard years ago, the Romulan Empire underwent yet another in an ongoing series of expansions, and claimed Kevratas in the name of whoever was praetor at the time.

The rights of the Kevrata were restricted in accordance with the needs of the Empire. Public communications were all but eliminated. Curfews were established. And personal fortunes were seized—purportedly because the

Kevrata no longer required them as wards of the Empire, but in truth because the Romulans wished to add to their coffers.

The Empire assumed control over the planet's three major industries—trading, mining, and the manufacture of curiously beautiful native artifacts. All but the tiniest fraction of profits went straight back to Romulus.

For the Kevrata, the loss of personal freedom was a cut to the bone. But the loss of wealth cut them even deeper. They had measured their worth as individuals by how much they could give to others. Suddenly, they had nothing to give . . . and therefore, no worth.

A sad state of affairs indeed. And yet, the Kevrata were enduring Romulan rule a lot better than other subject peoples.

Anyone who wears such coats has to harbor hope, Picard thought. *It must be in their nature.* And if his mission were successful, the Kevrata would get what they were hoping for.

He turned to Decalon. "Which way?"

The defector looked around for a moment, making an effort to get his bearings. After all, it had been a long time since he lived on this world, and the snow made it difficult to discern one building from another.

Finally, he pointed and said, "This way."

Picard again took stock of his companions. It was tempting to see Joseph and Greyhorse as he had seen them on the *Stargazer*—as subordinates who would reflexively carry out his commands.

However, decades had passed since they served under

him. They were no longer the men they had been. And Decalon was an even bigger question mark.

But this was the team assigned to the captain, and this was the team he had accepted. "Let us proceed," he said.

And they set out through the storm for the dwelling of a Romulan named Phajan.

7

HUNKERING DOWN AGAINST THE COLD, PICARD AND
his comrades waited in the lee of a well-appointed stone
building just off one of the city's main thoroughfares.

The snow had stopped for the moment, but the sky
looked bruised and battered above them, and it promised
another blast of weather before too long. The captain
frowned behind his flap of thermal protection. *Yet another
reason it would be good if someone answered the door.*

Finally, they heard a voice say, over the whistling of
the wind, "What is your business here?"

Decalon moved closer to the grid beside the door,
which appeared to be part of an audio-only intercom system. "I have come to see an old friend," he said. "His
name is Phajan."

The voice that said the words was Decalon's. Obviously, he had disabled the mechanism that made him
sound like a Barolian.

"You sound familiar . . ." said the individual on the other end of the intercom conversation.

"I should," said Decalon. "Or have you forgotten the night we spent drinking ale at the foot of the firefalls?"

A pause. And then: "Decalon . . . ?"

"The same," said the Romulan. "Though as you will see, I do not look like myself these days."

A few seconds later, the door was flung wide, and a Romulan came out as far as the threshold. He was tall and thin, with hair graying at the temples and eyes that seemed to have witnessed a great deal of sadness. When he saw what Decalon looked like, his mouth fell open, letting out a wisp of frozen breath.

"I told you I do not look like myself," said Decalon.

His friend swore softly. Then his eyes moved in the direction of Picard, Pug, and Greyhorse, and he asked, "Who are *they?*"

"I will vouch for them," said Decalon.

Phajan hesitated—but only for a moment. "Come in," he said, "before we all freeze to death."

Picard didn't have to be told twice. As soon as he and his comrades were inside, Phajan closed the heavy wooden door behind them. Then he turned to Decalon.

"What are you doing back in the Empire?" he demanded.

Decalon smiled, contorting his features. "I am on a mission for the Federation." Touching the controls on his portable holosystem, he dropped his Barolian guise.

Phajan shook his head ruefully, but ended up smiling a little too. Then he embraced his friend.

"Idiot," he said. "It was so much trouble to get you out of here. And now you've come back."

"Unfortunately," said Decalon, "I cannot tell you what we are doing on Kevratas."

"I do not wish to know," Phajan assured him. "As always, the fewer who know such things, the better."

"Your family," said Decalon, "they are well?"

A shadow fell across Phajan's face. "My mother died last year. But my sisters and their families still live on the homeworld."

"Are they content?"

Phajan nodded. "Reasonably so."

For a moment, there was silence between the two Romulans. Then Decalon said, "It has been a long time."

"Too long," said his friend.

Phajan was one of the disaffected Romulans who, more than a decade earlier, had helped spirit defectors like Decalon out of the Empire. Decalon had spoken at length of Phajan's dedication and courage during the *Annabel Lee*'s flight across the Neutral Zone.

Picard had no reason to doubt the accuracy of Decalon's memory. Nonetheless, there was a great deal riding on the success of his mission, so he had consulted the Starfleet database downloaded to Pug's ship back in Earth orbit.

It corroborated Decalon's claim: Phajan had indeed been a big part of the Romulans' underground railroad, helping some fifty-five defectors escape to the Federation.

Why Phajan himself had chosen to remain in the Empire had been left unsaid. Of course, he was hardly the only Romulan who had enabled others to reach freedom without pursuing the possibility on his own.

"Do I know your companions as well?" asked Phajan.

He regarded Picard and the others, who were still disguised as Barolians. "Oresis, perhaps? Or Achitonos?"

"I'm afraid not," said Decalon. "Both Oresis and Achitonos are back in the Romulan colony we established in the Federation." He gestured to the captain. "This is Jean-Luc Picard, captain of the *Starship Enterprise.*"

"Ah," said Phajan, his eyes lighting up, "I have heard of Captain Picard. In fact, if I am not mistaken, he and I have worked together—though he probably never knew it."

"If you were one of my contacts in the Empire," said the captain, "I did *not* know it. For your protection, we were never apprised of any of your names."

"A wise policy," said Phajan, "which no doubt enabled many of our number to survive long after our operation outlived its usefulness and dissipated."

Indeed, the once-torrential flow of Romulans who had wished to escape the Empire diminished sharply after the first year of the underground railroad, and soon after stopped altogether. No one in the Federation could ever understand why.

Nor could Romulans like Decalon shed any light on the matter. It was as if their rejection of the Empire and her ideals were no more than a fad, which had its time in the sun and passed.

"And these," Decalon continued, indicating the doctor and their pilot, "are Carter Greyhorse and Peter Joseph, both former officers in Starfleet."

Phajan took them in at a glance. "You are welcome in my house. As welcome as my friend Decalon."

"It is kind of you to say so," Picard told him.

Phajan dismissed the notion with a wave of his hand. "It is the least I can do for those who gave Decalon and others a life beyond the Empire."

"I did not contribute to that effort," said Greyhorse, a strange burr in his voice.

The remark came out of nowhere. Had it been articulated by a man without a record of criminality and psychological instability, the captain might have overlooked it. As it was, it put him on his guard.

Joseph, looking a little concerned, put his hand on the doctor's shoulder and said, "It's all right, Doc. I didn't get that opportunity either."

"However," Greyhorse went on, as if his colleague hadn't said a thing, "I wish I *had* contributed. There is nothing more important than freedom."

Picard looked for Phajan's reaction. But all the Romulan did was say, "I agree."

He had failed, it seemed, to notice anything off-center about the doctor's comments. However, there was no way to know what else Greyhorse might choose to say, or at what critical juncture he might choose to say it.

Picard began to wonder if it had been a good idea after all to put the doctor in such a crucial situation. Not that there was anything he could do about it now, except keep an eye on Greyhorse and hope for the best.

Perhaps sensing Picard's discomfort, Decalon changed the subject. "You live well," he observed of Phajan.

Their host looked around at the furnishings—a collection of sleek, overstuffed chairs and boldly wrought wall hangings made of burnished metals. They *were* rather opulent-looking, especially by local standards.

"One of the advantages," said Phajan, "of being a tax collector. In fact, the *chief* tax collector."

"You collect taxes from the Kevrata?" Greyhorse asked, and not in an especially kindly tone of voice.

Their host turned to him, his features strained. "Do not presume to judge me."

"That is not his intention," said Picard. He looked pointedly at the doctor. "Is it?"

Greyhorse looked lost for a moment. Then he said to Phajan, in a softer voice, "I apologize if I gave you that impression. People do what they must to survive."

"They do indeed," said Phajan, relaxing a bit.

"We appreciate your hospitality," said Decalon, again cutting in on an awkward moment, "but we don't want to stay long. Every moment we remain here places you in danger."

Phajan shrugged. "You need not be concerned about that. Now sit down and tell me how I can help."

Opening their thermal suits, they deposited themselves in their host's overstuffed chairs and waited while he brewed them a drink—a tart, clear beverage called *cijarra,* which Picard had sampled in his time on Romulus. Then, as they sipped the steaming *cijarra* with unanimous regard for its subtleties, Decalon told his friend what they required of him.

"We need a way," he said, "to contact the underground."

Phajan's brow bunched above the bridge of his nose. "Easier said than done."

Decalon frowned with disappointment. "I thought, perhaps—"

"That I would know, since I was once part of an under-ground myself?" Phajan shook his head. "That was a different time, my friend, and a different life."

"Then you cannot help us?" asked Picard.

Phajan considered the question for what seemed like a long time. "If it were easy to find the underground," he said at last, "Commander Sela would have done so by now."

The captain felt a pit open in his belly. "Did you say . . . Commander *Sela?*"

"Yes," said Phajan. "She took over the administration of Kevratas a few weeks ago. Do you know her?"

"I have run into her," Picard confirmed. "More than once, in fact." He didn't go into Sela's relationship with Tasha Yar, seeing no point in it. "She is formidable, to say the least."

"So it would seem," said Phajan. "I have lived on Kev-ratas for decades now, and I have never seen it governed so strictly—or so cruelly. The natives speak of Sela with fear in their voices."

"Then she has not changed," said Picard.

"And the underground?" asked Decalon. "Is there no way to let them know we are here? Without alerting Sela as well?"

"I have an idea," said Phajan. "I have long suspected that one of my servants has contacts in the underground—though of course, she has never said anything about it. If you wish, I will pursue the matter with her. *Carefully,* you understand. And with some luck, I may succeed."

"We would be most grateful," said the captain. "There is a great deal at stake here."

Not the least of which was the fate of Beverly Crusher. And only after Picard's team brought a cure to the Kevrata could they turn their attentions to finding her.

"I understand," said Phajan. He crossed the room and got a dark green thermal suit off a wall hook. "One way or the other, this will not take long."

Worf gazed at the desktop monitor in front of him, which hadn't been hooked up until the day before, and took in the sight of Captain Idun Asmund.

"You look well," she told him.

"So do you," he said.

It was not a lie. Had Worf not known better, he would have believed Asmund to be ten years younger than her chronological age. But then, as a student of the Klingon martial arts, she exercised vigorously on a regular basis.

Some years earlier, when she and some of Picard's other former colleagues visited the *Enterprise,* the ship was plagued by a series of vicious murder attempts. In time, the evidence seemed to point to Idun Asmund.

Worf, who was Picard's security officer at the time, was forced to place the woman in the brig. Still, he became the only one who would heed her protestations of innocence.

But then, he was a Klingon born and she—despite her blond hair and unmistakably human features—had been raised as a Klingon on Q'onoS. Worf could see beyond the appearance of guilt and conclude that Asmund was telling the truth.

Though no one would listen to him, she told him she was grateful for his efforts on her behalf. Later, of course, she was proven innocent of the charges. But being a Klingon, she would not have forgotten Worf's faith in her.

Hence, his decision to contact her under these circumstances. If any of the captain's former colleagues might consider helping him, it would be Idun Asmund.

"Congratulations," said Worf, "on your promotion to captain."

Asmund smiled a tight, controlled smile. "That happened several months ago, and you did not see fit to contact me then. To what do I owe the honor now?"

Worf wasn't surprised by her directness. Klingons weren't in the habit of mincing words.

"I have a question," he said, "that you may be able to answer."

The captain nodded. "Go ahead."

"Doctor Crusher has been declared missing in action and Captain Picard—along with some of your old colleagues—has been assigned to find her. I thought you might know where the captain's mission was leading him."

Worf had barely gotten the first sentence out when he saw the look of surprise and concern on Asmund's face, and knew by that sign that she wouldn't be able to help him. If she hadn't heard yet about Beverly's disappearance, she certainly wouldn't be able to point Worf in the captain's direction.

"I am sorry to hear about Doctor Crusher," said Asmund, who had served with the physician's late husband on the *Stargazer*. "Unfortunately, I have heard nothing about this mission, so I cannot be of help to you."

"I understand," said Worf, containing his disappointment.

"But missing-in-action reports are not always as final as they appear to be. Doctor Crusher may yet turn up unharmed."

"That is our hope," said Worf.

But he could tell by Asmund's tone that she wasn't optimistic, despite her words of encouragement. In her view, no doubt, the doctor was as good as dead.

Of course, she didn't know Beverly the way Worf did. "I will not take up any more of your time," he said. *"Qapla',* Captain."

Asmund inclined her head. *"Qapla',* Worf, son of Mogh." A moment later, her image on the screen was replaced with that of the Federation logo.

Expelling a sound of disgust, Worf sat back in his chair. Asmund had turned out to be a dead end. But surely, there were other avenues he and Geordi could pursue.

He just hoped one of them bore fruit.

Worf's sleep had been interrupted by a vision the night before, a dark and unsettling drama in which he learned that the doctor had perished on some obscure and foreboding world trying to help a species oblivious to her efforts. In the dream, it fell to Captain Picard to bring her body home, just as he had done with Beverly's mate decades earlier.

At the doctor's funeral, the captain said that only *one* thing could have saved Beverly from death—the intervention of the Klingon warrior who had been her comrade. Unfortunately, said Picard, Worf had not made an effort to reach out to her. He had forgotten about her, allowing other matters to command his attention.

To a greater degree than most other species, Klingons

put stock in dreams—and for all his exposure to humans and Starfleet, Worf was no exception. If Doctor Crusher perished, it would *not* be because he had forgotten about her.

With that in mind, he asked the computer for Geordi's location on the ship. He had to tell his fellow conspirator that his conversation with Captain Asmund had availed them nothing.

And that they were back to square one.

Picard had spent much of the time since Phajan's departure thinking about Beverly Crusher, and what hardships she might be overcoming at that juncture. But as the seconds ticked away, something else rose to the surface of his mind.

Not a thought, exactly. More of a feeling.

He had made decisions based on feelings before in the course of his career, and seldom did he have occasion to regret them. Eventually, they all turned out to be based on something—a half-remembered fact, an unconscious observation.

But at the times they first came to him, they seemed only to be feelings—faceless, formless, and yet compelling all the same. *This,* Picard told himself, *is one of those times*.

Even as he thought this, he saw Pug sit down on the chair opposite his. The former security chief seemed concerned—perhaps as concerned as Picard himself.

"What's wrong?" Pug asked. "And don't tell me nothing. I've seen your shoulders bunch that way before."

You know me too well, the captain thought. "I have a bad feeling about this, Pug."

"How bad?"

Picard frowned. "I think we should leave."

"I beg your pardon?" said Decalon, who was standing at the far end of the room.

"I think we should leave," the captain said a little louder, drawing Greyhorse's attention as well.

"Why?" asked the doctor, still cradling in his powerful hands a dusty metal curio he had picked up from an end table.

Picard turned to him. *Why indeed?*

"Phajan has been gone a long time," he said. "Too long, it seems to me. The more I consider the situation, the less inclined I am to trust him."

Decalon cursed beneath his breath. "Phajan's character is beyond reproach. He was an integral part of the underground railroad, trusted implicitly by your Federation."

Picard acknowledged the fact. "Despite all that," he said, thinking out loud, "Phajan never left the Empire himself. What kept him here all this time?"

"He didn't want to abandon his family," said Decalon. "He was attached to his mother and sisters."

"Who live on the homeworld," Picard pointed out, "while Phajan lives here on Kevratas. Not a terribly strong attachment, I would say."

It was a good point. What's more, the Romulan didn't have an answer for it.

"And now he is a tax collector," the captain continued, "helping the Empire to exploit the Kevrata."

"These are not easy times," said Decalon. "It is difficult for people to find employment."

"Perhaps," said Picard. "However, I cannot imagine that this was the only position available. The most lucrative, possibly, but not the only one."

Decalon straightened. "It is not Phajan's fault that he is paid well for his services."

"Those who live in comfort," said the captain, "are seldom eager to take risks. I have seen it over and over again. And Phajan very definitely lives in comfort."

The Romulan's face darkened. "He risked his life for me and others like me. He is a hero."

"Was," said Picard. "But by his own admission, he has changed. He is no longer the person you knew. And now we are sitting here—at Phajan's insistence—relying on him to help us. But will he? Or will he betray us?"

Decalon made a gesture of dismissal. "Wild speculation. Where is the proof to support it, Captain? Where is the evidence so overwhelming that we should cast Phajan aside, and with him our best chance of contacting the Kevratan underground?"

It was a fair question. And Picard was certain that if he pondered it long enough, he would find an answer. But there was no time for that. If there was even a chance that Phajan would violate their trust, they had to move quickly.

"When you became part of this mission," Picard told Decalon, "you agreed to follow my orders. This is one of them."

Exasperated, the Romulan turned to Greyhorse for help. "Reason with him," he said.

But the doctor was already on his feet. "I would say I'm the wrong person to speak of reason, having exhibited certain deficiencies in that area."

Decalon looked at Greyhorse askance. Having never been apprised of the doctor's difficulties, he could not have known what Greyhorse was talking about.

Peremptorily, Picard asked, "Are you coming, Decalon?"

The Romulan regarded him again and shook his head. "This is madness. Phajan will return and wonder what became of us."

"Which, I believe," Greyhorse said as he put the dusty curio back on its table, "is the captain's intention."

Decalon looked disgusted. However, as Picard had pointed out, he wasn't the one in charge of their mission.

"Let's go," said Pug.

Reluctantly—because Phajan really *had* been their most promising lead—Picard pulled his thermal suit back on, hood and all. Then he opened the door to Phajan's house and led the way outside, where a stinging, lashing sleet had begun.

The captain bent into it. He didn't need to glance over his shoulder to know the others were following him— including Decalon, however grudgingly.

Picard had likely seen his last of Phajan, so he would never have his assessment of the Romulan validated. Once, in the earliest days of his captaincy, that would have bothered him. It didn't bother him any longer.

He wasn't in this for the satisfaction. He was in it to see his mission accomplished and Beverly brought home again.

With those two very important objectives in mind, he left Phajan's house behind.

Sela and her troops had put down at the last square large enough to accommodate their hovercraft, and continued the rest of the way to Phajan's house on foot.

After all, in the seemingly perpetual storm that plagued Kevratas, the hovercraft couldn't run as silently as it was supposed to, and the commander didn't want her prey to suspect that something was wrong. If even one member of the Federation party heard the craft's deep, metallic moan, he and his comrades would be seeking a new hiding place.

Sela wasn't looking forward to a house-to-house search of the city. Not when night would be falling soon and the already low temperature would be dropping even further.

As the house loomed out of the rush of ice and snow, Sela signaled for half of her troops to surround the place—in case her prey tried to escape through a window or the rear exit. With a dozen centurions slicing through the weather to carry out her order, the commander glanced at her informant.

"Four of them, correct?"

"Yes," Phajan confirmed, his voice muffled by the part of his garb that covered his mouth.

And not just any four, Sela mused.

One of them, beneath his holo-disguise, was a Romulan traitor. And two others were former Starfleet officers.

But the prize, in this case, was Jean-Luc Picard, Sela's longtime nemesis, the human she loathed above all others. She had any number of scores to settle with the captain, and she knew oh so many ways to settle them.

When the commander first heard from Phajan about his guests, she speculated that Picard had crossed the Neutral Zone specifically to rescue Beverly Crusher—a typical human gesture. Surely, that would have been enough to explain his appearance on Kevratas.

Then Phajan told her that one of Picard's companions was a doctor—leading Sela to the conclusion that the captain wasn't just there to retrieve his chief medical officer. Like Crusher, he meant to provide the natives with a cure for their plague.

One they would never receive—though without question, a vaccine would have made Sela's job a good deal easier. The fear and misery caused by the disease had rendered the most desperate of the Kevrata even more so. With little or nothing to lose, they had become bolder, more vocal in stirring up the masses.

Were there a way for Sela to take credit for a cure, she might have allowed Crusher to pursue one. Certainly, it would have placed the Romulans in a different light, presenting them as benefactors rather than occupiers and oppressors. Under those circumstances, the rebellion would have swiftly lost its appeal.

But the rebels knew of Crusher's appearance on their world. And they knew also that the Romulans had proven quite ineffectual in fighting the plague—both this time and on that other occasion, when Sela was but a child and had yet to hear of Kevratas.

If Sela were to offer them a cure, they would suspect it was the work of the human physician. Instead of the

Empire receiving credit for an uncharacteristic act of kindness, the Federation would be identified as the natives' benefactor—and far from dampening the fires of revolt, Sela would find herself fanning them.

So the Kevrata would remain at the mercy of their disease. And if that created more of a mess for her to clean up, so be it.

Squinting against the assault of the weather, Sela watched her centurions take their places around Phajan's house. "Your vigilance," she told the tax collector, "is to be applauded."

"I only did my duty," said Phajan. "May the Empire vanquish all her enemies."

Sela nodded in approval of the sentiment. Picard was certainly an enemy worth vanquishing.

As for Phajan . . . it was not so long ago that *he* had been an enemy himself. Now he was reduced to a tool, to be used by whoever was in charge on Romulus.

More than a decade earlier, Phajan had been part of a scheme to smuggle defectors to the Federation. Both the Imperial Defense Force and the Tal Shiar had become aware of the operation at about the same time.

Fortunately, the Defense Force got to it first. The smugglers it took into custody were given a choice: they could give up the identities of their comrades or they could die a crushingly painful death. Most of them opted for death. Only Phajan and a couple of others chose to live as turncoats.

For a while, they continued to accept overtures from potential defectors, who expected to obtain passage to the Federation like those before them. Thanks to Phajan and the other traitors, these people were instead seized and destroyed.

Eventually, the truth about their fates must have leaked out. The flow of overtures slowed to a trickle and then stopped altogether.

With the ring disabled, there was talk in the Defense Force's inner circle of turning Phajan and his cohorts over to the praetor, who would almost certainly make examples of them. Then Shinzon took over and the discussion was set aside.

Because of that turn of events, Phajan and the others were allowed to live. Sela was glad of it, considering the opportunity it was even now presenting her. But then, traitors often managed to come in handy.

Come in handy . . .

It was one of her mother's expressions. Sela felt like spitting—and would have, were it not for the flap of garb that kept her face warm. She wanted nothing to do with her weakling of a mother. It was bad enough that she had inherited some of Tasha Yar's genes when it came to her appearance.

Inside, she was a Romulan—and she would kill the individual who said otherwise.

"Commander Sela," said Akadia, her second-in-command on Kevratas. "Your centurions are in place."

Sela nodded. "Then let us root out these intruders."

"As you wish," said Akadia. He turned to Phajan, looking down on the tax collector with the hauteur of a career military officer. "Come with me."

Without a word, Phajan did as he was instructed. They were followed by the rest of the troops Sela had brought with her, except for the two Sela had designated as her bodyguards. As Akadia's party approached Phajan's front door, his centurions fanned out on either side of it.

Sela couldn't hear Akadia's instructions to Phajan over the incessant hissing of the storm, but she had an idea of what he was saying: something along the lines of "Open it."

The tax collector punched a code into a narrow strip beside the door, which sat just below a communications grate. The security system was of the type Sela had ordered installed in all Romulan domiciles. In fact, it was one of the first commands she had issued after her arrival on Kevratas.

After all, these were dangerous times. Romulan citizens had to be protected from the vagaries of the natives.

As she thought that, Phajan's door opened and Akadia led the charge into the house. Phajan remained outside, his face turned away, his back pressed against a wall lest he be struck by an errant disruptor beam.

It is merely a matter of time now, Sela told herself, and pulled her hood further down over her face.

But as the seconds passed, nothing happened. And the longer the commander waited, the stronger became her suspicion that something was amiss. Then Akadia appeared in the doorway shaking his head, and she was sure of it.

Picard and his comrades were no longer in Phajan's house. *Most unfortunate,* the commander thought, tamping down her disappointment.

Tramping through the snow, oblivious of the cold, Sela made her way past Phajan and Akadia and took a look inside the house herself. It was painfully and undeniably empty.

When she emerged, she went straight to the tax collector. His brow knit as he saw the expression on her face.

"There is no sign," said Sela, working hard to keep her voice free of emotion, "that Picard was ever here."

"Commander," said Phajan, his voice rising in pitch, "I swear that what I told you was true. Picard and the others were here less than an hour ago."

Sela gave him a long, hard look. He appeared to be telling the truth—and indeed, she couldn't imagine why the fellow would have lied to her.

Unfortunately, it didn't matter whether his intentions had been honorable. The results were unsatisfying, and to the commander's way of thinking, results were all that mattered.

"They were here," Phajan insisted.

"Of course they were," said the commander. "We were simply too late to apprehend them."

Phajan's fear seemed to drain from his face. "I am glad you understand, Commander."

She didn't say anything more. She simply turned and walked in the direction of her waiting hovercraft, leaving Phajan standing there by his open door.

I don't like being disappointed, she reflected as the sleet slanted into her face. *Especially in front of my centurions.* So far from Romulus, she needed the unmitigated trust and cooperation of everyone who served under her at all times. Anything less could be her undoing.

Fortunately, Sela had someone to blame for this disaster. Despite what she had said to Phajan, the turncoat had to at least suspect that she was not pleased with him, and that his days among the living were numbered.

After all, Romulan commanders weren't renowned for their stores of patience, and Sela was even less patient than the rest of her ilk. It was, as she had been told on more than one occasion, one of her better qualities.

8

———

PICARD HAD KNOWN FROM THE MOMENT HE AND his team abandoned the shelter of Phajan's house that there were drawbacks to their Plan B. *Significant* ones.

On one side of the ledger, they knew where the rebels had hidden themselves—in an elaborate network of catacombs below the fortresslike edifice that, in ancient times, had housed the region's royal family. In fact, everyone possessed this bit of information, including the occupying Romulans.

But that didn't mean they could easily make use of it. The catacomb complex was so expansive and confusing that it could conceal a moving target indefinitely—which was why Sela's centurions had yet to snare a single member of what was, quite literally, the Kevratan "underground."

"With all due respect," said Decalon, a little more than

two hours after they had entered the tombs via one of the tunnels exposed by the Romulans, "we should have remained with Phajan."

The captain frowned. He was leading the way through the frigid darkness, his palmlight probing just a little deeper than those of his comrades. "I believe," he returned, "that you have expressed that opinion several times already."

The Romulan fell silent again. But if he wasn't saying the words out loud, it didn't mean he wasn't saying them to himself. And Picard had yet to demonstrate that his backup plan was capable of bearing fruit.

After all, the rebels had to have lookouts positioned in the tunnels surrounding their encampment. And if they had eluded the Romulans to that point, they also had to be able to relocate at a moment's notice.

For all the captain knew, their presence underground had already triggered such a move, and they would run out of supplies before they got near the rebels a second time. That was one possibility. Another was that the underground would confuse them with the Romulans and decide to ambush them.

If that happened, Picard and his companions wouldn't stand a chance. They would be outflanked and outnumbered before they knew what was happening.

The third possibility was even worse: that they would encounter a Romulan search-and-destroy patrol, which was likely to show them even less mercy than the Kevrata would. *Hardly a pleasant prospect in the bunch,* Picard conceded.

He was still hoping for the fourth possibility—the one

in which they stumbled across the rebels before too long and were greeted without violence. But as he made his way from tunnel to cold, dank tunnel, that seemed less and less likely all the time.

The tricorders they had brought down to Kevratas with them could have made their task a good deal less difficult. Unfortunately, they were fouled most of the time by the same mineral deposits that made it impossible to beam to the planet's surface.

Joseph came up beside the captain, his eyes darting everywhere. "We'll find them," he said. "Just watch."

Picard had to smile. "I miss your optimism, Pug."

"Still have that marble?"

"Of course," said the captain. "It is in a safe place in my quarters on the *Enterprise.*"

Joseph had given his lucky marble to Picard to help him through a competency hearing more than thirty years earlier, shortly after the captain took command of the *Stargazer*. It didn't let Picard down that day, nor had it let him down since.

He had offered to return it on more than one occasion. However, Joseph had always refused to take it back, saying that Picard needed it more than he did.

"Well," said Joseph, "that explains why we're still wandering around in these tunnels. If you had brought the marble, we would have been toasting marshmallows with the rebels by now."

"Forgive me," said Picard.

"Not a chance," said Joseph.

The captain glanced at him. "I don't remember your being so insubordinate when we were on the *Stargazer.*"

"Back then, you were a god to me. Now you're just a guy who forgot his marble."

Picard sighed in mock frustration. It was good to have Joseph alongside him again. *Damned* good.

He glanced back at his other former comrade, who had been silent since they left Phajan's house. Greyhorse was inscrutable as he searched the beam-shot darkness of the tunnel, his thoughts very much his own.

Picard preferred that to what the doctor was saying earlier. It was not a comfortable thought that the man most indispensable to the success of their mission might also be a little insane.

The administrator of Greyhorse's penal colony had said he was capable of taking part in a mission. She had *assured* the captain of it. But he feared now that she had been wrong.

And if that was the case, it wouldn't matter if they found the rebels or not. It would all be for nothing if Greyhorse couldn't focus enough to come up with a cure.

"I am sorry," Decalon said suddenly, "but this is futile." He gestured to the length of tunnel behind them. "We should turn around and return to Phajan's house. He may have made contact with the underground by now."

"The captain's already told you," said Joseph, "we're no longer pursuing that option."

Picard put his hand on his friend's shoulder. "I can speak for myself, Pug." He turned to Decalon. "We are not going back. We are moving ahead. *Now.*"

The Romulan regarded him for a moment. "This is a mistake."

"Perhaps," said the captain. "But again, I remind you

that when you undertook this mission, you agreed to follow my orders."

"That," said Decalon, "was before I realized how fallible you are. As fallible as any other human."

"And Romulans aren't?" asked Joseph. "If you dust off your memory a little, you'll remember it was we humans who—"

Picard didn't hear the rest, because suddenly he realized why he had pulled them out of Phajan's house. For a reason he couldn't articulate at the time, but a valid one nonetheless.

"The dust," he said.

Pug and Decalon looked puzzled. Greyhorse too. "I beg your pardon?" said the Romulan.

"Phajan's house was full of it," said the captain. "And yet he told us he had servants. If that were true, why wouldn't they have dusted the place?"

His question echoed in the frozen air of the tunnel. Pondering it, his companions looked at him and at each other, but more than anyone they looked at Decalon.

"Romulans are meticulous housekeepers," Picard noted. "Surely, if Phajan had even *one* servant . . ." He allowed his voice to trail off, leaving the rest for his companions to fill in.

Decalon's eyes went flat and stony. He remained that way as he considered the captain's insight, no doubt looking for a loophole in its logic. But in the end, he seemed unable to find any.

Finally, the Romulan lifted his chin. "As you have deduced," he told Picard, "Phajan was attempting to deceive us. I regret that I did not see it. And I regret even more that I was so foolish as to question your judgment."

The captain nodded. "Then let's go on." But before he could lead them deeper into the embrace of the catacombs, their tunnel was filled with long, seething needles of emerald fury.

Disruptors! he thought. But what he yelled was "Down!"

It was too late to help Joseph, who took a shot square in the chest and went skittering backward. But Picard and the others were able to douse their palmlights and flatten themselves against the rough stone floor.

"We are not Romulans!" the captain called out, hoping that it was the underground they had encountered rather than one of Sela's patrols.

But there was no answer and no respite in the enemy's volleys. *So much for that,* Picard told himself.

He couldn't tell if Joseph was still alive, but he didn't have the luxury of worrying about it. Pulling out his phaser, he aimed in what seemed like the right direction and returned fire.

A moment later, Decalon and Greyhorse did the same, their ruby beams clashing violently with the green ones of their adversaries. Unfortunately, Picard and his comrades were compelled to fire blindly, obtaining only glimpses of their intended targets in the flash of energy fire, so they had no idea if their blasts were hitting anything.

Suddenly, the captain heard a cry—deep and resonant with pain. *Greyhorse,* he thought with a pang of concern. There was a reason the doctor hadn't been brought on a great many away missions: he was a decided liability in a firefight.

"Doctor?" Picard called out.

"Here," said Greyhorse, though it sounded as if he were responding through clenched teeth.

But at least he was alive. That meant they could still carry out their mission, as long as they could beat the odds and maneuver their way out of this mess.

Simplicity itself, the captain thought.

Even though it was left to only Picard and Decalon to carry on. Even though it was clear they were vastly outnumbered, given the number of beams erupting at them.

The captain was desperately trying to come up with a method of escape when his adversaries did the last thing he would have expected—*they stopped firing.* At first he thought it was just a momentary respite, but it stretched on. And on.

In the eerie silence, Picard was left with one burning question . . .

Why?

Geordi had every reason to be happy as he stared at his monitor screen. After all, he had added another important piece to the puzzle of where Captain Picard had gone in pursuit of Beverly.

But all he could do was sit there, his mouth as dry as the deserts of Kolarus III.

Worf, who was standing beside Geordi with his hand on the engineer's chair, was the one who finally said it out loud: "The Romulan Empire . . . ?"

Geordi wasn't a big fan of the Romulans. Sure, he had worked with his share of them during the Dominion War, when they were officially allies of the Federation. But he couldn't forget what they had done to him years earlier, capturing him and programming him to murder a Klingon dignitary.

He still shuddered when he thought about it, and not with fear. There weren't a lot of things that made Geordi angry, but that was one of them.

And now an old comrade from his days on the *Victory,* who had been transferred recently to a Starfleet monitor station, had responded to his request for data on the *Annabel Lee.* Without question, her course was taking her into the heart of the Empire.

"Looks that way," said Geordi, in answer to his friend's question.

"But why would the Romulans call for the doctor?" asked Worf. "Unless—"

"Unless it wasn't the Romulans," said Geordi, "but one of their subject worlds. One in need of medical expertise."

Worf nodded. "That makes sense. But we do not know *which* world, and there are scores of them."

The engineer frowned. "I could swear Beverly once said something about treating people from a Romulan outworld." He glanced at Worf. "Sound familiar?"

Worf considered the question, then shook his head. "It does not."

Geordi leaned back in his chair. "Maybe if I go over a list of the outworlds, one of them will ring a bell."

"With that sort of information in hand," said Worf, "all we would need is a spaceworthy craft—and we have enough of them in the shuttlebay to take our pick."

The engineer nodded. "I just have to remember."

Calling up a list of the worlds in question on his monitor, he went to work.

The silence around Picard was so deep and vast, it seemed he could lose himself in it and never be found. *What is going on?* he asked inwardly.

"Who are you?" came a voice, cascading suddenly through the corridor.

The question hadn't come from a Romulan—the captain was certain of that. The tongue that fashioned it was too rough, too guttural to be anything but Kevratan.

Picard's unseen adversaries hadn't answered his remark earlier, perhaps because they couldn't distinguish between a human voice and a Romulan one. But clearly, he had planted a seed of doubt in their minds.

"We are not the enemy," said the captain, hoping to grow the seed into a certainty.

"Then who are you?" asked one of the Kevrata—a different one, Picard thought.

"A team from the Federation," said Picard. "We are here to help you defeat the plague."

"You are not the doctor," observed the first Kevrata, making it sound like an accusation.

"Doctor Crusher is not among us," the captain conceded. "But I have brought you another physician—one who studied the plague at Doctor Crusher's side."

The Kevrata exchanged muted comments. It seemed to Picard that one of them was doing his best to overrule the others.

"How do we know you are telling us the truth?" a Kevrata asked.

There was but one way to convince them. Putting his phaser away and deactivating his holodevice, the captain got to his feet in the darkness. Then he switched on his palmlight and turned its radiance on his undeniably human countenance.

More comments, as muted as before. But this time, there didn't seem to be as much controversy.

Finally, a light went on among the Kevrata and a single figure rose from their midst. He seemed exceedingly tall for one of his species, nearly two and a half meters by Picard's reckoning. The disruptor in his hand looked strangely toylike.

Giving his weapon to one of his companions, the Kevrata stepped forward, his hands extended with their palms up. "I am Hanafaejas," he said, "leader of these people."

Picard imitated the gesture. "Jean-Luc Picard, captain of the *Starship Enterprise*. I come as an emissary of the Federation."

"Welcome to our home," said the towering Kevrata.

The captain's thoughts turned to Joseph. "One of my people was hit hard by your weapons fire. He will need medical attention—if he is still alive."

Hanafaejas dismissed Picard's concern with a wave of his massive furred hand. "Our weapons were not set to kill. Your comrade will be all right."

The captain felt a wave of relief. "I am glad to hear that."

"Hanafaejas!" called one of the other Kevrata, his voice strident with urgency. "It is a trick!"

Suddenly, a beam of light illuminated Decalon's face. The Romulan squinted but tolerated it without comment.

"A Romulan?" asked Hanafaejas. He turned to Picard, his expression a wary one.

"Decalon is a member of my team," said Picard. "He lived on Kevratas once. He knows his way around."

Hanafaejas considered the Romulan for a moment. Then he held up his hand, calling for restraint from the other Kevrata. "We will treat him as we treat our other guests."

The captain was glad to hear that also. He said so.

By then, additional lights had been activated, and Picard could see that Greyhorse—despite his own injury—was running a tricorder over Joseph. After a moment, the doctor turned to Picard and said, "He is suffering from a mild concussion, nothing more. Unfortunately, I have no stimulants with which to wake him."

"We do," said Hanafaejas.

At his signal, one of the other Kevrata produced a small bag made of what looked like natural fibers and gave it to Greyhorse. The doctor opened it, sniffed its contents, and then placed it under Joseph's nose.

With a groan, Joseph regained consciousness and looked around. Seeing the Kevrata standing about him, he tried to sit up—and grimaced at the pain it cost him. Clutching his head, he asked, "What happened?"

"You were hit with a directed-energy beam," Greyhorse explained, "but you sustained no serious damage."

"Also," said Picard with a glance at Hanafaejas, "we appear to have located the Kevratan underground."

"We will take you back to our place of concealment,"

said the giant. "We have medicines there that can assuage your comrade's disruptor shock."

Picard nodded. "Thank you."

The giant made a snuffling sound and said, "I regret from my heart that you will find our lair inadequately provisioned. We would very much like to be better hosts, but we labor under the burden of a long, bitter occupation."

"I assure you," said Picard, "we do not feel slighted in the least. To tell you the truth, I am far less interested in feasting than I am in information about Doctor Crusher. Have you heard anything about her?"

Hanafaejas hesitated for a moment, giving Picard the impression that he had unhappy news to impart. The captain bit his lip as he braced himself for it.

"Unfortunately," said the rebel, "I cannot help you in that regard. We have no current intelligence concerning the doctor. All we know is that she escaped the tavern where Commander Sela burst in on her."

Picard frowned. "It was Sela herself who took Doctor Crusher prisoner?"

"Yes," said Hanafaejas. "She took charge of Kevratas only recently, but she has already proven to be a most unpleasant individual."

"I know," said the captain. "I have made her acquaintance."

9

BEVERLY HAD SEEN A PARADE OF CENTURIONS COME down the corridor outside her cell and check on her at intervals. However, the one who had whispered to her hadn't been among them.

She couldn't help wondering if something had happened to him. Had he gotten hurt in a skirmish with the underground—maybe even killed? Or had Sela caught him in an act of disloyalty and thrown him in another cell?

Of course, his absence might have meant nothing. However, he was Beverly's only hope of escaping this place. That made his welfare a subject of more than passing interest to her.

Finally, on the third day of her captivity, she caught sight of the centurion in question. He was as alive and well as she had hoped. Sitting forward on the side of her bed, she wondered if he would say something to her again.

But when he stopped at her cell, he didn't look her in

the eye. He just examined the emitters that maintained her barrier, as if that were his only concern.

Maybe it is, Crusher thought. *Maybe he only said those things the other day to get my hopes up. To tease me.*

No. The centurion had been in earnest—she was certain of it. If he wasn't talking now, he had a reason. She would just have to accept it and remain silent as well.

Just as she made that decision, the Romulan did something none of the others had done. He moved to the control pad on the wall beside her cell and tapped in a code.

What's he up to? she wondered.

Before Beverly knew it, she got her answer—as she saw her plasma barrier fizzle away. Suddenly and unbelievably, the mouth of her cell was unbarred.

"Come," the centurion said, gesturing for her to get up and follow him. *"Now."*

By the time the doctor went through the open doorway, her benefactor was a third of the way down the corridor. Her heart pounding, she did her best to keep up with him on legs that hadn't been stretched in too long.

No one stood in their way as they reached the end of the corridor. And no one intervened as they negotiated the next corridor, which doglegged off the first.

Beverly was incredulous. There was a Romulan garrison in this building, with who-knew-how-many centurions. And yet it seemed they were about to walk out without a fight.

Until they neared the end of the second corridor and heard voices. There were Romulans around the bend—more than one for certain, and maybe as many as three or four.

Beverly looked to her companion, wondering what he would do. He seemed strangely calm, despite the considerable peril into which he had placed himself.

She wished she could say the same. Her blood was pounding so loudly in her ears she could barely hear anything else.

Gesturing for Beverly to stay back, her companion seemed to gather himself. Then he swung around the corner, launching himself into the midst of his fellow centurions.

The doctor trusted her unexpected friend, but she couldn't do as he had requested. Needing to get a sense of what was happening, she poked her head past the corner of the rough, stone wall.

What she saw was an antechamber with five violently clashing centurions. Unfortunately, her benefactor was surrounded by the other four.

At first, Crusher thought she and her ally were done for, and likewise her chances of escape. Then he showed her that he was as skilled a fighter as she had ever seen.

As she watched, amazed, he slammed one of his adversaries into a wall face-first. Then he ducked a blow from a second and sent a third one reeling with a kick to the chest.

Over the years, the doctor had been exposed to several kinds of martial arts—a couple of them under Worf's tutelage—and in her companion's repertoire she detected elements of all of them. Clearly, this was an individual who had studied widely, well beyond the boundaries of the Empire.

Each blow he landed was precise and eminently effective, each evasive maneuver smooth and economical. Before long he had leveled all four of his opponents, each of whom seemed as surprised by his prowess as Beverly was.

The moment the last of the centurions hit the floor, the doctor's benefactor looked back in her direction—and scowled. After all, he *had* gestured for her to hang back.

But he didn't take the time to scold her. All he said was, "Come," and crossed the antechamber in the direction of a high, arched doorway.

Beverly followed him. But as she picked her way among the unconscious forms of the guards, she saw one of them open his eyes and look up at her.

There was no time to stop him from grabbing his disruptor. It was too close at hand, right there on the floor beside him. And there was even less time for her to warn her benefactor.

So Beverly did the only thing she *could* do. She took a quick step and launched her booted toe into the guard's jaw. It snapped his head around, not hard enough to break his neck but more than hard enough to knock him out again.

Her companion must have heard the impact, because he stopped and looked back over his shoulder. But he didn't congratulate her. He just turned and kept going, with the obvious expectation that she would fall in behind him.

Which Beverly did. Having gotten *this* far, it would have been the height of foolishness—not to mention ingratitude—to do anything else. But first she knelt and picked up an ownerless disruptor, just in case.

The centurion paused just before the arched doorway, then slipped through it. The doctor went after him and found herself in a narrow, high-ceilinged corridor, which led to yet another arched doorway.

Beyond it there were other voices. *More of them than before,* Beverly thought. As she caught up with her bene-factor, he made another sign for her to stay back. But this time she grabbed his arm, and when he turned to her she shook her head.

She was a commander in Starfleet and an experienced if not exactly accomplished combatant. It didn't make sense for her to stand by a second time—especially when the odds were so heavily stacked against them.

The centurion looked into Beverly's eyes for a moment, as if to gauge the depth of the resolve he saw there. Finally, he nodded. Then, removing his disruptor from his hip holster with his right hand, he used his left to count down: *One. Two . . .*

Three.

Without a hint of hesitation, he went charging into the room. And Beverly, her weapon clenched in her fist, dove right in after him.

She saw instantly why her benefactor had drawn his disruptor, though an energy discharge would almost cer-tainly set off an alarm. The room was too big for hand-to-hand combat, their opponents too scattered. And their goal, an enormous set of wooden doors at the far end of the chamber, was too far away.

Fortunately, they had the advantage of surprise. The Romulans in the room—as many as seven of them, the doctor estimated—might have expected an attack from the Kevrata outside the building, but never from within.

Before they could react, Beverly and her companion

had blasted two of them off their feet. As the rest groped for their disruptor pistols, the intruders took down a couple more of them. Then the confrontation turned into bedlam, a wild, flashing web of fire and return fire.

It turned out that the doctor's companion was as good a marksman as he was a close-quarters fighter. As Beverly struggled to keep her adversaries in sight, her ally sent two more of his colleagues crashing into walls.

When Beverly cut down a Romulan running for the door, there was just one guard left standing. He managed to squeeze off only a single errant shot before an energy bolt folded him in two.

That left the wooden doors conveniently unguarded. And on their far side was freedom, if the sparkle of snow in the crack between them was any indication.

But Beverly wasn't dressed for the frigid Kevratan weather, and neither was her companion. She couldn't imagine them getting far before the cold seeped into their bones and they fell victim to irreversible hypothermia.

She was about to mention this when the centurion reached into his chain-mail tunic and produced something square and white. Saying, "Put this on," he tossed it to her.

As it flew through the air, it unfolded a little. Once Beverly had it in her hands, she saw it was a garment of some kind, compressed for ease of concealment.

Finding a hooded hole for her head, she slipped the garment on. Mercifully, it reached all the way down to her knees, with a belt that could be tightened at the waist. While it didn't do anything for her feet, it did have glovelike appendages for her hands.

Her companion had a second such garment for himself. Pulling it on, he motioned toward the doors. They attacked the task together, sliding a black metal bolt aside and then pushing one of the doors as hard as they could.

The thing was heavy, making them work. And when it finally swung open, it gave them a faceful of snow for their trouble. Brushing it out of her eyes with her free hand, Beverly tried to get a glimpse of what was ahead of them.

All she could see was blowing whiteness. But at least there weren't any guards out there.

Her benefactor leaned close to her, close enough to be heard over the hooting of the wind. "Stay with me," he barked. Then he showed her his arm and pointed to it.

She got the message. They were all in white—an advantage when it came to their escape. But if she let him get too far ahead of her, she would lose sight of him.

"I will," Beverly assured him.

She had barely gotten the words out when a shaft of green fury pierced the air between them. Recoiling from it, she almost fell on the slippery surface underfoot. But with an effort she righted herself and peered back into the building to see the centurion who had unleashed the beam.

Unfortunately, he wasn't the only one in the chamber. As others poured in and discovered the prone forms of their colleagues, they added to the barrage. Their blasts were like emerald flames erupting from the maw of a wooden-toothed serpent.

"Run!" bellowed Beverly's companion, grabbing her arm to pull her after him.

Knowing she could be skewered at any moment, she

turned from the guards and pelted after her benefactor. The Romulans' disruptor bolts buried themselves in the storm on either side of her, but somehow none of them found their mark. And after a while, they stopped coming after her.

Sparing a glance over her shoulder, the doctor could barely make out the form of the building in which she had been imprisoned. It would be even harder to spot a couple of fugitives, even if they weren't dressed all in white.

As for where they were going—Beverly had no idea. And even if she did, she would never have been able to get them there. She could barely keep her eyes open without exposing them to the slash of wind-driven snow.

Her companion, on the other hand, seemed to know exactly where he was going. *How?* she wondered. Romulans had inner eyelids that protected their vision from sudden changes in their environment, but they were opaque. If the centurion's had descended, he wouldn't have been able to see at all.

Maybe a com beacon, or something similar? Her companion could have planted it at their destination so they could home in on it, storm or no storm.

Beverly imagined she would find out eventually. That is, if Sela didn't find them first.

As Worf sat in the shuttlecraft he had selected for himself and Geordi and ran a diagnostic routine, he found himself wishing his comrade's memory were better.

Though to be truthful, he reflected, *I do not believe I*

would have remembered a passing reference either. It was impressive, he supposed, that Geordi recalled the incident at all.

Unexpectedly, his combadge beeped. Tapping it, he said, "Worf here."

"It's Geordi," came the response. "There's a shuttle requesting access to the bay."

"A shuttle?" the Klingon echoed. "I do not recall scheduling anything of the sort."

"Well," said the engineer, "someone's here. I think you ought to see who it is."

"Of course," said Worf. He added: "Any luck?"

Geordi sighed. "I've got it narrowed to three worlds. At least, I *think* I have."

"Keep trying," said the Klingon. Then he moved to the bay's freestanding control station, which would be manned around the clock once the ship was fully repaired—and confirmed that there was a craft requesting entry.

Hailing it, he asked its occupants to identify themselves. When they complied, it made him wonder what the purpose of their visit was. However, considering with whom he was dealing, that was a question best asked face-to-face.

It took a moment for the craft to pierce the semipermeable barrier that separated the shuttlebay from the vacuum of space. The moment it set down on the deck, Worf approached the door built into its starboard side.

As it slid open, it revealed a woman in a black and gray Starfleet uniform. She was slender, almost dainty from a Klingon perspective, her hair pulled back on one side in keeping with the style of the day. However, with her broad forehead and piercing gaze, she radiated authority like few other officers of Worf's acquaintance.

Stepping out of the craft, she said, "Commander. It's good to see you again."

"Admiral Janeway," said the Klingon. "We were not expecting you."

The admiral smiled. "I apologize for dropping in without warning. I promise I won't do it very often."

That begged the question of why she had chosen to do it *now,* but Worf chose to let it go for the moment. "Will you be staying long?"

"As long as I have to," Janeway told him.

He didn't know what to make of that.

"You see," said the admiral, "repairing a ship isn't as simple as it looks. Take the parts problem, for instance."

"The parts problem?"

"That's right. You think you've got them all at hand, just where you expect them to be, and suddenly some of them disappear on you. It's rather frustrating."

Worf had the feeling that Janeway wasn't talking about parts at all—that, in fact, she was talking about personnel, and certain personnel in particular.

Had she somehow discovered what he and Geordi were up to? It made the Klingon's guts squirm like serpent worms to think so. With Janeway breathing down their necks they would never be able to identify the captain's destination, much less join him in his efforts to rescue Beverly.

Or was he reading something into the admiral's remarks that wasn't there? *Yes,* he told himself, *that is certainly possible.*

Janeway looked around the shuttlebay. "You're just itching to get out of here, aren't you?"

Worf stiffened. "Admiral?"

"It's understandable," said Janeway. "You've spent all this time in drydock. You want to get out there and put the *Enterprise* through her paces."

"Uh . . . yes," said Worf. "Of course."

"But you can't rush a job of this magnitude. You've got to give it time. And you can't stick your finger in every little detail, as much as Mister La Forge would no doubt like to. As I used to tell my first officer, 'Relax, Chakotay. Everyone will do the job assigned him. Just make sure you do *yours*.'"

As she said it, she arched an eyebrow at the Klingon. "I trust we are in agreement on that point?"

The blood rushed to Worf's face. Now he was *certain* that the admiral knew. And he was just as certain that she would keep an eye on him and Geordi, twenty-four hours a day if necessary.

They would never get off the *Enterprise,* even if the engineer *did* recall what planet Beverly had mentioned. Worf's nostrils flared, but he otherwise contained his frustration.

"Admiral," he said, knowing he was taking a chance in asking such a thing, "is it possible that some parts may turn out to be superfluous here on the *Enterprise*—and therefore more advantageously deployed elsewhere?"

Janeway regarded him for a couple of seconds before speaking. "I'll concede," she said at last, "that it's possible. But it's also possible they'd just get in the way. Our record in these matters isn't perfect, Mister Worf, but we usually know what we're doing. If I were you, I'd give us a chance."

"Aye," he said grudgingly.

But he had a terrible feeling that without his help, Doctor Crusher would die as she had died in his dream.

Beverly's hood kept out most of the snow but every now and then, when she turned her head and the wind came at her from the wrong angle, she felt a splash of cold against her neck.

She tolerated it, just as she tolerated the fact that she could barely feel her feet anymore. No matter the hardship, it was still better than passing the hours in a prison cell, waiting for Sela to decide what to do with her.

Beverly didn't know how long they had been making their way through the storm. *An hour,* she guessed. *Maybe more.* It was difficult to say.

Time lost its meaning in the face of such elemental violence. It felt as if she had always been plodding through the snow this way, and might do so forever.

For all Beverly knew, they were going in circles, impossibly lost. But the Romulan didn't seem the least bit uncertain of himself. Leaning into the wind, he planted one foot after another. And not wanting to lose sight of him, she made sure to keep up.

Suddenly, as if by magic, a building rose up in front of them—a huge thing, strong and ancient-looking. It was made of black stone, which provided a stark contrast to the whipping veils of snow, or the doctor might have missed it.

Her companion came close and shouted something in her ear. But between her hood and the howling of the wind, she wasn't able to understand him.

"What?" she shouted back.

This time, she was able to make out the word: "Inside!" And for emphasis, the Romulan pointed to an arch in the building's façade that looked as if it might house a door.

Trudging through hip-high drifts, they received a respite from the wind once they got inside the arch. It was only then that Beverly realized how green her companion's cheeks were, the blood in them having risen to the sting of the cold.

As she had surmised, there was a door recessed within the arch. Like the ones she had opened in her escape, it was made of a single, heavy-looking piece of wood—but in this case, there was no obvious way to swing it open.

Beverly was about to remark on the problem when her companion pulled his protective garment up and drew something else out of his tunic—a device no bigger than his fingernail. Depressing one of the studs on its face, he turned to the door.

Nothing happened.

The centurion pressed the stud again. Still nothing. But his expression didn't change. He just kept pushing, looking at the door, and pushing again.

Beverly couldn't believe it.

The whole way here, she had managed to endure the cold because she was generating heat with her exertions. Now that she had stopped, she could feel the storm reaching into her, weakening her. If she remained in place much longer, she would grow sleepy and finally succumb.

"Is there another way in?" she asked.

"None," said her companion.

"We could use our disruptors," she noted.

"We could," he agreed. "But then the cold would follow us in. And Sela's centurions as well, if their sensors take note of our disruptor fire."

All right then, the doctor thought. *No disruptors.*

But they couldn't just stand there pressing her companion's device. That wasn't an option either.

Finally, just as Beverly was starting to conclude that the thing wasn't working, or that the door had frozen into place, she heard a creak and the slab of wood swung inward. Without a moment's hesitation, she and her companion moved inside.

A blast of snow followed them into a foyer and scattered itself over a black marble floor. Then the door closed behind them, sealing them off from the weather.

The silence was almost shocking after the clamor of the storm. Beverly pulled her hood back and basked in it.

And it felt even better to be out of the cold. As she rubbed her hands together to get the feeling back into them, she followed her companion into a much larger room, which had cascades of wooden seats descending from its gray stone walls.

"What is this place?" she asked.

"It used to be a government hall," her companion informed her, removing his hood and then his gloves. "But the Kevrata haven't been allowed to assemble here since the beginning of the occupation. And when Commander Sela arrived, she posted notice that anyone seen congregating *anywhere* would be imprisoned."

"Naturally," said Beverly. "That's what all tyrants do."

Her benefactor shot her a smile to acknowledge her comment. But it was a guarded smile, typical of what she had come to expect from his people. Romulans always reserved a part of themselves, even when they *weren't* risking their lives by betraying their superior.

She explored the place some more, leaving the centurion behind. "What made you decide to help the Kevrata?" she asked.

He didn't answer. All Beverly heard was a slithering noise, like a blacksnake making its way through the loose dirt of the Arvadan hills.

Turning around, she found herself looking down the barrel of her companion's disruptor.

Beverly looked up at him. "What's this?"

"What does it look like?" he asked.

She shook her head in mock reproach. "You mean you weren't just helping me out of the goodness of your heart?"

"No Romulan would."

"Then why bother freeing me from my cell?"

He chuckled dryly. "I needed to make sure Commander Sela didn't profit from your capture."

An internecine conflict, then. Between Sela and who else? And what's at stake? "Why is that important to you?"

The Romulan didn't say.

"So what now? You're just going to kill me?"

"I am afraid so," he confirmed. He adjusted his disruptor to its most powerful setting—one that wouldn't leave a trace of her. "Nothing personal, you understand."

The doctor gauged the distance between them. She would be taking a chance if she tried to rush him, considering his superior strength and the prowess he had demonstrated as a fighter. But what did she have to lose?

Beverly was about to spring at the Romulan when she noticed something—and realized she might have a better card in her hand after all.

"When did you get those lesions?" she asked.

Her companion looked at her. "Lesions?"

"The ones on the back of your hands."

Warily, the Romulan examined each hand in turn—and saw what Beverly was talking about. There were bumps on the backs of them, small but a dark and distinctive green in color.

"Do you know what those are?" she asked. When her captor didn't answer, she said, "They're symptoms of the disease that's afflicted the Kevrata."

That got the Romulan's attention—to an even greater degree than Beverly had hoped. He looked up at her, his eyes narrowing. "You're lying."

She shook her head. "Not a chance. I've seen them more times than I care to say. They're definitely a sign of the disease."

"But I'm not Kevratan."

"I'm afraid the virus isn't that choosy. Of course, your species might be more resistant to it. You might not get as sick as the Kevrata—or it might kill you in a matter of hours. At this point, I can't say."

The Romulan looked like the sort who suspected lies everywhere. But all Beverly was doing was telling the truth.

"What I *can* say," she continued, "is that if you've got

the plague, other Romulans will get it too. And considering the merchant traffic that goes through Kevratas, it will almost certainly spread to other worlds in the Empire."

Her companion's face drained of color.

"Of course, that also creates an opportunity," said Beverly, "because anyone who produces a cure for it will be doing both himself and his people a great service."

The Romulan scowled. "And you can accomplish this, I suppose."

"I did it for several humanoid species," the doctor said. "I don't see why I couldn't do it for the Romulans."

Her captor still looked suspicious, but he wasn't calling her a liar anymore. He licked his lips—a sign of indecision in a number of species, Romulans among them.

"I need to get you offworld," he said, thinking out loud. "Preferably back to Romulus."

Beverly didn't comment. The centurion was on the right track—why say anything that might derail him?

"That will involve a transport," he noted. "It will take time to arrange such a thing."

If you say so, she thought.

"And what will I do with you in the meantime?" asked the Romulan. "How will I keep you from running off?"

"I promise—" Beverly began.

But her captor held his hand up for silence. "What kind of fool do you take me for? Did you really think I was going to take you at your word?"

"Maybe not," she allowed.

"But what is the alternative?" asked the centurion. He cast a glance over the room. "There is nothing at hand I can use to bind you. I will need to look for something."

The Romulan adjusted the setting on his disruptor again. This time, he turned it to the lowest one.

Beverly was about to ask what he had in mind. But before she could open her mouth, he fired at her.

Manathas watched the human crumple to the flawless marble floor, her hair pooling around her like molten copper.

Then he looked at the back of his hand again, no longer constrained to conceal his panic and revulsion. Once Crusher pointed out the lesions, he remembered that he had seen such things on Kevratan corpses. But the bumps had been black, not green, or he would have made the association sooner.

Manathas couldn't stand the thought that some alien germ had invaded his body and was slowly wreaking havoc inside him. It made him want to retch.

Calm yourself, he thought, exercising a discipline he had honed over the long years. *Now.*

The Romulan's anxiety ebbed, slowly but surely, until it was little more than a vague discomfort. But he didn't know how much longer he could maintain this level of control.

He had to get Crusher to another world, where she could work on a cure for the Romulan variant of the disease. Only then would he breathe easily again.

As for the reward he might receive . . . it was a motivating factor as well, as the human had rightly pointed out. But it was nothing compared with the abatement of his fears.

Dragging his eyes away from his hand, Manathas pulled his hood back on and prepared to go out into the cold again. The doctor would only be unconscious for a short time, after all, and he had work to do before she came to.

"Gone?" Sela echoed disbelievingly, her words careening in her office from one stone wall to another like a flock of suicidal avians.

Akadia frowned. "Yes, Commander."

"How?" she demanded.

"She had help," said the subcommander. He looked as if his uniform had suddenly become a size too small. "From one of *us.*"

Sela felt her anger rise into her throat, threatening to choke her. By force of will, she tamped it down. "Who?" she growled.

"Jenophus, Commander. He was a much more accomplished combatant than anyone suspected."

Sela shook her head in disbelief. "You're saying Jenophus alone was responsible for the human's escape? With all the guards that stood between him and the front gate?"

Akadia nodded. "Yes, Commander. That is the consensus of everyone who opposed him. It was Jenophus alone. And the prisoner, of course. She was of some help."

Sela's teeth ground together. "Find them," she told the subcommander. "Both the prisoner and Jenophus. Go door to door if you have to, but root them out—or you and your men will have reason to regret it."

He withdrew from her presence. "As you wish, Commander."

Sela waited until her subordinate had left the room. Then she tapped a code into the portable com device on her desk, opening a channel to her orbiting warbird.

Whoever had gotten into the compound and escaped with the human might have had a plan for leaving Kevratas. The commander needed to stymie it.

The response from Tresius, the officer in charge of her warbird, was almost instantaneous. He asked how he could serve her.

"Be alert," Sela said, "for suspicious vessels. Our prisoner has escaped and she may try to leave Kevratas."

"If she does," Tresius responded, "I will prevent it. Rest assured of it, Commander."

Sela approved of his attitude. She always had. "If you do," she said, "there will be a substantial reward in it for you. Rest assured of *that.*"

"You are too generous," said Tresius.

No, she replied inwardly, *I'm exactly as generous as I have to be—no more, no less.* "Sela out."

Next, she deployed extra forces to the spaceport, and promised the officer in charge there the same reward she had promised Tresius. He too assured her that he would catch the fugitive.

Finally, Sela sat back in her chair, knowing she had done all she could. In time, she assured herself, the doctor would be caught in her web, along with Jenophus and the Federation team that had to that point eluded her.

But in the meantime, Sela's discontent would slither inside her like a hungry serpent.

10

Captain's log, supplemental. With the help of our friends the rebels, Doctor Greyhorse has set up a small lab here in the tunnels below the ancient castle, and is taking blood samples from Kevrata who are showing symptoms of the disease. He seems confident that his research, combined with what he learned at Starfleet Medical, will enable him to develop a vaccine in a relatively short time. For the sake of Hanafaejas and his people, I sincerely hope Greyhorse's confidence is not misplaced.

Decalon was neither a physician nor a biologist, so he could do nothing to help Greyhorse in his efforts to develop a vaccine. Nonetheless, he constantly found himself drawn to the tiny alcove where the doctor had set up his laboratory.

The rebels, for all the primitiveness of their existence,

had supplied Greyhorse with a computer, a biomolecular scanner, and the rest of the equipment he had requested. In their midst the doctor seemed like just another part of the system, as tireless and methodical as a machine.

At times he said strange things, or merely said things at strange times—making the Romulan so uncomfortable that he felt compelled to change the subject. If Decalon hadn't known better, he might have questioned the doctor's sanity. However, he didn't think the Federation would have dispatched a lunatic on such an important and difficult mission.

Besides, Joseph didn't seem especially concerned. In fact, he appeared to take pleasure from seeing his old colleague in such a workmanlike frame of mind.

That is, when he wasn't accompanying the rebels' scouts on reconnaissance expeditions. But then, Joseph had been a security chief on Picard's old starship, and he had navigated enough subterranean tunnels in that capacity to develop an affinity for them.

Picard, by contrast, spent most of his time with Hanafaejas, planning a distribution network for the delivery of the vaccine to the Kevrata. After all, it availed them nothing to devise a cure if they had no way to get it to the victims.

During those sessions with Hanafaejas, the captain seemed energetic and engaged. But in the moments between them, he seemed to withdraw inside himself and brood over something. Decalon had wondered what it might be—until Joseph cleared up the mystery for him.

Apparently, Doctor Crusher had been a close friend of Captain Picard. In Joseph's estimate, it was she who occupied the captain's thoughts.

Decalon knew what Romulans did to their prisoners. He wasn't optimistic that they would find the doctor alive, much less with her psyche intact.

However, Crusher's status wouldn't become an issue until they had completed their mission on Kevratas. Until then, there was no point in arguing the reality of the doctor's situation.

Besides, Decalon had his own distraction to deal with, his own set of disappointments and regrets. But in his case, they revolved around his friend Phajan.

The night before, a rebel named Kito—a newcomer to the ranks of the tunnel dwellers—had confirmed in the streets of the city precisely what Picard had suspected. Shortly after they left Phajan's house, a contingent of centurions had descended on it.

Had Decalon and his comrades still been inside, they would have been killed—or at the very least taken prisoner. Their mission would have ended as abruptly as Doctor Crusher's. And the Kevrata would have been no closer to salvation than the day the Federation learned of their plight.

Phajan, the Romulan thought. The name was like a dagger in his side, causing him pain with every breath.

How could he have been so wrong? How could he have misjudged his friend's character so badly? *And how vehemently I argued when Picard insisted on leaving Phajan's house.* If the others had listened to him, they would have ended up cursing him.

Decalon needed to redeem himself somehow, to prove that his inclusion on the team hadn't been a mistake. He could only hope he got the opportunity.

———◆———

Making sure no one could see or hear him as he huddled in the doorway of an old warehouse, Manathas removed a device from an inner pocket in his thermal suit.

It was small but powerful, as powerful as the communications transponder on any warbird. Had his employer been any less influential, he would never have been able to get his hands on such sophisticated equipment.

Fortunately, his employer was the single most powerful individual in the Empire. However, she was also the most demanding, and what she wanted was information.

Which Manathas would now give her. Opening a channel on a prearranged frequency, he kept his mind focused on his message—and not the disease that was running rampant inside him—and began transmitting to Praetor Tal'aura.

"Glory to the Empire," he said, "and the praetor, and all she does on the Empire's behalf." It was the ritual opening expected of him; to skip over it would have been impolitic, to say the least.

"We have captured a human physician," he said, "an agent of the Federation sent to cure the Kevrata of their plague." He glanced at his hand, where the lesions seemed to be growing in number and intensity. "Unfortunately, it is no longer solely the problem of the Kevrata. A strain of the disease has begun to affect the Romulan population here as well."

Manathas neglected to mention that he was one of them. If he did, Tal'aura might wonder if he was placing his own interests before hers.

"The human has given me reason to believe she can cure the Romulan strain of the disease. This, it seems to me, may be even more important to us than crushing the rebellion on this world.

"Yet Commander Sela appears not to grasp this possibility. She still wishes to destroy the physician. Fortunately, I have removed the prisoner from Sela's grasp and hidden her where the commander will not be able to find her. All I need now is a vessel on which to transport the physician to Romulus."

It was a reasonable request—one he was certain the praetor would grant. It was just a question of how long it would take for the vessel to arrive from some nearby world—one already in Kevratas's star system, if luck was with him.

Had Tal'aura been Manathas's only patron, he would have put the communications device away at that point. However, Eborion was waiting to hear from him as well.

Keying the device to another channel, the spy repeated some of what he had told Tal'aura: that he had wrested the doctor from Sela and hidden her where the commander wasn't likely to find her. Then he added that he had undermined Sela's influence with Tal'aura in accordance with Eborion's wishes.

He refrained from discussing the Romulan variant of the plague. It was the kind of information that Eborion might let slip, and if he did, the praetor would be interested to know where the nobleman had heard it.

"I will keep you abreast of further developments," he told Eborion. Then he *did* put the device away.

Earlier in his career, Manathas would have choked on

the idea of serving two masters. And if one of them was the praetor of the entire Empire? He would have recoiled from the notion as from a Vobilite rock-serpent.

But not now, he thought.

It was a dangerous game he was playing, no question. More dangerous than any he had ever played before.

However, it was critical that he secure a future for himself while he was still able to do so. And that meant accepting as much as he could as often as he could, from whoever was willing to offer.

Ironic, wasn't it? Tal'aura had hired him to keep an eye on Sela, whose loyalty—at least on the surface—was beyond reproach. But it was really Eborion whom the praetor should have hired someone to keep an eye on.

And yes, Manathas conceded, *on me as well.*

He wouldn't have put it past Tal'aura to do that—to hire a second spy to look after the first. But he couldn't let the possibility bother him, or he would lose sight of more certain challenges.

After all, it might be days before a ship arrived for Manathas and his captive. If they were to survive, they would need food and drink, and extra clothing. And Manathas had to obtain those items now—disease or no disease—before Sela's spreading net of centurions made it too difficult.

With that in mind, he left the shelter of the doorway and set out for the nearest Kevratan supply house.

Beverly woke with her face pressed against the cold marble floor and her hands tied tightly behind her back. Her feet, she discovered, were bound as well. It seemed her centurion "friend" had found something dark, strong, and rubbery, though she couldn't say exactly what it was.

He had done her one favor, at least. The ache in her head wasn't as bad as it could have been, so he must have kept his disruptor impact to a minimum. *I'll have to remember to thank him,* she mused.

But it would be infinitely better if she could escape before the Romulan came back, and to do that she would have to at least free her feet. Unfortunately, there was no way she could get her hands in front of her—not with her wrists so securely bound together.

Pursuing her only other option, Beverly bent her legs up behind her and reached down with her hands until she could feel her ankles. Then, though she couldn't see any of the knots, she started digging at them with her fingers.

It was slow work under any circumstances, but the gloves she wore made it even slower. Despite the protection they offered her, she pulled them off finger by finger. Then she resumed her task.

And she reminded herself that whatever hardships she had to endure, whatever prospects she had to look forward to, they were nothing compared to the plight of the Kevrata.

There might have been a hundred thousand of them in the capital alone, all dying horrible deaths. Some were dying quickly, some so slowly that it might have seemed they were immune. But all of them were dying, just as surely as Jojael and her comrades had died years earlier on Arvada III.

Beverly remembered how awful it had been to watch

them yield to the bloodfire. One by one, moaning and wheezing, crying out for help the colonists couldn't provide. She recalled the look in their eyes, the sorrow and the dread, but most of all the surprise—because they had truly believed the Federation could do for them what the Romulans would not.

Doctor Baroja had been wrong about the medical supplies—as it turned out, they were more than sufficient to take care of the Kevrata. But that was because the last of them died so quickly, medicines or no medicines—more than a dozen of them in the space of one wild and hideous night.

Normally, Beverly would have been asleep by then. But she was too busy running from bed to bed, delivering hyposprays or trying to comfort the Kevrata as they battled the monster eating them from within. The last of the aliens went under a couple of hours after dawn, claimed by the disease he had brought with him from his homeworld.

Jojael had been among the earliest to succumb. However, her travail had been less painful than most. Beverly was grateful for that.

Zippor, the botanist who served as administrator of the colony, looked at the bodies of the Kevrata with tired, red-rimmed eyes and muttered something about the Federation medical vessel assigned to the crisis. With the aliens no longer in need of the team's services, Zippor intended to contact the ship and tell their captain to turn back.

But he didn't—because Doctor Baroja was wrong about something else, besides the sufficiency of the medical supplies. Before noon of the same day, Bobby Goldsmith's father found a collection of tiny bumps on the back of his hand—bumps that weren't there before the arrival of the Kevrata. And to the horror of everyone in the medical dome, they were a lot like the bumps the crash victims had displayed before they died.

A tricorder scan confirmed it: Bobby's father had contracted the disease. And if one human could catch it, they all could. And theoretically, so could the nonhumans in the colony.

Doctor Baroja, who seemed to turn to stone at the news, whispered that the virus must have mutated—that what had seemed so common and relatively harmless to his species had overnight become something potentially deadly.

So it was no longer advisable for Zippor to tell the medical ship to turn back. The only question at that point was whether the colonists would survive to see it—because the medicines they had used to treat the Kevrata were now indeed in short supply, much too short to keep an entire colony alive.

Doctor Baroja had already begun to discuss the allocation of those medications—and whether they should go to the youngest and strongest or the worst afflicted, because they couldn't go to everyone—when Beverly's grandmother guided her out of the medical dome into the thick, oppressive heat of morning.

At first, Beverly thought it was because the talk inside the dome was getting too grim. But that didn't make much sense. She had already seen things far grimmer the night before, things none of the other kids in the colony had seen.

Then Beverly realized that her grandmother had something else in mind, because she didn't stop when they got outside the dome. They kept going in the direction of their house.

Beverly asked why her grandmother was taking her home, and Felisa Howard said it would become apparent in a moment. When they reached their domicile, the older woman didn't go to the front door. She skirted the structure and went out back, where her garden was glistening in the glare of their star.

"A long time ago," said Felisa Howard, in words Beverly would never forget, "long before synthetic drugs and hyposprays, our ancestors treated their problems with tubers and leaves. That's what *we're* going to do."

Beverly had never known such a thing was possible. As it turned out, she wasn't alone in that regard. No one else in the colony put any credence in Felisa Howard's idea.

But the woman proved that her notion was based in wisdom. In the dark days that followed, she studied the medicinal uses of herbs and roots. Then she ravaged portions of her garden, ground their contents into pulp, and administered it to those colonists who began to show symptoms.

They used the remaining supply of medicines too, of course. But it wasn't long before they were relying exclusively on what Felisa Howard could dig up.

It wasn't enough—not nearly. Colonists died slow, agonizing deaths. Bobby's father was among the first. Then Bobby himself caught the disease.

Beverly tended to him every chance she got, day and night. Mostly, he complained of being chilly, of feeling the cold invade his bones the way it had on Sejjel V.

As bad as he felt, Bobby seemed to like all the attention

Beverly gave him. He told her how much he wanted to get better, so he could take another walk with her at dusk.

But that wouldn't happen. The day before the Federation medical team arrived, Bobby died—with Beverly holding his cold, cold hand in her own.

She went on holding it until someone took it away and embraced her, and sent her outside to collect herself. But even in the hot Arvadan sunlight she could feel the chill of Bobby's hand, a piece of the winter he had carried inside him.

Beverly had sworn then that no one would die that way again if it was in her power to prevent it. And over time, she managed to keep that promise.

But now she had another promise to keep. *And I can't do it until I untie these damn knots. . . .*

Pug Joseph stopped for a moment to shift the weight of the biomolecular scanner on his back, then fell back into his plodding forward rhythm.

The scanner had been heavy from the moment he picked it up. But now that he had lugged it around some cold, dank tunnels for an hour, it seemed that much heavier.

"When was the last time you moved your camp?" he asked Jellekh, the Kevrata trudging along beside him.

"Three days ago," came the response. "But that's a long time for us to remain in one place."

"How often do you *normally* move?"

The Kevrata shrugged. "Every two days. Sometimes less, if we think the Romulans are getting too close."

"We have no choice," said Kito, the Kevrata just up ahead of them. "Unless we want the resistance to die a bloody death."

Kito was new to the group. He tended to be a little more graphic than Jellekh and the other veterans.

"Have they *ever* found you?" Joseph asked.

"Once," said Jellekh.

But he looked away, obviously less than eager to talk about it. Sorry that he had made his companion uncomfortable, Joseph dropped the subject.

Looking back over his shoulder—an awkward maneuver with the scanner strapped to his back—he spotted the captain in the back of the procession. Picard was walking backward, his phaser trained on the darkness behind them.

But then, the rebels were terribly vulnerable while they were laden down this way. They needed a little firepower fore and aft, in case they ran into trouble.

Joseph couldn't see Picard's face, but he had studied it enough over the last few days to know what was on the man's mind—in addition to a Romulan ambush, of course.

He was thinking about Beverly.

When Joseph visited the *Enterprise*-D, he was too wrapped up in his alcoholism to notice Picard's feelings for the doctor. *Or maybe back then, they just weren't as obvious.*

But here and now, they were hard to miss. Every time Beverly's name came up, the captain's expression changed. And it wasn't just a matter of concern for a longtime comrade.

Pretty clearly, it was more than that.

Joseph wished he could ease Picard's mind. He wished he could say with something more solid than blind optimism that Beverly was alive, and that they would get her back.

But all he could do was root for Greyhorse to finish the job assigned to him—because the sooner he did that, the sooner they could start looking for their friend.

11

───◆───

BEVERLY'S FINGERS WERE STIFF AND RAW BY THE
time she unraveled the knots that had held her feet, and
her legs were cramped so badly she couldn't imagine how
she would ever walk again.

But she didn't have the luxury of taking a breather. Not
when the centurion might come back at any minute.

Taking a deep breath, she forcibly put her discomfort
aside. Then she planted her hands on the floor, swung her
legs into a sidesaddle position, and with a jerk rocked
herself onto her knees.

It should have been easy to get up at that point. But she
had tortured her legs so, it wasn't. It took perhaps ten seconds
for her to lurch to her feet.

Moving on trembling, uncertain legs, she made her way
across the floor and through the foyer to the door. It had
taken a remote control device to get her and the centurion
in, but she didn't think she would need one to get out.

As it turned out, Beverly was wrong. The door wouldn't budge, no matter how hard she pushed against it. Apparently, her "friend" had the only "key."

She slumped against the wooden surface and heaved a sigh. *All right,* she thought, *I can't get out. But I can free my hands before he comes back.*

The centurion was a magnificent fighter, but anyone could be taken by surprise. *Anyone,* the doctor insisted. And if that was her only chance of helping the Kevrata, she would take it.

But she would need something sharp to slice her bonds, she thought, as she retraced her steps into the main room. A cursory scan of the place didn't show her any likely objects, so she took a closer look.

Finally she found it—a place where one of the stones in the wall had partly cracked away. The jagged edge it left was a little higher than Beverly would have liked, forcing her to get up on her toes to raise her wrists to the right height. But once she did that, she was able to begin sawing away.

It wasn't easy. The edge wasn't very sharp, and her bonds were tougher than she would have imagined. But she worked at it as diligently as she could, and as she worked, she found herself looking back on her life.

It wasn't because Beverly expected to die, though she knew that was certainly a possibility. It was more because she had been penned up and frozen and bludgeoned about, and she wanted to go somewhere more pleasant for a while.

Where she could gather her thoughts. Where she could *reflect.*

Funny, she thought. For a long time she had been too *busy* to reflect, too absorbed in her work to examine the entirety of her life and achieve some kind of perspective.

But it hadn't always been that way. Beverly hadn't been anywhere near that busy when Jack was alive. She had spent hours with him, even days, doing nothing at all.

Just being with him. Just living.

When Jack died, everything changed. She had always been strong, equal to any challenge. But she couldn't accept what had happened, couldn't meet it head-on.

She needed distractions—and she found them. Work, first of all, and plenty of it. And raising Wesley. And when he started to take care of himself, she found other ways to fill her time—writing and directing plays, practicing dance routines, research, correspondence with other medical officers.

But never just living.

The closest she had come to it were her breakfasts with Jean-Luc. She had looked forward to them with such eagerness, each one a refreshing oasis in a wasteland of hard work. And no two of them were exactly the same. In fact, she and her breakfast partner had dedicated themselves to finding unusual dishes, which they would then serve to each other and wait for a reaction.

Most often, it was positive—an expression of delight. But not always. The *durien,* for instance, that Ensign Jaiya had recommended, which ended up tasting like rotten eggs—that was definitely *not* one of Beverly's fonder breakfast memories.

But she could still taste her favorites—especially the uttaberry pudding, a specialty of Betazed. Sweet, pungent, and bitter by turns, it seemed to excite every taste bud in her mouth before it was done.

She wished she had some now. *Hell,* she thought, *under the circumstances I might even give the* durien *another try.*

But it wasn't just the food that made those breakfasts so wonderful. It was the company.

For a short time each day, she could just be herself. Not a highly regarded researcher, not a doctor with a ship full of patients, not even a high-ranking officer on a starship. Just a woman with a normal complement of quirks and weaknesses and out-and-out failings.

Because she was with Jean-Luc, she could let all that show. She had known him so long and had grown so comfortable in his presence, she could say or do anything.

They were precious times—Beverly had acknowledged the fact even then. But now, as she fought for her life on a dark, cold world, they seemed that much *more* precious.

Donatra had been so intent on her fleet's latest round of weapons diagnostics, she forgot to eat her dinner and then missed her regularly scheduled meeting with her chief engineer.

But she didn't forget the opportunity that presented itself only once every twenty-six hours, when the rotation of Romulus brought the capital closest to her ship's coordinates.

Activating a com link, Donatra stared expectantly at her monitor screen. However, it insisted on showing her the imperial insignia of a warbird with its wings outstretched, grasping Romulus in one talon and Remus in the other.

Then the predator vanished, leaving in its wake a different image altogether—that of a tall, broad-shouldered man who had once had many warbirds under his command, but had chosen for the moment to bind himself to the ground.

Donatra couldn't help smiling, her heart was so full of pride and longing. "Braeg," she said.

He smiled back at her. "Even when you are only an image on a viewscreen, you take my breath away."

"You're well, I take it?"

"Well enough," he said, "considering how little sleep I get these days. There is too much to think about, too many plans to make, too many people with whom I must speak. Every morning as I watch the sun come up, I promise myself I will sleep for a week—just as soon as the praetor has been overthrown."

"Take care your sleeplessness doesn't turn into carelessness," Donatra warned him.

Braeg's expression told her it wasn't a possibility. "I've been sleep-deprived before, haven't I?"

She chuckled. "As I recall, you have. But it was I who kept you awake, not some worm of a praetor."

"Ah yes," he said, "I remember now. A secluded villa in Ch'rannos, wasn't it?"

"It was. I wouldn't mind taking you back there some time—perhaps in the wake of Tal'aura's defeat. That is, if you're not too busy taking a nap."

"For that," said Braeg, "I would stay awake indefinitely."

Donatra checked the time on her chronometer. It wouldn't be wise to converse much longer. Tal'aura would almost certainly be monitoring communications with the surface.

"We need to say good-bye," he observed.

"Again," she sighed.

"But not forever," Braeg reminded her.

"Say the word," she told him, "and I will descend on Romulus like vengeance itself."

"No," said Braeg, a note of concern in his voice. "Tomalak *wants* you to rush in. Whittle him away little by little. And then, when he's good and—"

He stopped himself. "Listen to me—giving advice to the commander of the Third Fleet."

Donatra shook her head in mock derision. "Always the admiral."

"Not now," he told her. "Now I'm just a rabble-rouser. It's you who must seize victory."

"And I will," she assured him.

Then, with infinite reluctance, she cut the link. Once again, the warbird insignia dominated the screen.

Sitting back in her chair, Donatra closed her eyes and breathed deeply. Then she had her com officer contact Suran, so they could go over the latest data on Tomalak's forces.

Tal'aura stood on her north-facing balcony, looked down at the geometrically perfect web of streets below, and mulled what she had learned from the spy's communication.

"Interesting," she breathed, knowing no one would hear her.

But not pleasant. Not even remotely so.

Federation intervention. A variation of the Kevratan disease that could affect Romulans. And no end to the natives' resistance movement. Rather than getting better under Sela's hand, the situation appeared to be deteriorating.

I am losing my grip on the outworlds, the praetor admitted, if only to herself. *Braeg is right.*

And he hadn't missed an opportunity to say so. He had been everywhere in the last couple of days, rallying the citizens of the capital against her.

To that point, Tal'aura had refrained from crushing the admiral beneath her heel, though it was well within her power to do so. But that was before she received Manathas's report, when she still believed Sela was defusing the rebellion on Kevratas.

Now she was less confident in that regard. And if events on Kevratas unfolded as she feared, Braeg would gain momentum from them—making him too much a factor to be ignored, regardless of how his death might turn him into a martyr.

A praetor dared not display even a glimmer of weakness. She would have to deal with the general . . . and soon.

Beverly was warm . . . *ever* so warm.

She was in her grandmother's house on the green planet Caldos, a lovely old place with a stone hearth, and in the hearth blazed a merry golden fire. Bathed in its heat, she didn't have to wear anything more than a robe.

She was content, at ease, unthreatened, and she could have stayed that way for the rest of her life. Especially with such a tall, handsome fellow sitting beside her, adding his warmth to that of the fire.

She snuggled into the hollow of his shoulder and said, "I'm so glad you're here." And some other endearments, of which she was barely aware.

He whispered something in return and stroked her cheek. Then he took a step back and turned into a shimmering green mist. A moment later, the mist entered her, making use of her every pore. And with it inside her, she felt a dark and undeniable passion.

Beverly's eyes closing, she gave into it without reservation. "I had no idea I could feel this way," she murmured.

"We're nearly merged now," said the tall, handsome man, whose name was Ronin—or was it the glowing green mist? "As two candles join to form a single light . . ."

She didn't hear it all. She was too caught up in the emotions running through her. But she did hear him say he loved her, and she said she loved him in return.

Just as she was about to merge with him forever, she heard a knock on the house's wooden door—a hard, abrasive knock that roused her from her lover's embrace. Before she realized it, the door was open.

And Jean-Luc was standing just inside the threshold.

Beverly pulled her robe around herself and got to her feet, feeling vaguely ashamed. But why? She hadn't done anything of which she should be ashamed.

"I'm sorry for startling you," said Jean-Luc, his features

hard and suspicious. "I knocked, but there was no answer."

"What do you want?" she asked, surprising herself with her curtness, her eagerness to be rid of him.

"I hoped to meet your new friend," he said, his eyes searching the room.

"He's not here," Beverly said quickly, knowing of course that it was a lie.

"Well," said Jean-Luc, "if you don't mind, I'll wait. I'm anxious to meet this remarkable young man . . ."

"Jealousy doesn't become you," she told him.

It was a hurtful thing to say. A vicious thing. But she longed so much to be left alone with the tall, handsome man, she would have done and said things that were even crueler.

"This is my life," she spat. "I've made my decision and I'm not going to change my mind, so leave me alone."

Jean-Luc looked at her for a moment. Then he shook his head. "No. There is something wrong here. This is about more than just an obsessive love affair." And he asked why no one had seen her lover except her.

Just then, he appeared—the tall, handsome man she had come to love, whose name was Ronin. "All right," he told Jean-Luc. "Here I am."

Beverly moved to him, took his arm.

"And," said her lover, "I believe Beverly asked you to leave."

But Jean-Luc stubbornly remained where he was. "So you're Ronin. It's a pleasure to meet you." And he asked where Ronin was from, and how long he had lived there on Caldos.

"All that matters," said Ronin, "is that I'm here now.

And that Beverly and I plan to be together for the rest of our lives."

"That's a very romantic notion," Jean-Luc observed, "especially for two people who have just met. Don't you think perhaps you are rushing into things a bit?"

Ronin's expression turned as hard as rock. "I think you're a jealous man who can't bear the thought of losing a beautiful woman like Beverly."

"How did you come to Caldos?" Jean-Luc pressed. "What ship did you arrive on?"

"Jean-Luc," Beverly said, "leave him alone—" But as she said it, she felt like a traitor.

After all, she and Jean-Luc had been friends for a long time. They had been through a lot together.

Yet she couldn't help herself. She wanted Ronin, needed him. . . .

Jean-Luc went on despite Beverly's pleas. "Answer the question," he told Ronin. "What ship? I would like to look at the passenger list. Where have you been living here on Caldos? What is your position here? Who are your neighbors?"

Ronin's eyes flashed in anger and he lifted his hand. A flash of green energy emerged from it, enveloping Jean-Luc, snaking around him as if it meant to crush the life from him.

"Beverly," he groaned as he fell to the floor, "you have to get out of here . . . !"

Seeing the pain her friend was in, her concern for him overcame the feelings she had for her lover. Rushing to Jean-Luc's side, she took him in her arms and tried to protect him, to save him from the evil that was killing him.

Suddenly, it turned cold in the room—cold and dark.

Beverly turned to the hearth and saw that the fire had gone out. And it wasn't all that had disappeared.

Ronin had vanished as well, and so had the emerald energy he had unleashed. The only thing left in Beverly's house was Jean-Luc. And as she looked on, heartbroken, he faded from her embrace.

She sat there on the floor, looking at her empty arms, and shivered. It was cold, so cold. . . .

It was then that she woke up.

Beverly was sitting on a marble floor, her back propped up against a stone wall, her hands bound behind her. But she didn't know how she had gotten there.

Then, with a start of panic, she remembered.

It had taken longer to cut her bonds than she had expected, and finally her calves had cramped from standing on her toes. The pain had forced her to sit down for a moment, to put her back against the wall and give her legs a rest.

Just a second or two. At least that was what Beverly had promised herself. Obviously, it had been longer than that, though she couldn't say *how much* longer.

A tired curse escaped her lips. It echoed briefly, then died.

Struggling to her feet, she again felt the pain in her calves. And in her hamstrings. And in her shoulders—especially the one that had absorbed the disruptor bolt when she was captured.

The doctor was sore and stiff and cold to the bone, and she would have dearly loved to lie down and get some *real* sleep. But if she did, her body temperature would continue to drop and she might never wake up again.

Can't let that happen.

Finding the cracked stone in the wall, she backed up to it and started sawing again. The exercise got her blood pumping, but she was immensely hungry and weak as a result.

At least, she thought, *Jean-Luc isn't at the mercy of that energy creature.* What she had dreamed had actually happened, of course. She had fallen in love with Ronin only to discover that he was a parasite, preying on generations of Howard women, and finally on Beverly as well.

She had forgotten how brave Jean-Luc had been—how willing to place himself in deadly jeopardy in order to bring her to her senses. *Forgotten consciously, that is.* Her subconscious, apparently, had recalled the incident quite well.

Beverly smiled to herself, despite her misery. What she wouldn't have given to see her friend right now, breaking down the door with a squad of security officers in his wake.

But that wasn't likely to happen. If Jean-Luc was there at all, he would be helping the Kevrata. And by the time he got around to helping her, she would be long gone.

Which was why she would have to help *herself.*

12

GREYHORSE SAT BACK FROM THE EYEPIECE ON HIS biomolecular scanner, closed his eyes, and massaged the bridge of his nose with his fingers. Then he reached for the mug of *pojjima* Kito had left him and took a sip from it.

The *pojjima* was bitter, but not nearly as bitter as a Klingon dish Gerda had once shared with him. He couldn't recall its name, but he recalled with perfect clarity the expression on her face as she watched him eat it.

One of triumph, for Gerda had taken another step toward molding Greyhorse into a Klingon warrior. But also one of impatience, because he couldn't make the transformation as quickly as she would have liked.

In only one regard had Gerda approved of the doctor from the start, and that was his ability to absorb punishment without complaint. In truth, he had endured his share of it during his stint on the *Stargazer,* only part of it at the hands of his lover.

The one whose dishonor and death Greyhorse had taken so badly. The one he had hoped to avenge by committing murder on the *Enterprise*.

Gerda had been wrong in some respects—he saw that now. But she had been right to honor him for carrying his burdens without a whimper, for that wasn't just the hallmark of a good warrior. It was also the hallmark of a good doctor.

The ability to stay with a task, even when it meant going without sleep . . . to maintain one's focus, even when conditions were less than optimal . . . these were virtues in the medical profession. Indispensable virtues, if one was to remain true to one's oath.

Greyhorse had possessed such virtues. *But that,* he noted as he put down the *pojjima, was a very long time ago*.

Feeling a wave of panic coming on, he took a deep breath and held it, exactly the way his therapists had taught him. Then he let it out, as slowly as he could.

When a problem seems overwhelming, he had been told, *consider what you know about it. Break it down into its most rudimentary components, its most basic facts.*

All right, he thought. *I will.*

Most vaccines were essentially just pieces of dead virus. Exposed to them, an organism's immune system would come up with a new category of antibody, which would then fight off the living virus when it launched its invasion.

However, the virus afflicting the Kevrata was toxic to their species—so much so that even in an attenuated form, it was certain to kill its host before an immune response could be triggered. This was what made it so difficult to arm the Kevrata against the ravages of the plague.

Back at Starfleet Medical, Beverly had begun her research into the virus with a sample of her own blood. After all, it contained something precious—antibodies that had enabled her to survive as a teenager when so many of her fellow colonists had perished.

Without her grandmother's herbal remedies, even her natural ability to produce these antibodies might not have been enough to keep her alive. However, the herbs worked to bolster her immune response, enabling her to destroy and expel the virus.

In her laboratory at Starfleet Medical, with Greyhorse's assistance, Beverly had extended her biological advantage to other Federation member species—first humans, then Vulcans, then Andorians, and so on—by splicing the antibody-producing portion of her genetic material with their DNA. This circumvented the toxicity problem, and effectively girded the Federation against further exposure to the plague.

It was too late for Beverly to help those who had succumbed to the disease on Arvada III. However, she had seen to it that those colonists hadn't died in vain, and that appeared to have been a great comfort to her.

Greyhorse had never been exposed to the virus directly, but—like all space-traveling citizens of the Federation—he had been immunized against it. Therefore, he carried the key to the virus around with him the same way Beverly did.

All he had needed to do was obtain blood samples from the Kevrata, isolate the appropriate portion of their

DNA, and combine it with the appropriate portion of his own. Not a terribly difficult task, just one that necessarily took a while.

And he had very nearly come to the end of it. After many long hours, the vaccine was practically within his grasp. Or rather, he *thought* it was.

But it had been a long time since Greyhorse had worked with lab equipment, and even longer since he had held so many lives in his hands. He couldn't help asking himself questions.

What if I fail? What if I give the Kevrata hope, only to kill it when they see the vaccine doesn't work? What if I'm not as good as I think I am?

What if I never was?

More than once in the last several hours he had felt unreal, like a wraith haunting his own instruments. He had drifted, unable to keep from mulling things that had nothing to do with his research. Like how quickly a disruptor beam could kill him if the Romulans discovered the rebels' camp . . .

Or how quickly he could snap the neck of the centurion who attempted it.

I have to hang on, he told himself. *I am the only chance the Kevrata have.* And Beverly's only chance as well, since they couldn't look for her until the Kevrata were saved.

Greyhorse wished desperately that he were someone else—someone more at peace with himself, more predictable. Someone who wasn't carrying so many burdens.

But he was what he was. He could only hope that would be enough.

Beverly slumped against the stone wall, but it didn't mean she was ready to give up. She wouldn't allow herself to do that with so much at stake.

Unfortunately, the material the centurion had used to tie her wrists—which had been relatively easy to untangle from her ankles—was proving almost impossible to cut through. And at this point, every up and down motion of her hands sent excruciating bolts of pain through her shoulders.

Beverly hadn't eaten or had anything to drink in a long time—at least a day and maybe two. Her throat was as dry as she could ever remember it, so dry that she could barely swallow.

The cold was getting to her too, stiffening her joints and numbing her extremities. But more important, it was affecting her ability to think, and she needed to be able to do that if she didn't want this place to become her tomb.

It wasn't so much the centurion Beverly was worried about—not anymore. In fact, she was beginning to grow certain she would never see him again. For him to have been gone so long, he must have been caught by Sela's men or attacked by a resentful crowd of Kevrata, or in some other way gotten himself injured or killed.

That meant she alone was responsible for getting herself out of there. And she couldn't do that with her hands tied behind her back.

Get back to work, the doctor told herself. *Do it now.*

But if the centurion was no longer part of the picture, her need was no longer quite so urgent . . . was it? She could rest another few seconds. She could try to get her strength back.

Again, she wished Jean-Luc were there with her. He would have known what to say, what to do. He would have found a way to make everything all right.

That's what happened when they were trapped in an underground cavern on Minos, after Beverly had suffered a broken arm and leg and multiple lacerations. She was getting sleepy, slipping into shock from loss of blood. But Jean-Luc applied a tourniquet and kept her conscious until their colleagues could find them.

She could still hear him, his voice thick with concern as it echoed through the cavern: *"Come on now, stay with me. Come on now, stay awake—that's an order!"*

Beverly was cold that time as well, her teeth chattering, her skin turning clammy. At one point, she actually asked Jean-Luc if he had a blanket—or so he told her afterward.

What I wouldn't give for a blanket now, she thought. *Or a steaming cup of breakfast tea. Or some hot scones, like the ones Jean-Luc gave me this morn—*

No. It wasn't that morning that he had given her the scones. Of course not. *It was on the* Enterprise, *a few days ago. Or . . . was it a few weeks?*

It was hard for her to remember, so very hard. And all she wanted to do was lie down and get some sleep. That wasn't so much to ask, was it? Just for a few short minutes?

"Come on now, stay awake—that's an order!"

Startled, Beverly opened her eyes and looked about, expecting to see Jean-Luc kneeling over her. But he wasn't there. She was alone.

And she needed sleep.

"Come on now, stay with me!"

This time, Beverly didn't bother to look around. She was too weary, too firmly lodged in the embrace of encroaching slumber. It felt so good to finally give in to it . . .

And to set the voices aside.

Akadia shoved his fellow centurion into the unyielding stone wall of their barracks, to which they had returned after a long day of searching. Then he snarled, "I do not care to hear that spew a second time!"

His victim, a rangy fellow named Retrayan, glared at him. "With all due respect," said Retrayan, his voice rank with sarcasm, "you *will* hear it—if not from me, then from a dozen others."

Retrayan held out his hands, the backs of which were liberally adorned with tiny green spots. They were the same sort of marks displayed by the Kevratan corpses so routinely found frozen in the snow.

Until a day and a half ago, they hadn't been seen on a Romulan. Suddenly, it seemed *everyone* had them—Akadia included.

"Then I will see to it," said Akadia, "that those dozen others are graced with cells in this very building. That is the reward of those who defy Commander Sela."

The other centurions in the room—all twenty or more of them—appeared to take the warning with the seriousness Akadia had intended. But he feared it was only a matter of time before their panic overcame their good sense.

All the more reason to find the human doctor, and to do it quickly. If she could devise a cure for the Kevratan version of the plague, why not the Romulan one?

"On the other hand," said Akadia, "they who carry out their assignments without complaint will be the first to receive a cure when we obtain one."

That got their attention, he noted, seeing the glimmer of self-interest in the centurions' eyes. *Just as Sela said it would.* Nothing motivated a Romulan like the promise of advantage over his peers—especially when it was so intimately intertwined with his chances of survival.

"Of course," Akadia went on, "there will only be a cure if we find the prisoner." He glanced meaningfully at Retrayan. "And that will only happen if we keep our wits about us. Do I make myself clear, Centurion?"

Retrayan frowned but said, "Eminently so."

Akadia nodded. "Good."

After all, he had had ample opportunity to witness the suffering of the Kevrata. He wanted to avoid firsthand knowledge of it as much as anyone.

Eborion smiled to himself as he sat in front of his computer monitor and reviewed his family's weapons manufacturing accounts for the last several days. In point of fact, he had been smiling that way all morning.

But it wasn't his expertise at expanding his house's wealth that gladdened him so. He had reached the point where he could do that with his eyes closed. Rather, it was his investment on Kevratas that was giving him cause for celebration.

Manathas's communication to Tal'aura had discredited Sela's ability to command much more thoroughly than Eborion ever could have. Soon, the half-human would be no threat to him at all.

Engaging the services of Manathas had been a stroke of genius on Eborion's part. Unfortunately, it left a thread dangling. He couldn't take the chance that the spy would someday betray him or try to blackmail him.

So when this Kevratas affair was all over, he would arrange to have Manathas killed for his trouble. If all went well, the spy would be dead long before he got the opportunity to set foot again on Romulan soil.

And Eborion, the praetor's sole confidant, would go on smiling for a good long time.

Manathas slipped through the doorway of the government hall, placed his back against the wall beside it, and waited for the door to close behind him. Only after he heard the wooden relic lock into place did he allow himself to relax.

He had expected his fellow centurions to be a thorn in his side, an impediment and perhaps even an occasional danger to him as they scoured the city. But he hadn't expected them to be everywhere, as ubiquitous as snow-flakes.

Three times, they spied Manathas at the opposite end of a street and demanded that he identify himself. And when he wouldn't, they chased him, their beams vaporizing the falling snow.

At one point, he had been forced to conceal himself in a pile of Kevratan corpses—the result of a skirmish, perhaps, or possibly just the product of the centurions' frustration. Had the corpses not still been warm, he might have frozen to death.

It occurred to him as he lay there that the plague might still have been alive in them. But what did that matter? It was alive in him too.

Obviously, the spy had underestimated Sela's ability. The sting of her lash on the backs of her centurions was a more effective motivator than he had anticipated.

And the commander's net tightened after he was spotted, her troops concentrating on that part of the city. It became nearly impossible to secure the supplies he and the doctor needed. In the end, after eluding patrol after dogged patrol, he gave up on the clothing and the drink, and settled for the food alone.

But even that didn't assure Manathas of anything. On his way back to the government hall, just a few blocks from his goal, he found a squad of centurions blocking the street.

The only way to get past them was to scale a three-story building in a swirling, wind-driven snowstorm and come down on the other side. Half a dozen times, he slipped on the pitched roof and felt sure he was plummeting to his doom. But each time, he managed to arrest his fall and go on.

Had his only concern been his own survival, he wouldn't have taken such a chance. However, he had left the doctor in the government hall as long as he dared. Humans were not Romulans. They were weaker, more fragile. And, having told Tal'aura of the spreading plague and Crusher's importance in devising a cure for it, he could hardly show up on Romulus empty-handed.

Now that Manathas was back, he could only hope that Crusher hadn't yielded to the cold and the lack of sustenance. Dreading what he might find, he made his way through the foyer and emerged into the main hall.

But the human wasn't anywhere in sight. Cursing inwardly, he hastened to the center of the hall and spun around, searching its extremities.

That was when Manathas spotted her. She was sprawled next to the western wall beside its mounting ranks of wooden benches, her face concealed by a veil of her hair.

Rushing over to her, he saw that she had managed to free her ankles, and slowed down in anticipation of a trap. However, her hands were still bound behind her back.

Manathas knelt beside her, took a deep breath, and brushed the hair back from her face. She was terribly pale and her parched, cracked lips had a blue tint to them, but she was shivering—a sign that she hadn't yet perished.

Thanking his ancestors, he pulled her over to the wall and propped her up, then dragged his stolen sack of food off his back and opened it. By then, the human's eyes had fluttered once or twice and she had begun muttering something.

"What are you saying?" he asked, thinking it might not be a bad idea to get her talking.

This time it was intelligible, if only barely: "If you . . . find one, go."

"Find what?" the Romulan asked, removing a stiff, cold loaf of bread from the waterproof sack.

"An exit," Crusher groaned.

"I'm not going anywhere," he said, tearing the loaf in half and pulling out a puff of the softer bread inside.

His captive did something strange then—she smiled, despite the dryness and inelasticity of her lips. "You never do."

She's delirious, Manathas reflected. But what he told Crusher was "Eat." And he inserted the piece of bread into her mouth.

It was clear that she wanted to eat it because she began chewing furiously. But after a few seconds, she gave up and spit the bread out.

"What's the matter?" he asked.

"Water . . ." she whispered.

Manathas frowned. There was plenty of it outside in the form of snow, both on the ground and in the air. But as cold and debilitated as the human was, he didn't think it would be a good idea to let it melt in her mouth.

"Just a moment," he said.

Then he emptied the sack, took it outside, packed it half-full of snow, and returned. But before he gave it to Crusher, he treated it to a needle-thin burst of disruptor fire at his weapon's lowest setting—thereby turning the snow into warm water.

"Here," Manathas said, offering his captive a sip.

She gulped it down greedily, coughed it out, then gulped down some more. And she would have kept on gulping if he hadn't withdrawn the sack, concerned that she would harm herself.

"Easy," he told her. Then he reintroduced the water.

This time, Crusher tempered her enthusiasm. Before she was done, she had taken almost all the water in the sack.

"You drank more moderately at your wedding," Manathas said.

She looked at him, a little stronger now but still dull from her ordeal. "What . . . ?"

He grunted. "Nothing."

Again, he tried giving Crusher some bread. This time, he met with more success. Afterward, he took some himself—just enough to keep him going.

Then he turned his captive to one side and inspected her bonds. They were red with human blood and almost completely worn through. It was a good thing she hadn't severed them altogether, or he might have discovered her outside in the snow instead of in the shelter of the government hall. And then he would have had to explain her demise to the praetor.

Just then, his com device bleeted at him. Removing it from his thermal suit, he retreated to the far side of the hall and said, "Manathas."

"This is the vessel charged with taking you home," said a voice the spy didn't recognize, speaking in terms that wouldn't give anything away if his transmission were intercepted. "You have cargo, as I understand it."

Impeccable timing, Manathas thought. "That is correct. When can I expect you?"

"In six hours. Send me a signal on this frequency and I will transport you aboard. But make certain you're at a viable location. The magnetic fields on Kevratas—"

"I know," said the spy, wishing to keep their conversation as short as possible.

"I suppose you would. Six hours, then." A moment later, the com link was broken.

Manathas replaced the com device in his suit. Though it had looked bad for a moment, everything was in place.

It wouldn't be difficult to find a viable transport site; he had surreptitiously identified them all with Sela's instruments and made a mental map of them. However, getting Crusher to one of the sites would be a different matter entirely.

After all, Sela's men would be looking for two fugitives, one Romulan and one human. In their thermal suits, they would be difficult to miss.

So Manathas would have to sneak out and obtain some less obtrusive garments for them, a task he had been unable to carry out the first time. He shook his head as he considered the magnitude of the job—even for someone like him.

At least I won't have to worry about more food. For the next six hours, they could subsist on what they had.

Sighing, Manathas returned to Crusher's side. She was sleeping again, but the nourishment had brought some color back to her cheeks. In a little while, he would wake her and give her more food.

He would need her on her feet if they were going to make it to the transport site.

Beverly opened her eyes, saw the centurion's face come into focus, and shot backward in an attempt to get away from it.

Unfortunately, her hands were still bound behind her back, and the effort ignited rings of fire around her wrists. Clenching her jaw against the pain, she glared at the Romulan.

"I guess you're still alive," she said, her voice thin and harsh, and not at all like the one she was used to.

"I guess you are as well," said the centurion.

Then the doctor remembered: He had given her something to drink, hadn't he? And something to eat. When had he done that? An hour ago? A day? She had lost all track of time.

"Get up," he told her.

He seemed to be in a hurry. Her instincts told her to drag her feet, figuratively if not literally. "I don't think I can."

The centurion trained his disruptor on her face. "Then you put me in a difficult position. You see, there is a ship entering orbit at this very moment, sent here expressly to transport us off Kevratas. That can only be accomplished after we reach a location a few blocks away. But for us to get there, you will have to walk under your own power."

"Can't we wait a little while?" Beverly asked. "Until I'm stronger?"

"I'm afraid not. The ship will not linger—and I cannot remain here with Commander Sela combing the city for me. So rather than let my chance slip away, I'll get on the ship myself."

The doctor had no objection to that.

"Unfortunately," the centurion continued, "I will have to make certain before I leave that Sela doesn't get an opportunity to interrogate you."

"You don't want to kill me," Beverly said. "I'm the only one who can cure you of your disease."

"It is not my preference," he said. "But if I must, I will. I assure you, I have killed a great many others." He stepped to one side and showed her a pair of Kevratan coats lying on the black marble floor. "Including the two who wore these coats until less than an hour ago."

Beverly swallowed back her dismay and thought, *Bastard*.

The centurion used the barrel of his disruptor to indicate the door and said, "Now, let's go."

Obviously, she had pushed her luck as far as she could. With an effort, she got to her feet and allowed her captor to drape one of the coats over her shoulders.

As he fastened it in front, she wondered what it was like on Romulus. All she had to go by were the descriptions Jean-Luc had given her.

"What are the chances," she asked only half-seriously, "of your praetor sending me home after I've helped you?"

The centurion didn't answer. He just moved to the door, opened it, and led the way outside.

13

———◆———

FOR WHAT MIGHT HAVE BEEN THE TENTH TIME SINCE
Picard finished his meager, tasteless breakfast, he felt the
urge to look in on Greyhorse. And as on those other occasions, he resisted it.

True, Greyhorse had given indications that he might
not be as stable as his therapists believed. And on top of
that, he was working long hours under perilous conditions—a combination that could have cracked even the
sanest physician.

But the last thing Greyhorse needed was an unnecessary distraction. And that was exactly what the captain
would have been—a distraction.

For a while, Decalon had maintained a silent vigil in
the doctor's company, for reasons only he understood. But
after a while, even he had seen the need to leave Greyhorse alone.

It wasn't as if Picard didn't already have enough on his

plate. When he wasn't planning the distribution of the vaccine with Hanafaejas, he was taking his turn standing guard in one of the corridors. He didn't even have a moment to sit with Pug and reminisce.

But the entire time, he was thinking about one of two things. One was how quickly Greyhorse could come up with the Kevrata's vaccine. The other was how he would go about rescuing Beverly.

Picard was as certain as ever that she was alive. The question was where she was being kept. In a prison he and his Kevratan comrades could break into? Or some more secret place, of which even Hanafaejas might not be aware?

He wished he knew.

And he wished also that he could tell Beverly he was on Kevratas, moving closer to the moment when he could help her. It wasn't easy biding his time when he wanted to get out of the rebels' warren and find her.

As she, years ago, had managed to find him.

It was a time in his life he had tried hard to forget, though it still woke him in a cold sweat every now and then. For the first time, a Borg cube had invaded Federation space and Picard had been dispatched in the hope that he could stop it.

In the midst of an encounter with the cube, the captain was kidnapped off the bridge of the *Enterprise*-D and taken to a surgical alcove, where long, spidery probes planted mechanical prostheses in his flesh—the first step in his assimilation into the Borg collective.

Riker, who was left in command, beamed an away team over to the cube in an attempt to retrieve Picard.

When the Borg recognized the team as a danger, a wave of drones was sent to deal with it. Picard was one of them.

Beverly was part of the away team—and not just because she was the medical authority on the *Enterprise*. As Picard learned later, she had *demanded* to go. When she saw Picard on the Borg cube, with the bizarre appliance that had been attached to his hand and the eyepiece that had become part of his face, she gasped.

He was a monster, an unfeeling thing with only a vestige of humanity left to him. But the doctor wasn't so daunted she would give up on him. She started toward him, unmindful of her peril.

Fortunately, Data restrained her. Otherwise she would have received the same shock from Picard's energy shield that sent Worf flying backward. The tactical officer survived the experience, but Beverly might not have.

Then Geordi beamed the team off, before the Borg could overwhelm them. But the portion of Picard that was still human studied Beverly's face as long as he could, until the last of her molecules had departed.

In the end, she hadn't been able to rescue him. But she had made the attempt. She had *tried*.

It was that comfort he drew about himself afterward, trying hard not to relinquish it even when the collective stole all else from him. It was, above all else, what kept him from losing his sanity in the dark, screaming complexity of the Borg's biomechanical hell.

Eventually his people came back for him, and this time managed to spirit him off the cube. When they deposited him in sickbay, Beverly and Riker were waiting for him.

Even in his sedated state, Picard could hear the doctor talking, though she seemed very far away. But it wasn't what she said that caught his attention, for she was simply analyzing his altered condition. It was the sound of her voice, soothing him, providing an alternative to the madness of the collective.

Then Beverly injected him with a stimulant and he heard her voice again, stronger now and a good deal closer. In fact, it was right beside his ear . . . .

"Jean-Luc," she breathed, "it's Beverly. Can you hear me?"

There was more than compassion in her question. There was something so pure and bright it could pierce the relentlessly multiplying layers of machine-self and find his humanity huddling in a dim, cold corner of his consciousness.

In reply, Picard's mouth made the words "Beverly . . . Crusher . . . Doctor."

But through them he was crying out in gratitude, for she had bestowed upon him something precious without realizing it. She had retrieved him, in a way only she could.

"Yes," Beverly said, smiling because she recognized that a bridge had been built, however fragile it might be. "Don't try to move."

Picard didn't have to. He had *been* moved. And because of that, he could go on.

Now it was Beverly who was the prisoner of an implacable enemy, facing torture or death and terribly alone. Could he do less for her than she had done for him?

He would remain underground until Greyhorse gave the Kevrata their vaccine. He would do whatever it took to facilitate that outcome, for as long as it took.

But not a second longer.

Eborion ascended the broad stone steps that led to the praetor's palace, a boyish lift in his step. But then, he had ample reason to feel good about himself.

The spy had done his job, Sela had been diminished in Tal'aura's eyes, and Eborion had become the praetor's favorite. Had a plan ever been so perfectly executed as this one?

He could hear Tal'aura now: *I am disappointed in Commander Sela, Eborion. She has not performed up to my expectations. You will be interested to know that she captured a human—a doctor—sent to find a cure for the plague there. Unfortunately, she lost this human just as quickly.*

And so on.

Savor it, he told himself. *You don't know if you'll ever again taste a moment so delicious.*

A dozen fully-armed centurions stood at the top of the steps, eyeing Eborion as he approached. As a familiar figure at court, he knew they wouldn't bar his way. However, they also didn't move to notify the praetor of his arrival.

Obviously, she had left word with them to let him enter the palace unannounced. *A most agreeable privilege,* he mused.

The columned hall beyond the steps was populated by centurions as well—more than the usual number, given the unrest in the capital. But none of them reacted to Eborion's presence. They simply stood there and watched him go by.

I can get used to this, he thought.

He didn't encounter Tal'aura's *personal* guard, a cadre that wore black tunics instead of silver, until he reached the doors at the far end of the hall. Unlike their comrades, these centurions didn't merely watch Eborion.

They opened the doors to let him through. *Yes,* he thought, *I can* easily *get used to this.*

Beyond the doors, he encountered the stair that led up to the praetor's suite. He felt like taking the steps two at a time, but restrained his eagerness. He had to comport himself with dignity if he wanted to garner respect, not only from Tal'aura but from the rest of her court as well.

At the top of the stair there was another set of doors, a good deal more ornate than the ones below. They were open, inviting him into the chamber on the other side of the threshold.

As Eborion entered, he saw that Tal'aura was standing by a balcony—one of two that graced the chamber. It was something he had seen her do more and more lately, as if she hoped to find a solution to her problems out there.

He inclined his head. "You asked to see me, Praetor?"

"I did," she said. "Something has come to my attention that will be of interest to you."

He was flattered. Tal'aura had never before considered what might be of interest to him.

"One of my *advisors,*" she said, declining to identify the individual by name, "had occasion to intercept a message recently. It was from Kevratas."

Eborion felt a rush of blood to his face and smiled through it. "Kevratas?" he repeated numbly.

"Yes. It seems there is some treachery afoot there."

Eborion felt his guts soften. "What sort of treachery? Not against you, I hope?"

Tal'aura smiled a thin-lipped smile. "Actually, yes. It is very much against me. You see, I hired a spy to be my eyes and ears on Kevratas—a master in such things, called Manathas. Perhaps you've heard of him . . . ?"

Eborion's first impulse was to deny it. But Manathas was practically a legend. A great many people in his stratum of society had heard of the spy, though few had met him.

"Of course," he got out.

"Well, it turns out that Manathas is not only working for me. He is working for someone else as well."

The patrician swallowed back a hot spurt of fear. "A spy," he said, with lips that seemed not his own, "is not very useful if he cannot be trusted."

"Who is?" asked Tal'aura.

At first, he believed it was a rhetorical question. But the praetor didn't say anything more. She just looked at him, her eyes boring into his skull.

Finally, she broke the silence. "I asked you a question, Eborion. What good is *anyone* who can't be trusted? A citizen? A centurion? Even a counselor to the praetor?"

Eborion felt a whimper escape his throat. He hated himself for his weakness, but he hated himself even more for his stupidity.

He had been mad to think he could hide such a thing from Tal'aura. He had only one chance to save his life now—to fall on his praetor's mercy.

"Forgive me," he said, but it escaped his dry, constricted throat as little more than the rasp of twigs rubbing together. He fell to his knees on the hard marble floor and laid his chin on his chest. "I never meant to betray you."

"Yet you did," Tal'aura observed, her tone a sword's edge.

Eborion looked up at her and saw the fire in her eyes, and knew she had no mercy in her. So he tried one other approach, one last attempt to find a niche in which he could shelter his guttering hope of survival.

"My wealth," he said, "has been most valuable to you, Praetor. It can continue to be so."

Suddenly, Tal'aura laughed—as if he had said something funny. "No need to worry," she assured Eborion. "Your wealth will continue to serve me—long after I reveal your treachery to the Empire and seize your personal estate."

Then she tapped a com device on a table beside her and called out the names of her guards. A moment later, two of them came through the open doorway.

"What is your wish, Praetor?" one of them asked.

Tal'aura considered Eborion. "Put him in a cell, for now. I'll decide the manner of his execution at my leisure."

"No!" cried Eborion, his lower lip quivering uncontrollably. "At least leave me my reputation!"

He was part of a noble family, to which he had intended to bring honor. The prospect of dirtying its name was as bad as any torture Tal'aura could devise for him.

She gazed at Eborion from beneath hooded lids. "You ask me to let you take your own life?"

"I do," he said, his voice cracking miserably. Even

thieves and murderers were given the option of ritual suicide.

"By what means?" Tal'aura asked.

He licked his lips. "Poison."

"Fast-acting or slow?"

Eborion didn't want to push his luck too far. "Whatever my praetor wishes."

She nodded. "And if she wishes you to take your life here and now—by the sword?"

He felt as if he would retch. "Then," he moaned, "I will embrace that option."

Tal'aura considered him a moment longer. Then she said, "Your request is denied. When you die, it will be a public spectacle, an entertainment available to every Romulan. That is the punishment for treachery, Eborion."

Before he could plead any further, she made a gesture of dismissal and her guards advanced to grab the nobleman by his arms. Only as they dragged him out of the room did he began to appreciate the magnitude of what he had brought down on himself.

And of course, on his family.

Beverly trudged through freezing slush on pain-stiffened legs, her hands still bound behind her under a dead Kevrata's coat.

Snow was falling in heavy flakes from a dense, gray sky. It made for limited visibility, which must have been to the centurion's liking. The less noticeable they were, the easier their path to the transport site.

None of the Kevrata seemed to discern anything unusual about them. But then, they were too intent on their own troubles to give anyone else a second look.

Beverly and her captor passed a number of centurions as well, but Sela's men didn't take any interest in them. They were looking for a human and a Romulan, after all, not a couple of natives—and in their *nyala*-skin coats, natives were what they appeared to be.

The doctor had thought about running from the time they left the government hall, regardless of what shape her legs were in. But she knew it would only draw the Romulans' attention and get her thrown into another prison cell.

Besides, she had a disruptor pressed against her spine. One wrong move and she would be skewered by an energy bolt, her smoking corpse providing a distraction as her companion left the scene alone.

As he had said, he didn't want it that way. But if Beverly refused to cooperate, she would give him no choice.

So they plodded along, moving no faster than anyone else but steadily nearing their destination. Before long they would stop and the centurion would contact his ally in orbit, and their molecules would be seized by transporter beams. And soon after, they would begin their journey.

And she would live out her life, however long that might be, in thrall to the Romulan Empire. *Not exactly what I had in mind when I accepted the assignment.*

Beverly was still thinking that when she saw something she hadn't expected to ever see again. She closed her eyes for a moment to make sure it wasn't an illusion. But when she opened them, the coat was still there.

A blue coat flecked with silver—like the one her contact had worn in the tavern.

Was it possible he had escaped Sela in the melee, though Beverly could not? Or had he been working for the Romulans all along, helping them to bait their trap?

Or was it even the same Kevrata? With all the coats in the city, might not more than one of them be blue with silver flecks?

There was no way for Beverly to know. But if she played it safe, she would never escape her captor. She had to take a chance before the opportunity faded.

It wouldn't be easy to draw Blue Coat's attention—not with the Romulan's weapon pressed between her shoulder blades. She hoped he wasn't expecting any resistance from her, because if he was, she was a dead woman.

The doctor took a moment to gather her nerve. Then she stopped suddenly and dug her heel into her captor's shin as hard as she could. As he cried out in pain, she whirled and kicked him squarely in the mouth.

Before he could recover from the blow, she took off in Blue Coat's direction. "It's me!" she yelled, flinging her hood back with a toss of her head.

Blue Coat stared at her for a moment, his eyes wide with surprise and apprehension. But he had probably never seen a human, especially under such strange circumstances.

For what seemed like a long time, he gave no indication of how he would respond. Then he reached out and grabbed Beverly by the arm, and pulled her down the street.

"Quickly!" he rasped, casting a look back over his shoulder.

But Beverly had the heartsick feeling they weren't going fast enough. After all, the centurion still had a weapon in his hand, and she had seen how deadly accurate he could be with it.

Manathas put aside the pain in his shin, which was considerable, and went after Crusher. She had placed both him and his plan to spirit her off Kevratas in jeopardy, but he could still achieve his objective if he acted quickly.

Raising his weapon, which was set to merely stun, he aimed it at the doctor's back. But before he could squeeze the trigger, a Kevrata got in his way. He had no choice but to fire, sending the fellow sprawling in the snow.

Then he pelted after Crusher and the native who appeared to have befriended her. *A member of the rebellion?* the Romulan wondered as he began to close the gap.

He had almost caught up with Crusher and her newfound companion when a couple more of the Kevrata intervened. Obviously, they meant to stand there until they were cut down as well.

"Out of my way!" Manathas snapped, in a voice calculated to command respect.

Neither of the natives moved. A couple of quick blasts and they were no longer a problem.

But half a dozen other Kevrata appeared to block his path. And as the Romulan slowed his pace to deal with them, Crusher and her friend vanished around a bend.

Manathas started to take aim at the natives when he realized there were others closing in on him—not just from the front, but from all sides. And they were rasping curses at him, giving rein to their indignation.

He had seen indignant crowds before. He knew what they were capable of, once their anger gathered momentum, and he didn't relish the idea of being trampled to death.

Manathas had lost his captive. He had lost his chance to leave Kevratas with his mission accomplished. But he wasn't about to lose his life into the bargain.

Whirling in the opposite direction from the one Crusher had taken, he fired at the first Kevrata he saw. As his victim hit the ground, the Romulan leaped over him and ran down the street.

There was an uproar from the crowd, but it died with distance. And by the time Manathas turned the corner, he was among Kevrata who had no idea what had taken place.

Slowing his pace to a walk, he blended in with the stream of gaudily colored coats. There were cries of outrage behind him as his pursuers railed at him, but he didn't turn around. He was just another Kevrata going about his workaday business, inured to the violence fostered by the Romulan oppressor.

Of course, Manathas would miss his appointment at the beam-up site, and thereby forgo his ride back to Romulus. But he couldn't help that.

Regardless of what he had told the doctor, he couldn't leave Kevratas without her. Despite the danger, he preferred to remain there and attempt to retrieve her than to face the prospect of living—and dying—with a filthy plague inside him.

14

BEVERLY HAD NEVER BEEN SO APPRECIATIVE OF A hole in the ground as the one she stood contemplating now.

"As you can see," said Faskher, the Kevrata who had helped her escape the centurion, "you have insulation and heaters to keep you warm." He glanced back over his shoulder in the direction of his front door. "There is water down there as well, and some dried food. You may have to stay awhile."

"I understand," the doctor said.

Once Sela heard that a human female had turned up in the streets, she would send her men out searching door to door. But they wouldn't think to look for an underground shelter, the entrance to which was covered by a rug and then a bed.

Faskher turned back to her. "I wish I could be more generous," he said.

"You have been generous enough," Beverly assured him.

"It is kind of you to say so."

"How long," she asked, as she lowered herself into the hole with the help of a wooden ladder, "will it take to get word to my comrades?"

On the way to Faskher's house, he had informed her that there was a Federation team in the warrens below the old castle, and that it was close to producing a vaccine. However, not being in the warrens himself, he knew nothing more than that.

"It is difficult to say," he replied. "No one on the outside knows exactly where in the warrens your team is hidden."

By then, Beverly was looking up at him from the bottom of the hole. Something about being down there filled her with a great weariness. But then, it had been some time since she felt warm and well fed.

And safe.

"Just one other thing," she said, as her host began replacing the rug that had concealed the hole. "What happened to your companion? The one in the black coat?"

Farkner made a sound of disgust. "He died in the tavern."

Beverly was afraid he would say that. "I'm sorry."

"He would have felt better if he knew his death had enabled you to survive."

The doctor was touched by the sentiment—and regretful that she could no longer prove worthy of it. In the end, she had become nothing more than a liability.

But the Kevrata would get their vaccine. That was all that mattered.

———◆———

Were I in Tal'aura's place, Braeg reflected, *I would never have let it go this far. I would have crushed an upstart like me before I could finish my first speech.*

But then, he was used to thinking like a soldier. *I would have struck quickly and decisively, and demonstrated my impatience with those who questioned my authority.*

Fortunately for Braeg—and of course, the Empire—Tal'aura was not a soldier. She had yet to learn the difference between taking ground and holding it.

He looked out the window of the modest house in which he was hiding. Built on high ground just outside the capital, it had afforded him a clear view of the city the night before. This morning, however, a fog was obscuring the praetor's palace and most of the buildings around it, and would continue to do so until the sun burned it away.

As I will burn away the praetor, he observed. *It is almost time.*

Just then, he heard the trill that told him someone was at the door. *One of my lieutenants,* the admiral thought. His guards would not have allowed anyone else to get so close to him.

"Come in," he said, triggering the door mechanism.

As the door slid aside, it revealed Herran, one of the centurions Braeg had brought with him when he left the fleet. It was comforting to him to know he had surrounded himself with men he could trust.

"Good morning," said Herran.

Braeg tilted his head, as if to get a better look at his lieutenant. "You have that look," he noted, "the one that tells me you have good news."

"I do," Herran confirmed. "Eborion is dead. Hanged in the North Square."

Braeg leaned forward in his chair. "Truly?"

"Truly. Apparently, Tal'aura believed he had betrayed her and made short work of him."

The admiral stroked his chin. "Eborion came from a powerful family—one that must have been critical to the praetor's bid for power. Surely, she has weakened herself by cutting away so large a pillar of support."

"It would seem that way," said Herran.

Braeg eyed him, a smile pulling at the corners of his mouth. "Which would make this a good time to strike."

"I had a feeling you would say that."

The admiral considered the matter a moment longer. Then he made up his mind. "Contact Donatra as soon as you can. I want to tell her the battle is on."

Herran inclined his head. "With pleasure," he said, and went to see to it.

"Captain Picard?" said one of the Kevrata.

The captain, who had been drifting off to sleep on one of the encampment's extra cots, turned at the sound of his name and saw Hanafaejas kneeling beside him. The Kevrata's facial fur was matted with melted snow, a sign that he had recently come from the city above.

"What is it?" the captain asked, propping himself up on an elbow.

"I have news for you."

Picard felt his jaw muscles ripple. "Doctor Crusher?"

"Yes," said Hanafaejas. "She is alive."

The captain let out a breath he didn't know he had been holding. He had never heard better news in all his life. "Where is she?"

"At the house of a rebel—one who has chosen to remain aboveground, and serve as our eyes and ears."

"Will she be safe there?" Picard wondered.

Hanafaejas wrinkled the skin around his nose. "As safe as anywhere on Kevratas. If I were you, I would let her remain there until you leave us."

Picard considered the option, then nodded. "Thank your associate for his help, and let him know that Doctor Crusher will be his guest a little longer."

"I will see to it," said the rebel, and went to make good on his promise.

And Picard got up to tell his team the news. Beverly was alive. *Alive.* And if she had ever been in the hands of the Romulans, she was there no longer.

He would have preferred to have her join him in the warrens, but he trusted Hanafaejas's judgment. Besides, it would have been a risk to take her through the streets with Sela's men on the lookout for her—not only to Beverly, but to the rebels as well.

Better to exercise patience, he thought, as he set out to look for Pug. Now that he knew Beverly was alive, he could endure *anything.*

Commander Sela squinted against the blast of wind-driven snow, aimed her disruptor at the fist-sized stone sitting on the ancient wall, and squeezed the trigger.

A beam no wider than one of her pupils leaped across

the intervening fifty meters and vaporized the stone, leaving nothing but a puff of smoke in its place. Sela admired her work for a moment. Then she took aim at the next stone, a meter to the right of the first one.

Aim. Squeeze. *Poof.* Like its predecessor, the stone was gone but for a faint twist of gray.

It was a game to which Sela had challenged herself, up there on the roof of her borrowed fortress, every day since her arrival on Kevratas. She had missed her target only once in all that time—just after she learned of Doctor Crusher's escape.

She had been angry then, frustrated by her underlings' ineptitude. Little did she know how much more frustrated she would become—when her centurions began showing symptoms of the Kevrata's disease. Suddenly, it was no longer merely a local problem. It was one that might affect the rest of the Empire as well.

And the praetor would have read Sela's latest report by then, so she would know about Crusher's capture. It would only be natural for her to ask why the commander hadn't extracted the cure from her prisoner before matters got out of hand.

Sela took aim at another stone. A moment later, it was but a wisp of molecular debris.

Strangely, there were no indications that she had contracted the disease herself. Not even a single bump. One of the few benefits of mixed parentage, she supposed.

But other Romulans were not so fortunate. It was of the utmost importance to get her hands on a vaccine, or someone who could produce one. Someone like Doctor Crusher.

Or perhaps the other physician, who had come to Kevratas with Captain Picard.

Sela smiled to herself. No doubt the captain believed he was safe from her scrutiny. But he was mistaken. She knew exactly where he was—he and those who had come to this world with him.

They were in the warrens under the old castle, hiding like rodents. The physician among them had set up a laboratory there to provide the Kevrata with a cure.

As a matter of fact, he was making great progress. Before long, his work would be complete.

And how did Sela know all this? How was she able to divine the insurrectionists' intentions? She knew because she had a spy whose job was to keep an eye on the rebels for her—and the spy's name was Jellekh.

He wasn't a traitor by nature. However, he had a family that he loved very much, and that had made him vulnerable. One night, while Jellekh was away on insurrectionist business, Sela and a handful of centurions paid his family a visit.

When Jellekh returned to his house, the commander was there waiting for him—and his family was not. And she couldn't guarantee they would ever be back.

After all, as Sela was quick to point out, even she wasn't perfect. Despite her best efforts to "protect" Jellekh's wife and sons, there was no telling what kinds of accidents were liable to befall them.

It was a tactic that had worked for Sela in similar situations. It came as no surprise to her that it worked on Jellekh as well.

From that point on, he would have done anything she asked of him. But as it happened, Sela didn't ask very much—the occasional update on Hanafaejas and little more.

After all, Jellekh was a game piece she could play once and once only. She had preferred to wait for the time when playing him made the most sense.

That time was now.

With Jellekh's help, Sela would capture not only the Kevratan insurrectionists, but their Starfleet allies as well—Doctor Crusher included. And as a bonus, Sela would have the vaccine the other Federation physician had come up with—which, with a little work on the part of the Empire's best researchers, would help the Romulans who had contracted the disease.

All she had to do was wait for Picard and his people to leave the tunnels below the castle, and then follow them to Crusher's hiding place. At that point, it would be a relatively simple matter to seize them and end their adventure on Kevratas.

Then the furor on the colony world would die down and it would become just another Romulan possession again. And Sela, by virtue of her victory there, would again be catapulted back into the light.

She remembered what her father had told her when she was young: *Patience is an asset—spend it wisely.* Sela was proud to say she had done just that.

Pretending she was firing at Picard, she took aim and vaporized another stone.

———————

Like a great many other species, the Kevrata were partial to gambling. However, the object of their game—which involved three four-sided dice—wasn't to see who could amass the most wealth. It was to see who could give it away the quickest.

As Picard and his old colleague Pug Joseph looked on, the Kevrata named Kito finished wiping himself out—much to the chagrin of the other players. Grudgingly, they clapped him on the back.

"So," said Joseph, "I guess we didn't need it after all."

The captain looked at him. "It?"

"You know—my lucky marble."

"Ah," said Picard, "that."

"Of course," said Joseph, "we're not out of the woods yet. But it's looking pretty good right now."

"Better than it did before," the captain conceded.

"So what happens to him now? Greyhorse, I mean?"

Picard shrugged. "I don't know. Technically, he is still a resident of the penal settlement."

"You know," said Joseph, "I don't think he's right yet, and I don't think you do either. But I think he's probably right enough to get out of that place."

The captain knew what he meant. "Perhaps his performance here will be a factor in that decision."

"I sure hope so." Joseph smiled to himself. "Remember the time he was treating the Irhennian ambassador?"

Picard smiled too. "Yes. The one who insisted he had suffered internal injuries during the battle with the Gadraaghi? When all the while it was a—"

He stopped at the sight of Greyhorse coming down the

corridor. The doctor looked vaguely discomfited, as if he had eaten something that didn't agree with him. Suddenly, the captain wished he had brought the marble after all.

"Doctor?" he said. "What is it?"

Greyhorse turned to him as if he had never seen him before in his life. He stared for a moment, then said, in a voice full of disbelief, "It's done."

Picard looked at him. "You mean . . . you have a vaccine?" he asked hopefully.

The doctor hesitated for a moment, then said, "Yes. And a splitting headache. I forgot how difficult it could be staring into a scanner for hours on end."

"I am sorry to hear about your headache," the captain said, "but it was sustained in a very good cause."

Greyhorse blinked a couple of times. "You used to say things like that when we were on the *Stargazer.*"

Did I? "I am sorry I am not more original these days."

"It's all right," said the doctor. "I like hearing it. Those were good days, even if I didn't know it at the time."

They *were* good days. Greyhorse had been a trusted member of Picard's command staff then, and a respected medical officer—not someone trying to put his past behind him.

Not for the first time, the captain wished he had seen some sign of the doctor's transformation in time to do something about it. But like everyone else, he had missed it until it was almost too late.

"There will be good days again," Picard said. "I promise. In the meantime, we need to get your vaccine to the Kevrata."

Braeg looked out across majestic Victory Square, with its soaring fountains and its venerable statuary, where thousands of Romulans had assembled to hear him speak.

When he began his campaign against Tal'aura, he had been fortunate to draw an audience of even a hundred. Clearly, his popularity had grown, and that of his cause along with it.

Braeg smiled to himself as he ascended the sun-drenched stair before a statue of Pontilus, the Empire's revered first praetor. It was Herran who had suggested that, at this critical juncture, the admiral align himself with Pontilus in the people's minds. Judging from the enthusiasm of the crowd, the suggestion had been a good one.

But he wouldn't speak quite yet. *Wait another moment or two. Let their eagerness build to a crescendo.*

And it did, much to his delight.

The admiral had known this feeling on other occasions, after some long, carefully planned series of maneuvers had given him a strategic advantage over a formidable enemy. But then, he was going to fight a battle here, wasn't he?

A battle for the soul of Romulus. But he had plotted and deployed and maneuvered enough. It was time to attack.

"We have met in this square before," he said, his first words quieting the crowd. "We have shared our concerns about the waves of unrest threatening Romulus's stake in the outworlds. And we have talked about what this portends for the future of the Empire.

"When I commanded a fleet of warbirds against the Dominion, I took responsibility for my actions. After all, the decisions were mine. If they went awry, I looked to blame no one but myself. That is how a leader leads—by putting his pride and ambition aside and doing what benefits the Empire.

"Shinzon showed us what happens to those who put pride above all else. And yet Tal'aura insists on making the same mistake. She sees the numbers in which we gather, and she cannot ignore the strength we represent. But in her overwhelming pride, she continues down the path of ruin, and she takes us with her."

Suddenly, he raised his voice, lashing the crowd with his discontent. "No more! Let us show Tal'aura, once and for all, that the people are disgusted with her inadequacies! Let us tell her unmistakably that we have had enough of her failures!

"Let us act," he said, "in the name of our ancestors, who built what we have with their blood and their toil. Let us act in the name of our descendants, who deserve an Empire proud and strong. But most of all, let us act in the name of what is right—and tear this praetor down!"

Braeg had expected a cheer of approval. What he got was a storm of sound, so thunderous and sustained that after a while he feared for his hearing.

Clearly, he had the molten material he had hoped for. It was then a matter of forging it into a weapon that could pierce the heart of Tal'aura's regime.

And with his next words, he did just that.

Praetor Tal'aura stood before her viewscreen, icewater collecting in the small of her back, and watched Braeg whip the crowd in Victory Square into a frenzy.

She saw now that she had made a grave mistake. She

had been so careful not to make a martyr out of Braeg, and so confident that she could quell the uprisings on the outworlds, that she had allowed his affrontery to go too far.

Now he was calling for the people to oust her. *Unacceptable,* Tal'aura thought, *to say the least.* While she had eschewed the use of force to that point, she would now have to use force such as the capital had seldom seen.

Abruptly, the com device in her hand began chiming. She pressed a stud on it and said, "Yes?"

It was the commander of her troops in the capital. He asked her if she was monitoring Braeg's speech. She said that she was.

"I beg you, Praetor, allow me to cut him and his movement to pieces, while I still can."

Tal'aura gazed some more at the image of Braeg on the viewscreen. He was leaving her no choice but to eliminate him.

"You have my permission," she replied.

"Thank you," said the commander. "Long live the Empire."

The praetor had no doubt that the Empire would survive. Her reign was another matter entirely.

15

―――◆―――

KITO HADN'T BEEN ABOVEGROUND IN DAYS. BUT then, he had been standing vigil with Hanafaejas and the others, waiting for Doctor Greyhorse to give them what they needed.

Now, amazing as it seemed, he carried it in a pack slung over his shoulder—two hundred tiny vaccination kits donated by the owner of a medical supply house, and two hundred even tinier tubules of vaccine to go with them.

Kito could have lugged more, but he didn't want to arouse Sela's suspicions. Better to give the vaccine out little by little than to see the process grind to a halt.

The plan was to reach everyone in the city by nightfall, and Kevratas's other cities over the next few days. In a week's time, people would stop dying. And in another week, even the worst affected would be back on their feet.

After they had endured so much, it seemed too good to

be true. But Greyhorse was the one who had assured them of the timetable, and he appeared to know what he was doing.

As Kito understood it, the doctor had used his own genetic material in creating the vaccine. In a way, that meant every Kevrata on the planet would have a piece of Greyhorse inside him.

A lasting tribute, the rebel thought, *to one who has done so much for us.*

Then he stopped by the first house on his appointed route, a place not far from the alley where he had hidden from the Romulan hovercraft. Pounding on the door, he waited for the occupant to answer. A moment later, he heard a response from within.

"Please go away. We are afflicted in this house."

They didn't want to expose him to the virus if he hadn't been afflicted already. But just the day before, Kito had seen bumps on his hands. He had nothing to lose.

And the people within had everything to gain.

"It is all right," he told them. "I have something that can help you with your affliction."

A moment later, the door opened. The female standing beside it was suffering from an advanced stage of the disease, the bumps having spread to her face. Her eyes were dull with hopelessness.

"Nothing can help me," she said.

"Never spurn generosity," said Kito, quoting an old Kevratan saying. "If you let me in, I can tell you more."

The female hesitated, loath to open herself to disappointment on top of everything else. But in the end, she stepped aside and let him in.

It was time.

Donatra stood on the bridge of her ship, just in front of her command seat, and studied her forward viewscreen. It showed her a sweep of black space with Tomalak's force of some sixty warbirds emblazoned on it.

They were ready for her. And without a doubt, Tomalak was an accomplished tactician. However, Donatra felt good about her chances, and she had never been wrong in that regard before. She and her fleet would prevail, bringing Romulus out of its latest dark age into an enduring light.

"Give me a link to Commander Suran," she told her communications officer.

A moment later: "Link established, Commander."

"Suran here," said Donatra's mentor. "Is this what I think it is?"

"By now, Braeg has made his speech in Victory Square. But it will ring hollow if we do not follow with a statement of our own."

"Poetic," Suran observed dryly.

"Get your fleet ready," Donatra said affectionately, "and we will write the next verse together."

Her colleague chuckled. "Suran out."

Next, she had her com officer contact her group leaders. They logged on one after the other—first Macaiah, then Lurian, then Tavakoros.

"The moment has arrived," she told them. "Together we will shape the future of the Empire. Though these are Romulans we fight, show them no mercy, for they will show you none. And when the battle is over, Braeg will raise statues to you in Victory Square."

Her group leaders applauded the notion. They had been waiting for this moment without complaint—unlike some of their centurions. However, each was more eager than the next to put an end to the praetor's regime.

"Donatra out," she said, and had her officer sever the link.

Tomalak's force, ignorant of their plans, hadn't moved on the viewscreen. But they would move soon enough.

"Shields up," Donatra told her tactical officer. "Power weapons."

"Yes, Commander," came the response.

She turned to her helm officer. "Take us in. Half-impulse speed."

"As you wish, Commander."

As Donatra's warbird leaped ahead, she sat down in her chair and leaned forward. *Soon enough, my love. Soon enough. . . .*

Braeg wasn't surprised when he saw twin rivers of Tal'aura's black-garbed Capital Guardsmen come pouring into Victory Square. After all, he had finally committed treason, rallying the populace to overthrow the government.

He might have chosen that moment to flee and go into hiding. But he was a soldier, and he hadn't forged his reputation by running from his enemies.

Still, he didn't command anyone to help him. In fact, he didn't say anything at all. He just watched and waited.

And at precisely the right moment, Braeg's *own* centurions made their move.

They had positioned themselves on the edges of the crowd, looking like anyone else who had come to hear the admiral speak. And like anyone else, they had moved aside when the guardsmen came streaming into the square.

But unlike the other citizens in the square, they had disruptors concealed beneath their garb. And now that Tal'aura's men had rushed past them, they drew those disruptors and began to fire.

Confused, the guardsmen whirled and attempted to fire back. However, they were being attacked from too many directions. And their own forces were bunched together, making them ridiculously easy targets.

Of course, the greater part of the crowd—made up of true innocents—was unavoidably caught in the middle of the square. However, they were forgotten by Tal'aura's police and therefore left mercifully unscathed.

As Braeg looked on, he saw his men chip away at the guardsmen, cutting down one cornered rodent after another. *Which is what happens,* he noted, *when the Capital Guard tries to match wits with the man who beat the Wetraza at Crannac Oghila.*

And, producing a disruptor of his own, he added his fire to that of his partisans.

Tomalak eyed his viewscreen, where a tightly bunched squadron of enemy warbirds was plunging headlong toward the center of his formation, their disruptors painting fiery streaks on the void. Obviously, they intended to break through and attack the Defense Force from behind.

Not today, he thought, tapping a stud on his armrest to open a link to the group leader in charge of his center.

"Pontikanos," he said, "pull your ships back."

"But there is a squadron—"

"I am not *blind,*" said Tomalak, cutting Pontikanos short. "I see it too. Now do as I say."

Then Tomalak contacted two other group leaders and gave them instructions as well. *That should do the trick,* he thought, as he waited to see the results.

Pontikanos's ships retreated in accordance with his order, allowing the enemy to proceed through the position they had abdicated. For a moment, it seemed that Donatra's warbirds would pierce Tomalak's shield.

But when Donatra's vessels came shooting through, they found themselves confronted by defenders that had formerly fortified the extremities of Tomalak's formation. Outnumbered and unable to retreat, the intruders were trapped.

Tomalak was about to congratulate himself on the effectiveness of his reaction. Then two of Donatra's other squadrons darted through the positions his maneuver had abandoned—and went after his ships from behind, disruptors blazing.

Doing exactly what Tomalak had tried to prevent. And to address the problem, he had to release his stranglehold on the first squadron. He felt a rush of blood to his face.

It was a trap all along. Obviously, Donatra had taken the time to study his tactics. *I will have to be a bit more creative if I am to keep my reputation intact.*

A volley rocked his warbird, whipping him about in his seat. Tomalak calmly righted himself, tapped at his armrest again, and barked, "Skirmish clusters!"

After all, he had already been outflanked. His best chance was to collapse his formation into groups.

Of course, Donatra would be doing the same, and her commanders were by and large more skilled than his. But Tomalak enjoyed an advantage in that he didn't care how long the battle lasted; all he cared about was keeping the opposition away from Romulus.

Donatra, on the other hand, couldn't afford to waste any time. She had to carry the day and do it quickly, or Braeg's revolt would die on the vine.

"Avoid unnecessary risks," he advised over his com link. "Let the traitors fall prey to them."

As if I have to tell them that. The last thing they want to do is miss the praetor's next feast.

As Tomalak surveyed the battle, he saw that his commanders were following his orders. They were pursuing evasive maneuvers, forcing Donatra's ships to come after them—and thereby expose themselves to fire from unexpected quarters.

That's better, he thought.

Suddenly, an enemy warbird filled his viewscreen, her weapons batteries spitting emerald fury. *A would-be hero, hoping to cut off the serpent's head.*

But Tomalak wasn't inclined to cooperate. "Hard to port!" he snapped, and felt the shift in inertia as his helm officer complied.

The barrage bludgeoned his warbird and significantly weakened his shields, but it wasn't the killing blow his adversary had hoped it would be. And now it was Tomalak's turn.

"Helm," he snarled, "bring us about! Tactical, let me know when you've got a lock!"

On his screen, the enemy was wheeling as well. But Tomalak boasted the best helm officer in the Empire, just as he boasted the best weapons officer and the best engineer—so his ship came out of her turn a heartbeat sooner than the other one.

"Lock, Commander!"

Tomalak leaned forward in his chair. "Fire!"

His disruptor beams stabbed their target like a pair of long, green fangs. The enemy tried to twist out of the way, but Tomalak stayed with her, a hunter refusing to be denied his prey.

Finally, her shields gone, her hull battered and blackened, the vessel went up in an immense ball of flame.

Tomalak watched the few remaining pieces of debris fly outward in an ever-expanding circle. Then the spectacle was behind him and his helm officer was awaiting new orders.

He leaned back in his chair and—because he was who he was—ignored the instructions he had given his subordinates just a few moments earlier.

Smiling to himself, he said, "Find me another one."

Picard emerged from the catacombs at a different site from the one where he had descended into them.

Like the first spot, this was a jumbled, half-collapsed stone entryway lying unconcealed on the outskirts of the city. However, it was much closer to the place where the captain had arranged to rendezvous with Beverly.

A place where the planet's magnetic fields were all but absent. A place from which—with the help of the miniature pattern enhancers they had brought—Picard and his comrades could beam back to the *Annabel Lee* and return to Federation space.

With not four of them on board, but five.

Picard couldn't wait to see Beverly. It had been one thing to learn that she had survived her ordeal; witnessing the proof of it would be quite another.

Hanafaejas and a couple of his rebels had preceded Picard and his team onto the street, just in case there were any centurions around. As luck would have it, there weren't.

But there *was* a blizzard of white snow swirling about them. It cut down drastically on visibility and dampened sound. All the captain could hear was the whisper of flake on flake.

Joseph looked around as he followed Picard out of the tunnel, as alert as when he was the captain's chief of security. Then came Greyhorse, an imposing figure in his black thermal suit, with Decalon immediately behind him.

The Romulan had been quiet since he admitted he was wrong about his friend Phajan, gathering with the others in the corridors at mealtimes but contributing little to their conversations. Of course, he had almost hamstrung their mission, and that couldn't have been an easy thing to live with.

The only person with whom Decalon seemed comfortable was Greyhorse. But then, he had spent a good deal of time in the doctor's company.

Not being a scientist, the Romulan couldn't have made Greyhorse's work go any faster. However, his presence in the doctor's makeshift lab might have been a positive factor, giving Greyhorse unspoken encouragement or keeping his energies from flagging. It was difficult to say.

"Activate your holoprojectors," Picard said.

A moment later, he was in the company of three Barolians again. The rebels, who had seen the disguises before, appeared to take them in stride.

"This way," said Hanafaejas, indicating the way.

Picard fell in beside him, embarking across a landscape of long, generous drifts. The snow lashed his face, causing him to pull his hood forward a bit.

"Nice weather we're having," he told Hanafaejas.

The Kevrata glanced at him. "It will soon get worse."

Though Picard wouldn't have believed it possible, Hanafaejas was right. As the minutes passed, the storm seemed to intensify. He could barely see among its twists and tatters. Were it not for the rebel beside him, he would have been terribly and hopelessly lost.

"Yes," the captain said, his words all but snatched by the wind, "nice weather indeed." Lowering his head, he pressed forward, comforting himself with an assurance that they would be on the *Annabel Lee* within the hour . . .

He, his team, and the woman whose death he hadn't been able to accept.

16

THE PLACE WHERE PICARD WAS SUPPOSED TO MEET Beverly was a broad slope cut by deep, snow-choked gullies—in the midst of which sat a sprawling, opulent-looking Kevratan domicile that had at some point fallen into disrepair.

Despite the size of the place, the captain and his companions were almost on top of it before they saw it loom out of the storm. That was how dense the snow was.

Beverly wasn't in evidence yet. *Hardly a surprise,* Picard thought, as he shifted his grip on his phaser. He had insisted on arriving a few minutes early, reluctant to let her wait for him any longer than she had to.

After all, he had his team and a half dozen armed Kevrata with him. She was bringing only her host, wishing to minimize the possibility of a security breach.

Picard glanced at Pug, then at Greyhorse. They looked back at him from within their hoods, eager to simply secure Beverly and be done with it.

Suddenly, an image came to him out of the featureless white of the storm. . . .

Beverly standing on the deck of the medical Starship Pasteur, *her red-golden hair drawn back loosely into a knot, a captain's insignia emblazoned on the scarlet breast of her uniform. Frowning out of concern for him, her features softened by age, but as beautiful as when she first set foot on his* Enterprise.

Perhaps more so.

That Beverly was part of a future that would probably never exist, a future Picard had encountered years earlier while jumping helplessly through time. In it, he had married Beverly and then divorced her, but they still loved each other as much as ever.

Why think of that now? he asked himself.

"Captain," someone said, in the deep, stentorian timbre of a Barolian. "Look!"

Picard turned and saw that it was Joseph who had spoken. Following his friend's gesture, he discerned a figure through the veils of falling snow.

Beverly? he thought.

But it wasn't just a single Kevrata who accompanied her. It was a line of them. And the more Picard studied them, the more it seemed to him *they weren't Kevrata at all.* . . .

"Centurions," said Hanafaejas, who could see better in the storm than a human could. "Ten of them, maybe more."

Picard looked around and saw silhouettes behind them as well. In fact, they were closing in from every direction.

"We're surrounded," Joseph observed.

"Lay down your arms!" a feminine voice called out. "Otherwise, you will be destroyed!"

A moment later, Picard saw the one who had issued the ultimatum. Even if she hadn't distinguished herself from the other Romulans, he could have picked out her face across the span of a *thousand* snow-blown fields.

After all, he had loved it the way a father loves a daughter, and mourned it to the same degree when death claimed it. And when, years later, he saw it twisted with hatred and resentment in the trappings of a Romulan commander, part of him had recoiled in shock and disbelief—but another part had been grateful for the chance to bask again in Tasha's light.

"Sela," said Decalon.

She wants us alive, the captain thought. But then, they were more valuable that way—both to the Empire and to Sela herself.

Picard had no intention of surrendering. But before he could give the order to fire, the rebels beat him to it.

Their disruptor beams sliced through the falling snow, jackknifing a few centurions. But the others returned the favor without mercy, catching the captain and his comrades in a deadly, pale green crossfire.

Picard and his team fired as well, though it was difficult to see well enough to hit anyone. Fortunately the rebels didn't have that problem, striking almost every target they aimed for.

Sela still had the numerically superior force. However, if she waited long enough, that would no longer be the case. Anticipating her next move, Picard said, "Watch for a charge."

Right on cue, a wave of centurions came hurtling toward them. The captain fired into their midst, as did his comrades. But enough of the enemy got through to make it a hand-to-hand fight, in which the Romulans couldn't help but have the edge.

Ducking a punch that would have caved his skull in, Picard drove his elbow into his attacker's chest. Then he fired at a second one, sending him sprawling in the snow.

A third adversary fell short, stopped by someone else's disruptor beam. However a fourth one, only half-glimpsed, managed to hammer the captain from behind.

The impact numbed his shoulder and drove him to all fours, but he still had a grip on his weapon. Pivoting on his knee, he leveled a blast in what he believed was the right direction.

Unfortunately, the centurion was gone by then. And before Picard could regroup, another one hit him from the side.

Together they tumbled in the snow, a mess of arms and legs, but it was the Romulan who wound up on top. Drawing his fist back, he drove it into the captain's face. Then he did it again.

And again.

Picard was close to losing consciousness, the taste of blood strong in his mouth, his holoprojector disabled. But while the centurion was pummeling him he had been groping for his weapon, which had spilled out of his hand into the snow.

And now he had found it.

Pressing it against his adversary's side, he pulled the trigger and catapulted the centurion away. But as dazed as he was, it took him a moment to gather himself, to get his feet underneath him.

As it turned out, a moment was too long.

Still on one knee, he felt something hit him in the jaw, rattling his head about. Unable to stop himself, he slumped to the ground. As he looked up through swimming senses, he saw who had hit him—and who was standing over him now, her weapon leveled at him.

"Sela," he breathed.

She didn't say anything. She just smiled, as if this were revenge for the schemes he had foiled and the humiliation he had cost her. And in that smile, there was nothing of Tasha.

My luck has run out, he thought. There would be no escape this time, no last-second maneuver.

He had come to Kevratas to keep others from dying. But in the end, it was he who would perish. *Ironic, isn't it?* Steeling himself, he awaited the fatal impact.

Then something happened—a fur-clad body striking suddenly and unexpectedly, with an audible thud—and Sela, tangled with the newcomer, went tumbling down a steep, white incline into a gully.

It was a full second later, as Picard replayed the event in his mind, that he recognized the red-gold hair spilling from his savior's hood.

Beverly . . . he thought.

Braeg was so intent on firing across Victory Square at Tal'aura's outflanked centurions that he didn't give any thought to the shadow passing over him.

After all, what could it it be but a cloud? Then it slid

into his field of vision and he saw it for what it was—a type-six military hovercraft equipped with long-range disruptor cannons.

But, Braeg thought helplessly, *there aren't supposed to be any military hovercraft on Romulus.* In fact, there were laws specifically prohibiting them, enacted hundreds of years earlier.

Yet there it was. A well-kept secret, no doubt built in anticipation of just such an eventuality.

And it wasn't alone—because Braeg saw two more hovercraft wafting in pursuit of the first, and a moment later he realized there was a fourth one.

They stopped over the square in what the admiral now saw was a diamond-shaped formation, and spit fiery beams of disruptor energy into the corners where Braeg's men had positioned themselves. Suddenly the tide of battle began to turn, and not at all in Braeg's favor.

He cursed as he watched his men die, skewered on the ends of thick green energy bolts. They lashed back at the hovercraft, but to no avail. Their hand weapons didn't have enough power to be effective at that distance.

Nor was it only his men who were perishing. So were the citizens caught in the middle of the square. Those inside the hovercraft didn't seem to care who they were cutting down.

Braeg needed to do something before it was too late. But what *could* he do? He hadn't planned for this. And he didn't yet have Donatra's warbirds to back him up.

I'm a strategist, he insisted. *If there's a way out, I can find it. I* must *find it.*

But in the end, he saw there was only one strategy left to him, only one tactical maneuver he could use to stop the bloodshed.

And only Braeg could execute it.

Beverly hadn't thought about it. There wasn't time.

She had seen Jean-Luc lying on the ground at the mercy of Sela's disruptor and her instincts had taken over, sending her flying through the storm to plant her shoulder in Sela's side.

Then her momentum had carried them into this snow-filled gully, where each of them was now struggling to rise to her feet before her adversary could do the same.

Beverly won that battle. Still, she had barely braced herself before Sela fired a naked fist at her, both her weapon and her glove buried somewhere in the snow. The doctor managed to elude the attack, but lost her balance in the process.

So when Sela shot a boot at her, she couldn't ward it off. It hit her squarely in her half-healed shoulder, sending needles of fire through it and forcing a groan from Beverly's lips.

Smiling, Sela went after the same spot again. And though Beverly was ready this time, the attack struck bone nonetheless.

Go on the offensive, the doctor urged herself. Otherwise, Sela would hammer that wound all day.

Feinting with her left hand, she drove hard with her right. But Sela's response was lightning-quick, deflecting Beverly's assault. And without hesitation, she answered it with one of her own.

Dancing backward, the doctor avoided the first blow. But the second caught her in the jaw, dumping her unceremoniously in the snow. She tried to recover, to get her legs underneath her, but Sela followed with a roundhouse kick to the head.

Dazed, Beverly looked up at the Romulan. Sela just stood there, a smirk of triumph on her face.

"You can't win," she said, her voice like a whip. "You're weak, like the rest of your Federation. Like my *mother.*"

Beverly felt a gobbet of outrage lodge in her throat. Tasha had been a warrior, as courageous as anyone the doctor had ever known. She deserved a better fate than to be reviled by her only child.

"I knew your mother," Beverly said, anger spreading through her limbs like an elixir, "and she was a lot tougher than you think. But then," she added, somehow dragging herself to her feet, *"so am I."*

Before Sela could appreciate what she had ignited, Beverly launched herself across the space between them. Landing a shot to her adversary's jaw, she spun her around. Then she lashed out with her foot and swept Sela's legs out from under her.

The Romulan tried to get up, but the snow proved too soft and slippery—and Beverly took advantage of it. Plowing Sela into the ground, she smashed her in the nose with the heel of her hand—eliciting a bright green spurt of blood.

Sela struck back, but Beverly hardly felt it. She was too busy delivering blow after blow, doing her best to pound the fight out of her enemy.

"You will *not* beat me!" Sela gurgled, trying to heave her tormentor off her.

"Actually," Beverly spat through hard-clenched teeth, "I already have." And she administered a right cross that snapped Sela's head around, knocking her out as effectively as any sedative.

The doctor sat there on her adversary's chest for a moment, spewing steam from her nose and mouth. Then, certain that Sela wouldn't get up any time soon, Beverly rolled off her onto the blood-flecked snow.

Only to look up into the face of one of Sela's centurions.

Then she realized it wasn't just *any* centurion. It was the one who had tied her up in the government hall. He stood on the lip of the gully pointing his disruptor at her, his expression one of unconcealed delight.

"Doctor Crusher," he said, a deadly edge to his voice. "Imagine meeting *you* here."

Weary as she was, Beverly thrust herself to her feet. She wished she could say something that would keep the centurion from stunning her and making off with her, but she couldn't.

I was so close, she thought. *So very close.*

"Pleasant dreams," said her enemy.

Then someone loomed out of the storm behind him.

"Fire!" Donatra commanded.

The *Valdore*'s disruptor beams raked the flank of the warbird on her viewscreen, opening rents in her hull but failing to hit any critical targets. And before the commander could make another pass at her adversary, another one came after her.

Barking out an order, Donatra hung on to her seat and watched the scene on her screen slide to the right. Her helm officer was doing her best to get them out of harm's way, but the commander doubted they would slip the barrage entirely.

As if in confirmation, the *Valdore* shuddered. But fortunately, it was no worse than that.

A moment later, Donatra's viewscreen displayed her new adversary—right behind her, in excellent position to wreak havoc on the *Valdore*'s engines. But by the same token, the *Valdore* had a clear shot at her pursuer's command center.

And Donatra had to make use of every opening she got. "Target and fire!" she snapped.

Her disruptors plowed into the enemy, inflicting heavy damage on her forward shields. Had Donatra been the pursuer instead of the pursued, she would have ignored the volley and blasted her adversary's engines.

Instead, the warbird veered off.

Donatra swore under her breath. Every time she engaged the enemy, he evaded her. It couldn't be a coincidence. It had to be a strategy, instituted by Tomalak.

He knows we need a quick victory, she thought, *and he's doing everything in his power to prevent it.*

In his place, Donatra would have done the same thing. But that didn't keep her from wanting to snap Tomalak's neck.

"Commander?" said Oritas, her com officer.

Donatra wondered what Suran wanted. Perhaps to tell her the enemy was running from *his* ships as well.

But after a moment or two, Oritas still hadn't said why he called to her. She turned to him, a question in her expression.

"It is Herran," the com officer said at last, his expression as empty of emotion as his voice. "He has news of Admiral Braeg. Apparently, he has given himself up to the capital guard."

At first, Donatra thought she had misheard. Then she saw the stricken look on the face of her officers, and realized she had heard correctly after all.

"It's a lie," she spat.

But even as she said it, she knew she was wrong. Braeg trusted Herran with everything. He would never have reported such a thing if it were not true.

"What else does he say?" she asked Oritas.

He gave her the grim details—the speech Braeg had made in Victory Square, the arrival of Tal'aura's centurions, Braeg's counterstroke, and then the appearance of . . .

Hovercraft? Donatra swore to herself.

They had killed indiscrimately, not just Braeg's men but innocents as well. The ground had run green with their blood.

Unable to stop the craft any other way, Braeg had waded through the crowd and surrendered himself to Tal'aura's guardsmen. Seeing him give himself up, his men had turned and tried to escape. Many of them had made it, Herran included, though the praetor was in the process of hunting them down.

Donatra felt her throat constrict. Braeg had sacrificed himself for the good of those in the square. And now he was Tal'aura's prisoner, to do with as she wished.

She wouldn't allow him to live. She couldn't. He had proven himself too dangerous a foe.

Donatra had believed they would have all the time in the world some day. *But not anymore.* Clenching her fist, she smashed her armrest with it.

Braeg's only chance now was for Donatra to cripple Tomalak's defense forces—and to do it as quickly as possible. But Tomalak's tactics were designed to slow them down.

Which meant they would have to take more chances than ever. "Give me a link to Suran," she told Oritas.

"Commander," said her tactical officer, her voice taut with urgency, "there'a a warbird bearing down on us. It appears to be Commander Tomalak's."

Donatra's jaw clenched. Apparently, Tomalak didn't feel compelled to be as evasive as the rest of his commanders.

It was all right. She couldn't win without going through Tomalak anyway. He was simply making it easier for her to find him.

Of course, Tomalak was widely considered the craftiest commander of his generation. As good as Donatra was, Tomalak was reputed to be better.

She lifted her chin as she watched his warbird loom larger on her screen. *We will see about that.*

After all, Donatra had studied accounts of Tomalak's exploits, committed to memory his favorite maneuvers—which was how she had broken up his initial defense formation. All she had to do was see which approach he took, and then react to it.

"Lock weapons," she said. "Wait for my order to fire."

"Weapons locked," came the response.

Patience, Donatra told herself firmly, *no matter the urgency of the situation.*

And indeed, she waited as long as she could to see which way Tomalak would veer off. But the longer she waited, the more certain she became that he wouldn't veer off at all.

A direct attack, without subtlety or nuance? From someone as well regarded as Tomalak?

It didn't seem possible. And yet, the evidence was right there in front of her.

She couldn't wait any longer. In a couple of seconds, the enemy would ram her. "Fire!"

Finally Tomalak's vessel veered off, but not before he unleashed a barrage of his own. Donatra braced herself as her screen went pale green. A moment later, the impact sent her ship lurching to starboard. Behind her, a control console exploded.

"Report!" she barked.

"Shields down eighty-four percent, Commander!"

"Weapons and propulsion still fully operational!"

At the same time Donatra's screen cleared and she got a look at her adversary. Tomalak's ship couldn't have been damaged much worse than hers, but it was retreating as if the *Valdore* had made it impossible for her to fight.

Donatra didn't understand. Why would Tomalak attack her head-on—and then run? It wasn't at all the behavior of the master strategist she had studied.

Suddenly the answer dawned on her, sending a tingle of dread down her spine. But by then it was too late, because her tactical officer was already shouting a warning.

"Another warbird, Commander—coming up behind us!"

"Evade!" Donatra snarled.

The words had barely escaped her when she was catapulted forward. The next thing she knew she was piled against a bulkhead, one of her arms throbbing with pain.

Tomalak, Donatra thought.

He had tricked her, exchanging ships with one of his commanders. Then he had ordered that commander to attack her while Tomalak himself waited for an opening.

"Get us out of here!" Donatra exhorted her helm officer.

On the viewscreen above her, the enemy released another volley. She felt a second impact, worse than the first. In its wake another console exploded, sending up a geyser of smoke and sparks.

"Helm!" Donatra bellowed, dragging herself to her feet.

Then she saw that the helm was unmanned, her officer dead or otherwise incapacitated. Staggering across the bridge, she brought her good hand down on the controls and punched in a prearranged maneuver.

I may perish, she thought, turning back to the viewscreen in defiance, *but I will* not *go down without a fight!*

Decalon had caught a glimpse of Doctor Crusher as she went tumbling into a gully. However, he was too busy dodging disruptor beams to do anything about it.

Finally, one of them found him—or rather, found his weapon, blasting it out of his hand. But the Romulan who did it was leveled by the Kevrata, giving Decalon a moment's respite.

He used it to go after Doctor Crusher.

It wouldn't be easy to find her among the twisting curtains of snow, but Decalon was determined, and he had always had a good sense of direction. Finally, after staggering around for a while, he caught sight of something— a slash of purple that might have been part of a Kevratan overcoat.

It's her, he thought. *It* must *be.*

But before he could reach the doctor, someone beat him to it. One of Sela's centurions. And he had a disruptor lodged in his fist, which gave him a considerable advantage over Decalon.

There was no telling what orders Sela had given her soldiers—whether they were to recapture Doctor Crusher or simply kill her—so Decalon didn't have the luxury of sneaking up on his target.

Putting his head down, he covered the intervening distance as quickly as he could. *Thirty meters,* he thought. *Twenty. Ten . . .*

Finally, with a last desperate burst of speed, Decalon went bowling into the centurion. There was a flash of pale green energy—errant, he hoped—and they were skidding into the gully together, jockeying for position as they fell.

They wound up side by side, struggling for the centurion's disruptor—but not for long. Because just as Decalon thought he might wrest the weapon away, the centurion elbowed him in the face.

Decalon lost his grip for a moment—but that was all the time the centurion needed. Scrambling to his feet, he aimed his weapon at Decalon and fired.

Decalon was thrown backward, the air exploding from his lungs. But when he landed, he found he was still alive. Fighting hard to breathe, he thought: *Stun. It was set on stun.*

Through a haze of pain, Decalon watched Beverly tackle the centurion and try to take him down. But he backhanded her across the face, sending her flying backward, and aimed his weapon at her as he had aimed it at Decalon.

No doubt, he meant to knock her unconscious. Then he would take her to Sela, who would kill her or torture her for what she knew.

Either way, Decalon couldn't allow it. Doctor Crusher was one of those who had risked their lives to smuggle him to freedom. She wouldn't become a prisoner of the Empire as long as he was alive to prevent it.

Pushing himself up out of the snow, he took a step and dove flat-out across the gully.

But he was too weak, too starved for air. His dive carried him only as far as the centurion's feet.

Turning to Decalon, the centurion frowned in annoyance. Then, calmly and methodically, he reset his disruptor.

Decalon grabbed the centurion's leg and tried to push him back. But it was no use. He didn't have the strength. Without comment, the centurion trained his weapon on Decalon again.

And depressed the trigger.

Picard had to fight his fatigue and confusion as much as his enemy as he pulled back his fist and let it fly.

The centurion, who had been reeling already as a result of the captain's other blows, took this one on the point of the chin. He staggered for a moment, eyes rolling back in his head, then collapsed.

Finally, Picard thought.

Pouncing on the disruptor the centurion had dropped, he looked around. The battle had moved away from him for the moment, leaving him alone in the falling snow.

And giving him a chance to go after Beverly.

Shielding his eyes, the captain approached the gully into which Beverly had vanished, but couldn't discern anyone down there. Yet he was certain that Beverly and Sela had fallen that way. So with his borrowed weapon in hand he hastened down the incline, hoping he wasn't too late.

He had almost reached the bottom when he saw two figures lying there, either dead or unconscious. Then he noticed two others just beyond them, still on their feet—and facing each other.

One was a centurion, a disruptor pistol in his hand. And the other . . . was *Beverly*.

Picard felt a pang as he saw her, her hair flying free from the confines of her Kevratan hood. But he didn't dare call to her lest he alert the centurion.

Slowing his descent, he got within thirty meters of them—the maximum effective range of a disruptor. Then he stopped, took aim, and squeezed off a beam.

It went straight and unerringly to its mark. Or rather, where its mark had *been*.

Unfortunately, the centurion chose that moment to move forward and strike Beverly—effectively removing himself from the line of fire, and leaving the energy bolt to bury itself in the snow.

Instantly, Beverly's captor turned in Picard's direction. Before the captain could get off another shot, the centurion grabbed the doctor and used her for a shield. Then he put his disruptor to her head.

"Drop your weapon," he snapped, his voice audible even over the hiss of the wind, "or I will kill her!"

Picard knew that once he was unarmed, the Romulan would destroy him. But he had no choice. He couldn't roll the dice with Beverly's life at stake.

"All right," he said, "I am dropping it. See?" And he let the disruptor fall to the snow-covered ground.

"Step away from it," said the centurion.

His teeth clenched, the captain stepped away.

As he had predicted, the centurion's weapon swung in his direction. A smile spread across the bastard's face. He had Picard exactly where he wanted him.

But in the same moment, Beverly made a motion with her hand. Nothing too overt—just enough to let the captain know that something was coming.

He had known Beverly a long time. He knew what she would do as surely as he knew his name. And he knew also that the opening she gave him would only be a brief one.

Without warning, she grimaced and pumped her elbow into her captor's ribs. As the Romulan folded in pain, Picard dove for his weapon and came up firing.

By then, Beverly had freed herself, and there was nothing to protect the centurion. The captain's blast struck him in the shoulder, spinning him about.

Even then, the Romulan managed to get off a shot of his own. His beam cut a hot, steaming path in the snow, coming within a meter of Picard's elbow.

Refusing to give his adversary a second chance, the captain took more careful aim this time—and struck the centurion squarely in the chest, driving him backward head over heels.

Warily, Picard got up and regarded his enemy. However, it was clear that the centurion was unconscious, his eyes rolled back in his head.

Half-running, half-sliding, the captain covered the distance to Beverly in a heartbeat. Then, separated from her by mere centimeters, he drank in the sight of her.

In truth, she had looked more composed. There was a dark swelling under one eye and blood in the corner of her mouth. However, she had never seemed more appealing to him.

Folding her into his arms, he felt her slump against him, battered and exhausted and not embarrassed to show it. "By now," she rasped, "you should know I don't need rescuing."

He couldn't help smiling at the irony. And as he gazed into the depths of her glittering blue eyes, he couldn't help something else as well.

Lowering his mouth to her ear, he whispered, "I love you, Beverly. I have always loved you. And I always will."

It wasn't something she didn't know. However, Picard had never said it that way—so urgently, so fervently.

He withdrew a little, eager to see the look on her face. After all, she loved him too. She had said so. And at that moment, she had to be feeling the same way he did— clutching with all her strength what had almost been lost to them forever.

But when he saw Beverly's expression, it wasn't a happy one. She looked hesitant, uncomfortable. And by that sign, Picard realized he had blundered.

He had violated the unspoken laws of their friendship, upset its delicate balance, sent it whirling out of control. By striving to make something more of the feelings they shared, he had inadvertently made something less.

Slipping free of his embrace, Beverly moved to one of the other figures in the gully—one Picard recognized as Decalon. A curse escaped his lips.

Beverly knelt beside the Romulan's blackened, blasted corpse. Then she turned back to the captain. "The Romulan who came with you?"

"Yes," he said.

"He died trying to save me," she told him.

Picard recalled how introspective Decalon had been in the catacombs. As if he were just waiting for an opportunity to redeem himself.

And he had.

Then he saw the other figure lying in the gully, and he recognized that one as well. "Sela."

Picard hated to just leave her there, knowing she would be trouble again in the future. But he didn't dare risk taking her along with them.

Suddenly, he heard someone call his name from the top of the slope. It was Pug.

"Come on!" he yelled, beckoning them—signifying, no doubt, that the Kevrata had opened a window of opportunity for them. "Let's get out of here!"

Without looking at the captain, Beverly started up the slope. As Picard went after her, he wished he hadn't said what he said to her. He wished he had exercised more control.

But it was too late. And for all he knew, the damage was irreparable. *What have I done?*

17

⎯⎯◆⎯⎯

TAL'AURA WATCHED BRAEG RAISE THE BRONZE GOBLET
to his lips, his dark eyes full of pride and brash defiance—
unlike the trepidation others had displayed in similar
situations.

Without hesitation or stint, the admiral drained the
goblet's clear sweet contents. Then he put it down on the
marble-topped table beside him.

For a moment, there was no change in his expression,
not even the faintest crack in his composure. The praetor
found herself wishing he had not been her enemy, that he
could have served her instead of opposing her.

Then it was too late, because Braeg's handsome face
had already begun suffusing with blood, turning greener
than the homeworld's deepest seas. A heartbeat later, he
fell dead beside the marble table—the martyr Tal'aura had
not wished to make of him.

She sighed as her men dragged away the corpse. *A*

monstrous pity. And yet she could not have allowed Braeg's treason to go unpunished.

Wisely, she had kept the proceeding a private one, attended only by government officials. But Braeg had exercised his right of statement anyway, knowing his words would be recorded for posterity. He had spoken of Tal'aura's tyranny, of the purity of his motives in trying to overthrow her, and finally of Donatra.

Oh, how he spoke of her.

Even the praetor had been moved by his words—and, she conceded it now, made envious. For as long as she lived, she would never be loved as Braeg had loved Donatra.

Enough of this, she told herself. *Other matters require my attention.* Tapping a command into the control device in her hand, she called up a different image—that of the individual in command of her Defense Force.

Tal'aura saw Tomalak swivel in his chair to face her. He looked as if he had come from a refreshing sleep, not a battle with a rebel armada.

"Congratulations on your victory," the praetor told him.

"It was my pleasure to serve you," he said.

Not yet, she thought. Tomalak's pleasure would come later, after she had arranged for some of Eborion's lands and wealth to be transferred to the commander's name.

The rest, of course, would be given to Eborion's aunt Cly'rana. After all, it was she who had exposed Eborion for the traitor he was.

Suspecting her nephew was up to something, Cly'rana had arranged to monitor all his communications. Otherwise, his message from Manathas would almost certainly have gone undiscovered.

And why had Cly'rana torn the veil from Eborion's treachery? Out of loyalty to the praetor—or so she claimed. But she had not pleaded for the life of her nephew, who must have been a threat to her within her family, nor had she turned down the share of his wealth Tal'aura gave as a reward.

In the process, the praetor had learned a valuable lesson: that even the Hundred could be bought.

"Nonetheless," she told Tomalak, "it was a great achievement."

Of course, the odds had been in his favor all along. Only the rebels' fervor had allowed them to think otherwise. But it was left to the victors to say how treacherous a battle had been, and how courageous those who had fought it.

"We are going through the ships we captured," said Tomalak, "and sending their crews down to face charges of treason. Unless, of course, you would like us to address their actions up here."

In other words, Tal'aura interpreted, *kill them without a trial.* She appreciated the value of expedience, but even *she* wouldn't deprive the rebels of their right of statement.

"That will not be necessary," she told Tomalak. "I prefer to deal with them myself. Besides, you will have your hands full repairing their vessels—and your own."

"As you wish," the commander responded.

Unfortunately, nearly half of the rebels' fleet had gotten away, the ships commanded by Donatra and Suran among them. Tal'aura was forced to assume that both fleet commanders had survived the battle and were at that moment replotting her downfall.

Also, she had to deal with Sela and Manathas.

The latter, being a master of disguise, would be difficult to apprehend. However, it would be impossible for him to find work in the Empire, as no potential employer would want to incur the praetor's wrath.

Sooner or later, Manathas would make a mistake, and someone would identify him and turn him in. It was just a matter of time.

As for Sela . . . she had allowed the Federation to win the admiration of the Kevrata, and thereby fan the flames of rebellion on the outworlds. And into the bargain, she hadn't snared a single Federation agent.

Most disappointing, Tal'aura reflected. But Sela had at least been loyal to her, whereas others had not.

For now, she would leave the half-blood on Kevratas to wallow in her failure. Sela would hate that—and want more than ever to regain the standing she had enjoyed under previous regimes. And when the praetor needed her again, she would be ready.

But neither Sela nor Manathas was the worst of Tal'aura's problems—not since the Kevrata's plague had demonstrated an affinity for Romulans. With all the commercial traffic going in and out of Kevratas on a daily basis, there was no telling how many ships might already be carrying the virus, or how far it might have spread.

One thing was certain: It needed to be stopped.

The praetor had not previously felt a need to deploy research teams to Kevratas, since the disease had been a strictly Kevratan concern. Now, of course, she felt otherwise.

She just hoped her scientists could devise a cure before the virus reached Romulus. . . .

Back in his lair beneath the ancient castle, surrounded by his comrades in the artificial lights of their new camp, Hanafaejas sat on his haunches and lowered his head into his hands.

They had succeeded in their effort to buy Picard the time he needed. As far as Hanafaejas knew, all five of the Federation people had escaped to Pug Joseph's ship—not only Picard and his companions, but Doctor Crusher as well.

However, one of the rebels had perished in a blast of disruptor fire. Hanafaejas let his head loll on his chest as he keened the name of the dead one.

"*Jellekh . . .*"

His comrades responded in kind, filling the alcove with the thin, high sound of their mourning. But then, Jellekh had been the bravest and most dependable of them.

And he might still be alive if there weren't a traitor in their midst. Hanafaejas raised his head and regarded the comrades facing him in a rough semicircle.

Someone had told Sela where Captain Picard would be meeting Doctor Crusher, or those centurions wouldn't have known where to find them. Clearly, there was a leak in the rebels' camp, and Hanafaejas vowed not to rest until he found out who it was.

For now, however, he had a more urgent task. He had sworn to Captain Picard that he would send a brief, untraceable message to Sela's headquarters, letting her know that he was in possession of a vaccine for the plague.

And that he would part with it—for a price.

It wasn't the way of the Kevrata to make bargains with each other. When they gave something away, they did it unconditionally. However, when they dealt with other Kevrata, they could expect their largesse to be reciprocated.

In this case, unfortunately, they were dealing with their Romulan oppressors—the *other* plague ravaging their planet—which meant the rebels had to adhere to a different standard. Besides, Hanafaejas wasn't asking for wealth in exchange for a cure. All he wanted was something the Romulans owed the Kevrata anyway . . .

Their freedom.

To Picard, the journey to Kevratas had seemed painfully long. However, the journey back seemed even longer.

One reason, of course, was the loss of Decalon. It was unfortunate that he could not have escaped the Empire a second time. However, he had gone down fighting, repaying his saviors for the sacrifices they had made to liberate him.

There were worse ways to die.

The other reason for the tedium—from Picard's point of view, at least—was Beverly. She was acting as if nothing had changed, as if they were still the people they had been before.

But Picard knew otherwise. He could see it in her eyes, in her smile, in the distance she kept from him.

On the other hand, she seemed perfectly willing to converse with Joseph or Greyhorse. Especially when the alternative was to be alone with the captain.

It saddened him that it should be so. He wished he could change what he had done, erase every trace of it from Beverly's memory. But he didn't have that option. He could only take responsibility for his mistake and endure its consequences.

Eventually they received orders to rendezvous with the *Zapata,* a *Surak*-class starship that would take Beverly and Greyhorse to a starbase for debriefing. However, Picard would remain with the *Annabel Lee* the rest of the way to Earth.

He was grateful. It would be less awkward that way.

Days later, when they made contact with the *Zapata,* Picard and Joseph accompanied their comrades to the *Annabel Lee*'s transporter room. Feeling as if he were moving through a dream, the captain clasped Greyhorse's big hand and wished him well.

Then he turned to Beverly, hoping he would find in her expression some trace of what had existed between them. But it was as if he were looking at a stranger.

"Good-bye," she said, and gave Picard a hug. But it seemed lacking in enthusiasm.

"Good-bye," he responded.

"Don't forget," Beverly said as she pulled away, "you promised you'd come down for dinner sometime." But her eyes didn't sparkle the way they had when she first extended the invitation.

"I will not forget," he assured her.

And he wouldn't. But he had no intention of bringing

the matter up again. That way, if Beverly was just being polite, it wouldn't lead to any more discomfort.

Picard watched as she said good-bye to Pug. If anything, Beverly seemed more genuine with him, more earnest in her intentions to see him.

Joseph clapped the doctor on the shoulder. "Who knows, I may come by and see you too."

Greyhorse considered his old colleague. "I will look forward to it."

Beverly laughed. It was an easy laugh, the kind she had once shared with Picard. *But not anymore.*

Someday, he believed, that would change. She would get over what had happened and grow comfortable with him again. But he didn't know how long it would take, and in the meantime he felt a part of him was missing.

As Picard watched, the two doctors assumed their places on the platform. Then they were enveloped in columns of light, and gradually faded away.

"And there they go," said Joseph.

The captain nodded, staring at the emptiness.

"Come on," said his old friend. "I'll buy you a drink. Nothing alcoholic, mind you. I'm supposed to be past all that."

Picard wished he could have enjoyed the jest a bit more. Silently, he allowed Joseph to lead him out of the transporter room.

Geordi turned to Worf, as they stood there before the platform in Transporter Room One, and said, "Remember what Joseph told us."

The Klingon quoted the message they had received only minutes earlier: " 'Be careful with the captain. He is still a little shaken up.' However, he did not say by *what.*"

"Maybe," said Geordi, "he felt that was none of our business."

Worf made a sound of disdain. "If it is *his* business, it is ours as well."

The engineer felt the same way, of course. But before he could reply, a pillar of light planted itself squarely on the transporter platform.

It took a few seconds for something to take shape in the glow. But then, cargo haulers weren't known for their state-of-the-art transporter equipment.

Finally the column of light began to fade, and Geordi got a better look at the transport subject. The fellow looked familiar, though at the moment he was uncharacteristically out of uniform.

Stepping down from the platform, Picard looked at Worf and then Geordi, and said, "Don't tell me you have nothing better to do than supervise transporter operations."

The engineer smiled. "Some transporter operations are more important than others."

"Welcome back, sir," said Worf.

Picard smiled. "Thank you, Commander." Then, herding his officers along as he made for the exit, he said, "Tell me how the repairs are going."

Geordi was surprised, if pleasantly so. This wasn't at all the man Joseph had warned them about.

"Pretty well, sir," said the engineer. "There was some trouble with the plasma manifolds, but I think we've worked it out."

The captain nodded. "Excellent. What about the shield emitters?"

The spacedock crews had just begun to install them when Picard was called away on his mission—which Geordi still didn't know much about. However, he was sure he would hear about it before long.

"All the forward emitters and a couple of the aft emitters are operational," he said. "It'll be another few days before we get the rest of them online."

"Is the bridge in any shape yet?" Picard asked.

"Not exactly," said Worf. "The chairs still are not in yet."

"What, if I may ask, is the holdup?"

The Klingon scowled. "They sent us the wrong ones. However, they have taken them back."

"And," said Geordi, as they emerged into the corridor, "they tell me the right ones are on their way."

Picard sighed. "They *always* say that."

The engineer chuckled. "Yes, sir, they do."

"By the way, sir," said Worf, casting a glance at Geordi, "we received a visit from Admiral Janeway. She wanted to see for herself how the retrofit was proceeding."

The captain looked surprised. "It is rather unusual for an admiral to visit drydock. But then, Janeway is an unusual admiral."

"Right," said Geordi, hoping the subject could be brought to a close without any mention of their aborted rescue party.

"And," asked Picard, "what about the plasma manifolds?"

Geordi looked at him. "We went over that a moment

ago, sir. You remember I said there was a problem with them?"

A shadow seemed to pass over the captain's face. "So you did. My apologies. It appears I will need a little time to . . . decompress."

In the engineer's memory, the captain had needed that only a couple of times before. But that was after he had been turned into a Borg, or tortured by a Cardassian gul.

It told Geordi that Joseph had known what he was talking about. And it made him wonder what had thrown Picard off his game, despite his attempt to cover it up.

But the engineer wouldn't pry. If the captain wanted a sympathetic ear, he knew where he could find one.

"Take all the time you need," Geordi said. "I'll let you know if anything cries out for your attention."

Picard nodded. "Thank you, Commander. Carry on." He glanced at Worf. "Both of you." Then he left them standing there in the corridor and went on alone in the direction of his quarters.

Geordi watched him go for a moment. Then he turned to Worf. "More than a *little* shaken up."

Worf's brow creased with concern. "I will keep an eye on him, in case he needs assistance."

The engineer nodded. But he had a feeling this was something Picard would have to work out on his own.

Picard spent his first two days back by himself, doing his best to shake his malaise. But it was not an easy task.

On the third day, he finally said *to hell with it* and

shoved his personal problem aside. He had a duty to his ship and crew, after all. *It is time,* he thought as he left his quarters, *that I acted like it.*

But en route to the turbolift, something strange happened. The captain was wondering about the placement of an EPS relay when, out of the corner of his eye, he glimpsed a woman in a pale blue lab coat.

By the time he turned his head, she had gone down a perpendicular corridor. However, he had seen enough of her to be certain.

It was Beverly.

She was there on the *Enterprise*. But for what reason? And how was it possible he had not known of her arrival?

Hastening down the corridor, Picard peered around the bend of the perpendicular passage and caught sight of her again. But as he did, his heart sank in his chest.

It was a woman, all right. And she was indeed wearing a pale blue lab coat. But her hair was decidedly more blond than red. And now that he got a good look at her, she wasn't as tall as Beverly either.

Just another new person in the science section, Picard thought as he went on to the turbolift. *One whose name I will learn in time.* But definitely not the woman he had believed her to be.

In the lift compartment, he encountered a couple of new engineers and made small talk. Then he got out and crossed the bridge, which was still a mess of circuitry, to his ready room.

As the captain went inside, he wondered how he could have been so stupid. Beverly was elsewhere, either on a starbase or a ship or perhaps back at Starfleet Medical. But she was not on the *Enterprise* and might never set foot there again.

And the sooner I get used to it, the better.

Circumnavigating his desk, Picard took a seat and looked around the room. *Something is different,* he decided. Then he realized what it was: a new carpet. The same color as the old one, but cozier somehow. More cheerful.

The place was shaping up, he conceded. *And the rest of the ship along with it.* Before long, *Enterprise* would leave drydock and do what she was meant to do: plumb the mysteries of a vast and still largely unexplored galaxy.

The captain smiled a little at the thought. There were still adventures ahead. *A great many of them.* All he had to do was put the past behind him and look to the future.

As he had done as a boy, when he looked at the stars and yearned to be among them. As he had done as a young second officer, bringing a battered *Stargazer* back to Earth.

As he would do again and again, for as long as the fleet had need of him.

Just then, he heard a familiar voice over the ship's intercom: "Commander Worf to Captain Picard."

The captain looked up. "Picard here."

"Sir," said Worf, "the new chief medical officer has arrived."

Picard was taken aback. Had Worf alerted him to the imminence of this person's arrival? Probably—and he had been so distracted, he had failed to pay attention.

I am not ready, he thought. However, he would have to meet the fellow sooner or later. "Send him to my ready room."

"You mean . . . send *her* to your ready room."

Picard sighed. *It would have to be a woman, wouldn't it?* "Yes, of course. Send *her.*"

Suddenly, he didn't feel comfortable behind his desk. He yielded to a need to get up, to stretch his legs, and wound up in front of his observation port.

For once, there weren't any repair vehicles floating around. Just him and the stars. At least, for a little while.

Then he heard a chime, and a chill ran down his spine. "Come," he said, forcing certainty into his voice.

But he kept his back to the door. After all, until he actually saw Beverly's replacement, he wouldn't have to acknowledge the fact that she was really gone.

It was a bit rude, yes, and he had always prided himself on his manners. But he couldn't help it. *Funny,* he thought. He had faced all sorts of enemies and nightmarish circumstances in the course of his Starfleet career, but he couldn't bring himself to face his new medical officer.

Picard heard the whisper of the door as it opened, and then again as it closed. And by those signs, which cut him like knives, he knew that Beverly's replacement had entered the room.

"I apologize," he said, keeping his eyes on the stars as he gathered himself. "I was tied up, or I would have greeted you in the transporter room. In any case, I am glad to have you aboard. You are obviously highly qualified, or you would not have been selected for this assignment."

For the first time, he heard his new CMO speak. "I *requested* this assignment, Captain."

Had he heard only the words and not the voice, he might have marveled at the coincidence—because they were among the first words Beverly uttered when she came aboard the *Enterprise*-D. But hearing the voice, he knew it was no coincidence, because the woman who had uttered the words the first time was the same woman who had uttered them a second ago.

The captain turned from the observation port and saw Beverly Crusher standing before him, a sheepish smile pulling at the corners of her mouth. "I don't . . . understand . . ." he said, stumbling over the words like a schoolboy.

By way of a response, she crossed the room and took him in her arms. Then she raised her perfect mouth to his and kissed him—long and passionately.

Afterward, she said, "I've been a fool, Jean-Luc. I was given a second chance at loving you and I almost threw it away. Can you forgive me?"

Picard smiled and brushed a lock of hair from her face. "Perhaps in time. But then, we have plenty of that now, don't we?"

And he kissed her all over again.

Acknowledgments

After some sixty books, this is the central lesson I've learned about the writing life: Acknowledgments get harder all the time. Dedications aren't so bad, because there are always people you want to honor, but acknowledgments are a bear.

In this case, for instance, I want to thank my editor, Margaret Clark, for her insights into the *Trek* mythos, her creativity, and her recognition that writers are people with mortgages, dental appointments, and kids to pick up at the bus stop. And that's the sort of thing I would say about her, except I've already said it. A lot.

Take a look at the books I've written in the *Stargazer* series, all six of them (buy 'em, collect 'em, trade 'em with your friends), and you'll see I just keep thanking Margaret for this stuff.

Nor is she the only one. I heap a load of gratitude on Scott Shannon, my publisher, as well. So I could tell you he's a smart guy who always seems willing to go out on a limb for a good cause (i.e., me), but you've heard that song before. On the other hand, the guy deserves a few props for his efforts, so what am I going to do—ignore him?

And how about Paula Block, the *Trek* guru in Viacom's licensing department? I've already waxed poetic about how understanding she is and how much she contributes to a manuscript—sometimes even going so far as to reject a stupid idea and force me to come up with a better one, which is more or less what happened in the case of *Death in Winter*. And I've told you also how indebted I am to Paula for letting me cover unexplored *Trek* ground in books like *Reunion,* when that privilege seemed to be reserved for the TV shows.

But how many times can you listen to that? How many times can even *Paula* listen to it? It's embarrassing already.

Even my medical experts, Doctor Seth Asser of Rhode Island and Doctor Laurence Glickman of across the street, are guys I've thanked before. They're brilliant, they're exemplary human beings, and I couldn't have handled the bits of science in this book without them. But then, I couldn't have done those *other* books without them either, and I'm not going to thank them any better now than I did then.

So look, here's what I'm thinking. Just go out and buy my other books and read the acknowledgments in *them.* Believe me, they're a lot better than the acknowledgments in this one.

COMING NEXT SUMMER
FROM POCKET BOOKS

STAR TREK: THE NEXT GENERATION®
RESISTANCE

———◆———

J. M. Dillard

PROLOGUE

———

IT BEGAN AS IT HAD BEFORE: CLAUSTROPHOBIC dreams, a sense of impending evil, the shattering of sleep with a desperate, rasping gulp of air.

In darkness, Jean-Luc Picard threw back tangled sheets and rose. It seemed he had done so countless times: had risen in the grip of a vague terror and made his way, blind but knowing, through his unlit bedchamber. He entered the lavatory and paused in front of the mirror.

"Light," he uttered hoarsely, and there was light.

In the glare he winced at his reflection. He looked the same: clean-shaven, with lean, sharply sculpted features, a gleaming bald crown. Yet something was subtly different; something was subtly *wrong*. He studied his face intently, seeking explanations for his sense that he, that his entire world, had gone awry.

Beneath his left cheekbone the skin twitched. The movement was barely perceptible; Picard leaned closer, grasping the edges of the cool counter. Had it been his

imagination, the product of paranoia triggered by the elu-
sive, disremembered dream?

No. The muscle in his cheek spasmed again briefly,
then rippled. Alarmed, Picard placed a hand to it and felt
a hard object beneath the flesh, an object that was neither
tooth nor bone, but inhuman.

He withdrew fingers that trembled despite his efforts
to steady them. The object pushed hard, now, against the
inside of his cheek, like a child-sized fist trying to force its
way through his skin.

The sense of pressure mounted until it became nigh
unbearable. In horror, Picard watched as his cheek stretched
beyond all possible limits, until the hard, steadily lengthen-
ing cylinder emerged from within his body and erupted
through the flesh.

Astoundingly, there was no blood, only a single bright
flash of pain. A slender, gleaming arm of metal emerged
and extended itself a hand's breadth, then paused an inch
before the mirror. A whir: the servo's end bloomed and
opened, revealing skeletal fingers, razor-keen, deadly, fingers meant for grasping, killing, transforming . . .

"The Borg," Picard whispered. Flashes of the dream
returned: infinite rows of metallic honeycomb cubicles,
filled with the assimilated, mindlessly awaiting a direc-
tive; the surgical chamber, efficiently modern yet medi-
evally grotesque, its walls lined with prosthetic limbs,
eyes, sharp saws, burning lasers; worst of all, the queen
herself, no more than a disembodied head with shoulders,
her lips curved upward in the most wickedly smug of
half-smiles, her metallic black-bronze eyes full of promise
and threat . . .

We were very close, you and I. You can still hear our song.

Not again. Not again, not again, not again.

Shining metal fingers clicked and flexed inches away from his eyes, blotting out his reflection, his individuality. Picard sank to his knees, still gripping the counter. This time, his shriek was not silent. . . .

The sound—which emerged as no more than a loud groan—jarred him to full consciousness. In the instant of disorientation that followed, he pressed his palm to his cheek and discovered, to his profound relief, only human flesh. His breathing was shallow, rapid; he forced it to deepen and slow, and let reality reclaim its hold on him.

This was his bed, and *Enterprise*'s night. He was now, truly, awake.

"Jean-Luc?" A voice, soft, beside him; the sound of long, slender limbs sliding against sheets. "Jean-Luc, you're all right. You were dreaming."

"Beverly." His voice was hoarse with sleep; he cleared his throat. "Yes, of course, I'm fine. Just a dream."

She rolled onto her side. He could see her silhouette, though not her expression; she had propped her elbow against the pillow, then rested her head upon her palm. Her hair spilled down to brush his shoulder. "What was it about?"

He tensed slightly. He knew the nuances of her tone well; she was the doctor now, not lover or friend. And she was asking a question whose answer she already knew.

"I was talking in my sleep, then," he said flatly, wryly.

She nodded. He sighed as she persisted. "Feel like talking about it?"

"What's there to say? I don't know why I'm dreaming about them. It was all resolved long ago."

Even before she spoke, he read her skepticism in the way she slightly drew back her head. "A wound as deep as yours won't ever heal completely, Jean-Luc."

"Then help me forget." He took hold of the arm supporting her head and gently pulled; she didn't resist, but laughed and let herself roll toward him, almost on top of him. He gave her a swift kiss, and they smiled at each other in the darkness.

"I'm sorry it still troubles you," she said gently.

He shrugged. "It's not troubling me. It was just a . . . subconscious hiccup, that's all." He stroked her hair. "Sorry I woke you. Go back to sleep."

She yawned, then settled against him, her cheek nestled beneath his collarbone. In an instant, she was out again—a doctor's talent, learned long ago in medical school. He teased her about it, but it was a talent he envied, especially now that he lay staring up at the night ceiling fully awake, feeling the regular rise and fall of her breath against his ribs.

The dream left him troubled. He had not thought of the Borg in a very long time; he could not remember the last time he had consciously relived the horror of his existence as the human/machine hybrid named Locutus. He did not understand why such memories should surface now. More important, he did not know why they should prove especially disturbing.

In his ear, the faintest of whispers.

"What?" He tilted his chin down to glance at Beverly. She was sleeping soundly; he decided she had murmured while dreaming. He gazed back up at the ceiling, then closed his eyes, determined to dismiss all foolish anxiety and return to sleep himself. He drew in a breath, then released it as a sigh and let his body rely completely upon the bed for support.

Another whisper, too soft to be intelligible.

Picard opened his eyes. This time, he did not look down at Beverly; this time, he knew that she was not the source. For the solitary voice was soon joined by another, then another . . . until it became a faint, distant chorus of thousands.

You can still hear our song.

It was, Picard knew with a certainty he wanted urgently not to possess, the whisper of the collective.

It was the voice of the Borg.